THE SITUATION IN FLUSHING

GREAT LAKES BOOKS

EDMUND G. LOVE

The Situation in Flushing

W *WAYNE STATE UNIVERSITY PRESS DETROIT*

Library of Congress Cataloging-in-Publication Data

Love, Edmund G.
The situation in Flushing / Edmund G. Love.
p. cm. — (Great Lakes books)
Reprint. Originally published: New York : Harper & Row, 1965. With new foreword and pref.
ISBN 0–8143–1916–5 (alk. paper). ISBN 0–8143–1917–3 (pbk. : alk. paper)
1. Love, Edmund G.—Childhood and youth. 2. Flushing (Mich.)—Biography. 3. Flushing (Mich.)—Social life and customs.
I. Title. II. Series.
F574.F67L6 1987
977.4'37—dc19 87–17769
CIP

Half-title page illustration by Eric Blegvad.

ISBN-13: 978-0-8143-1917-8 (pbk.) ISBN-10: 0-8143-1917-3 (pbk.)

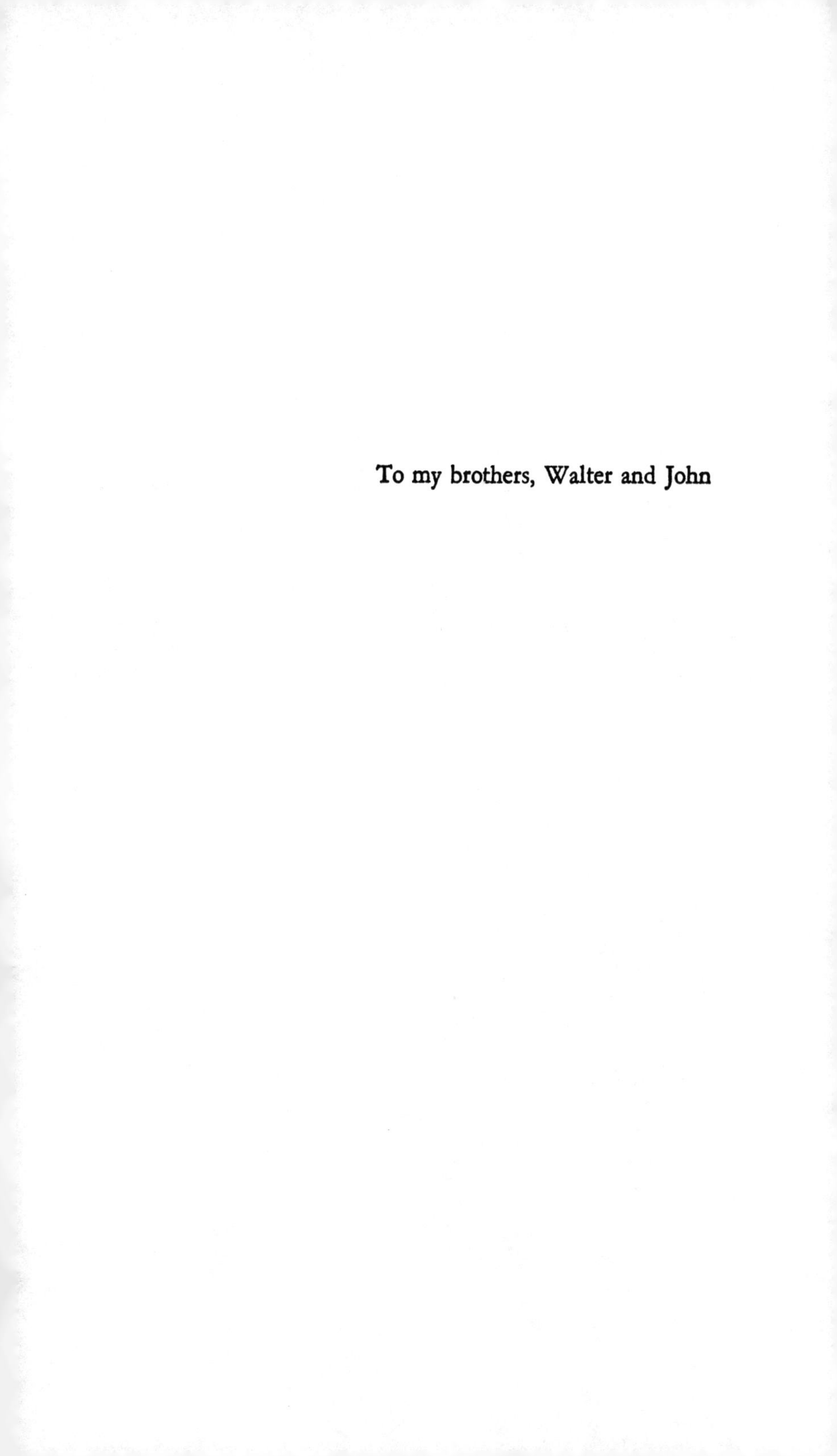

To my brothers, Walter and John

Foreword to the Great Lakes Books Edition

The Situation in Flushing is far more than visual entertainment. Edmund G. Love has given rebirth to the childhoods of countless readers, and particularly those who shared small-town backgrounds in the final years of America's age of innocence.

All of the marvelous incidents in this book occurred before the advent of World War I; before the intrusion of the automobile in massive swarms; and before the invasion of printed materials in such quantities as to hump the backs of postal workers. This book concerns a small town in Michigan which was still in charge of its daily affairs, and in a very real sense it is history with a tender touch, nostalgia with a loving embrace.

When *The Situation in Flushing* first appeared some two decades ago, I wrote that it was a better book than *Tom Sawyer*, and a recent rereading has done nothing to reduce this rather bold summation. For this is not only an engrossing account of a young lad's attempts to understand the adult world which was even then full of strange swirls and complications but also a great piece of reporting—of getting complicated facts in orderly array and presenting them in fascinating detail.

Some of these facts have been stored, no doubt, in newspaper files and the records of the village, but they have been buttressed, they have been given new life by the vivid memories of a boy who was barely six and one-half years old when the Armistice was declared. One catastrophe—an all-night village fire—occurred within my witness when I was approximately the same age, and I saw all of it, from the beginning fireball in the back of a garage to the explosion of a can of beans as an inquisitive native poked in the smoldering remains of a grocery store the next afternoon. The fire wiped out what little prospect of fortune my family had. Yet I would not be able to write of it with the clearness of Edmund Love, who stood on a street corner while much of the Flushing business area burned, leaving his post but twice. Listen, briefly . . .

"As darkness settled in, the sky became a brilliant red. People from as far away as Lennon, Montrose, and Flint could see it. Word had gone out to the towns by telephone and telegraph and many of the townspeople had already started for Flushing to help. As the glow in the sky further advertised the village's desperate plight, farmers and other people who had not yet heard of the fire became aware of it. People streamed along the roads toward Flushing in cars and on horseback and in buggies. The evening passenger train from Saginaw was held at Montrose for fifteen minutes while citizens of that village clambered aboard with fire extinguishers, axes, shovels, brooms, and pails. At Brent Creek another fifty fire fighters got aboard from the surrounding countryside. Later that evening the northbound train from Durand and Lennon brought a hundred fire fighters. The streets of Flushing were filled with running, shouting, grim-faced people. Long lines of men passed buckets up from the riverbank to put out smaller fires. Some of those lines were two blocks long."

That is excerpted reporting from the memory of a boy who stood by Fred Graves's barbershop while surroundings important to him were engulfed in flames. Chapter Six runs for fifteen fascinating pages, and if there is a better illustration of "remembering" how an event happened, and who did what when, and the cries in the night, and the concern, and alarm, and true grit of villagers and those who come to assist them—well, I haven't read it.

Chapter Fourteen is in much this same heroic vein, although it deals with the memorable day in 1921 when there was a series of train wrecks of varying degrees of intensity on the Grand Trunk railroad within the environs of Flushing. There is no justice in life. I lived an entire boyhood in Liberty Center, Ohio, hoping to see one mere derailment on the Wabash Railroad, whereas Edmund Love saw six in one day. Listen, again for the memories of a youngster who was obsessed with all phases of railroading . . .

"While the second special was taking water, northbound extra number 2265, which was to pull 2315 on the track, whistled for the crossing south of town. I went over to stand in front of the depot where I could see it better. It came slowly around the bend and drifted almost to a stop as it approached the Team track switch, its white flags blowing in the breeze. The head-end brakeman was hanging from the cab ladder and he dropped to the ground and ran ahead of the engine to throw the switch. When he raised his hand in signal there was a belch of smoke from the stack and the engine nosed slowly into the siding. Number 2265 felt its way through the weeds of the unused track, chugging leisurely downgrade, the fireman leaning far out his window and peering backwards to catch the signal of the brakeman when the caboose cleared the switch. The engineer had one hand on the throttle and one hand on the brake and his eyes were glued on the fireman, waiting for the relay of the signal. . . . Something made the engineer look around and he saw the depot looming up before him. He had run out of track. He jammed in his throttle and applied full brakes. . . . Unfortunately, there were weeds on that track and the weeds were slippery. When the brakes were applied, the wheels locked and slid along. There didn't seem to be any change of speed at all. The cowcatcher scooped up the tie from the end of the track and the engine and tender slid right out into the roadway that ran around the depot. It came to halt in a cloud of dust."

Thus, another snippet from a highlighted day in *The Situation in Flushing* involving brilliant reporting from memories preserved over long and eventful years.

There is much more to *Situation* that has endeared it to one generation of readers and promises similar enjoyment to owners of this reprint. It is a grand recollection of events, places, and implements no longer common in today's society. And it comes from the typewriter of an author who has always been sensitive to all facets of the American scene.

Wayne State University Press is to be commended for this revival, and others contemplated. A great president once told us that knowing where we had been was important to where we were going, and here in charming detail is a facet of our history.

Judd Arnett
Detroit Free Press
April, 1987

Preface to the Great Lakes Books Edition

Americans seem to have a preoccupation about small towns. Some of our best literature has been written about them. Mark Twain's *Tom Sawyer* and Thornton Wilder's *Our Town* are good examples. Both of these authors loved the places they wrote about. And the fascination has not worn off. In the last year or so *Lake Wobegon Days* has roosted at the top of the best-seller lists for many weeks.

The Situation in Flushing was written twenty years ago. I wrote it shortly after my father's death in 1962. He left me his papers and among them I found a picture I had drawn in 1921, when I was in the fifth grade. It was full of peculiar-looking little steam engines. It was not unique because I spent most of my boyhood drawing pictures of peculiar-looking little steam engines, but in this particular picture there were more of them and some of the little steam engines seemed to be in trouble. When I first saw this picture I wondered why my father had saved it all those years. After a while I began to wonder what had prompted me to draw it in the first place. So I methodically went to work jotting down all I could remember about one day from my boyhood. It soon became apparent that some of those little steam engines were indeed in trouble. And so had my father been in trouble at that moment. Shortly after the events were straightened out, I put them down in narrative form and showed the piece to my editor, Elizabeth Lawrence Kalshnikoff, of *Harpers'*. She wanted more reminiscences, and I wrote them. The original chapter eventually became Chapter Fourteen in the book and if you want to know what kind of trouble everyone was in, you'll have to read that chapter.

The Flushing that I knew and wrote about no longer exists. Like Mark Twain's steamboats, the little steam engines of the Grand Trunk railroad have long since disappeared from the scene. There are still a few farmers living within driving distance of the town, which is now called the city of Flushing, but I doubt if there has been a horse within the corporate limits for forty years. And I'm certain that no small boys have been allowed to ice down a hill in winter since I left. But this does not mean that Flushing has lost all of its charm. A tornado and the Dutch elm disease has taken its toll of the lovely trees that I wrote about, but the lawns are still green and there is a neatness and a serenity about Flushing that are gone from most of America.

I go back to Flushing often and I walk around the streets that I ran around when I was small. Within what used to be the village limits, the same houses still stand—most of them. The same buildings are still in place in the downtown although most of them now serve different purposes. Most of the growth has taken place in the area outside Flushing. The farm where my grandpa Perry and I burned stumps on Saturdays now supports ranch houses and split levels. But the railroad still runs through the town, although most of the sidings where Burt Emans used to switch back and forth with me ringing the bell have been dug up. The water tank where all the trains stopped is gone, too, and diesels go roaring through pulling a hundred cars or more, but I guess it is enough to know that this little old plug line is probably more prosperous now than it was in my day. I don't think it will disappear soon. And because it is still there a person can stand in front of the depot and see the same vistas I saw seventy years ago.

Flushing, which was born two years before Michigan became a state, is celebrating its birthday along with the state by publishing the second volume of its historical series and restoring the depot, which suffered a devastating fire a few years ago. Each year, for a long time now, the city has thrown open its more historic houses to the public. These have included the house where I was born and brought up. The chicken coop is gone from the back yard and the outhouse, of course, and someone has uprooted the old hitching block beside the back door.

The remarkable thing about Flushing is that the ghosts still watch over it. It was the people who lived there who made Flushing unique. Joe Gage and J. B. French and Tom McKenzie, the blacksmith, and John Egan and Ira T. Sayre all lived here and they are all buried up in the cemetery along with Roy Simpson and Sate Parmelee and my father and mother and Grandpa Perry. There was a lot of love and good will and humor in this little town and this is what I remember best about it and what I wish all the people who pick up this book and read it will remember about it.

Somewhere, sometime, sixty or seventy years from now, some American will sit down before his word processor and write another book about the town he grew up in. I hope his memories are as good as mine are and that his town will be as wonderful as mine was.

If I may be forgiven I should like to add one little footnote to all this. People often ask me how I came by the title for the book. At the time I was working on it, I was busy reading a book by Jean Paul Sartre in which he told about his boyhood growing up at his grandfather's place in Alsace. Sartre was as impressed with his grandfather's library and its books as I was with the Grand Trunk railroad and its engines. As I read Sartre's book, I kept thinking how different life was in Flushing and yet how similar it was because Sartre was beguiled by a fascination as deep as mine. He called his book *Situations*. It seemed appropriate to borrow it. It almost became a trend. When Thomas E. Dewey was working on his memoirs a few years later, he told me, he used the title *The Situation in Owosso*. He said it kept reminding him of what he was supposed to be writing. Bruce Catton, a good friend of mine, told me once that he was writing *The Situation in Benzie*. It turned out to be *Waiting for the Morning Train.* You can see how catching this idea of writing about growing up in small town is.

I hope a lot more small boys—and girls—grow up in small towns and write about it. It can be a pretty fascinating business.

Edmund G. Love
January 21, 1987

PHOTOGRAPHS

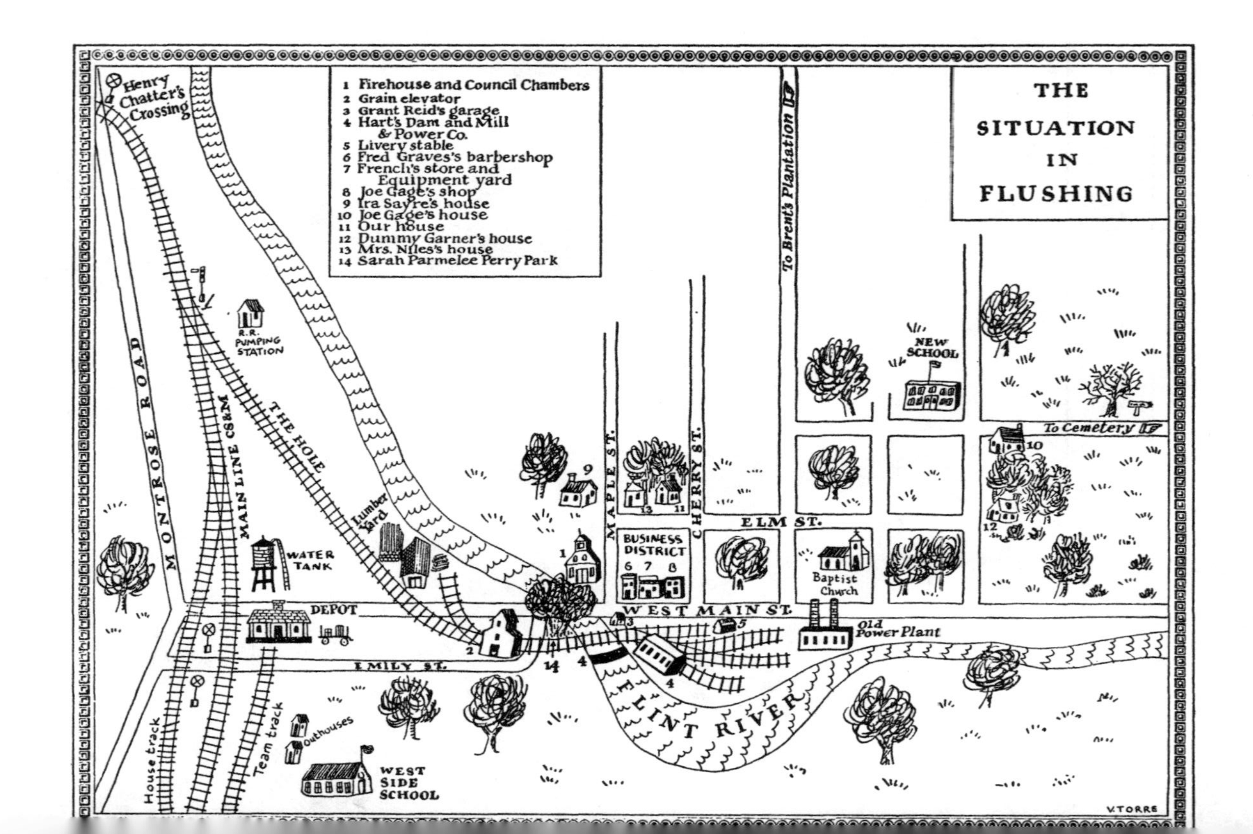
THE SITUATION IN FLUSHING
1 Firehouse and Council Chambers
2 Grain elevator
3 Grant Reid's garage
4 Hart's Dam and Mill & Power Co.
5 Livery stable
6 Fred Graves's barbershop
7 French's store and Equipment yard
8 Joe Gage's shop
9 Ira Sayre's house
10 Joe Gage's house
11 Our house
12 Dummy Garner's house
13 Mrs. Niles's house
14 Sarah Parmelee Perry Park
Henry Chatter's Crossing
MONTROSE ROAD
MAIN LINE CS&M
THE HOLE
R.R. PUMPING STATION
Lumber Yard
WATER TANK
DEPOT
EMILY ST.
House track
Team track
Outhouses
WEST SIDE SCHOOL
MAPLE ST.
CHERRY ST.
ELM ST.
BUSINESS DISTRICT
WEST MAIN ST.
Baptist Church
Old Power Plant
FLINT RIVER
To Brent's Plantation
NEW SCHOOL
To Cemetery
V.TORRE

Edmund Love at five years old.

Edmund Love's father standing next to the William Love Lumber Company in 1915, the summer he bought it from his father.

The famous wreck of number 2310. (Photo courtesy of the Railroad History Museum, Durand, Michigan.)

Walter, father Earl, John, and Edmund, Christmas 1919. Edmund was seven years old.

The West Side school, where Edmund went to school from the fourth to the seventh grade.

Engine number 2297, "a famous goat," pulled manifest freights through Flushing, usually at night.

Joe Gage at the command of the Flushing Fire Department, 1920.

THE SITUATION IN FLUSHING

CHAPTER ONE

THIS BOOK started out to be a story about locomotives and a small boy who wanted to grow up to run one. But when I began to write about my love affair with the railroad, it turned out to be impossible to disentangle the story of the town I lived in and the people I knew, so I haven't tried.

I was born into a world that ceased to exist almost as soon as I came into it. In the first twelve years of my life rural America was swept away as completely as though it was a picture on a blackboard that had been suddenly erased. The technological revolution that had been creeping into the large cities for some time flooded through the country. It came so suddenly and the changes were so thorough that most people didn't realize that the old way of life had gone.

At the time of my birth, in 1912, the village of Flushing, in Michigan, was still in the horse-and-buggy age. There were only five automobiles in the whole village. The coal wagon, the dray wagon, the milk wagon, and the grocery cart were all drawn by horses. The business block on Main Street was lined by iron hitching rails on which I used to play skin the cat and perform other gymnastics. It would be difficult for me to say just when it was that the automobiles outnumbered the horses and buggies on Main Street. The farm wagons disappeared one by one and the cars took their places, but I have always felt that I looked up one morning and found it all different. There were no horses and buggies left. Instead of five automobiles in the town there were five hundred.

It was only when I sat down to write this book that I realized that the change in Flushing coincided with the years I lived in the town, and that I couldn't write about those years without letting it creep in. Perhaps the most logical place to start is with Sarah Parmelee Perry, because she typified the spirit of the old world in Flushing.

Sate Parmelee Perry died in Arizona in April, 1916, and her body was brought home to Flushing for burial. Funerals were never sad affairs in the village. After the mourners returned from the cemetery, someone would always ask the inevitable question, "Who got stung today?" The pall of gloom would lift immediately as the memory of some dignified person swatting a bee was invoked.

The caretaker of the Flushing cemetery was a man named Roy Simpson. Roy was a kindly man, solemn of countenance and soft-spoken, as befitted a man of his calling. He had moved in from a farm to take the job of caretaker in about 1896 and he had brought his bees with him. He put the hives in long rows out behind his house which was adjacent to the cemetery. Flushing's cemetery was a pleasant place. It was covered with trees and flowering shrubs and every week people put out bouquets to mark the graves. It was certainly a great place for bees. The bees in Roy Simpson's hives shuttled back and forth to work among the blossoms and they thrived. Roy had a great feeling for those bees and he used to talk as though he understood them and knew each one by name. At some point he began to worry that they might be getting a little overworked. He decided to make things easier for them. So that they wouldn't have so far to commute, he got into the habit of taking a hive or two over to the cemetery each morning and leaving it there all day. As time passed he moved more and more hives and sometimes he would just leave them there overnight. It was natural that the bees came to believe that the cemetery belonged to *them*. Mourners at funerals began to be stung while they stood at graveside. At first one or two mourners would be stung, then three or four. When Sate Parmelee Perry got home from Arizona on her last trip she almost didn't get buried. There was an unusually large number of mourners at that funeral and some of them spilled over into the bees' domain. The bees declared war and several people were driven screaming from the premises.

Shortly after the near debacle at Sate Parmelee Perry's funeral, the village council summoned Roy Simpson to its weekly meeting and informed him that he would have to get those bees out of the cemetery. Roy reluctantly moved his hives back over to his house, but people kept getting stung at every funeral. For the next several years, the first item on the agenda at every weekly council meeting was Roy Simpson and his bees. He claimed that he had no way of keeping individual bees out of the cemetery, but it wasn't long before someone discovered he was moving a few hives over among the trees every time the village entered what seemed to him to be a particularly healthy period. He got caught every time because people were dying of heart attacks and other sudden onsets of mortality, even in those quiet days. For most of my boyhood the principal duty of Frank Wilcox, the town constable, was to go up to the cemetery on the night before a funeral and see if Roy had removed all the hives.

Roy Simpson never gave up the struggle for his little charges despite threats, warnings, cajolings, and orders. Every Saturday afternoon he would go down and stand on the corner by Fred Graves's barbershop near the iron bridge that crossed the river on Main Street. From that vantage point he would somberly look over the populace as they went about their business. All the families that looked in good shape could count on finding beehives in their part of the cemetery for the next week. Roy was as poor a prognosticator as everyone else, however, and it never ceased to be a risky business to go to a funeral in Flushing. It was the only town I have ever known where the funeral director regularly mounted a guard to keep the mourners from being wounded.

Sate Parmelee Perry was my grandmother and her husband, my grandpa Perry, lived to be ninety-one years old. When people used to ask him for the secret of his longevity, he had a stock reply.

"I don't *dare* die as long as Roy Simpson is running the cemetery," he said. "My friends would never forgive me for it."

Roy Simpson was only one of the individualists who inhabited Flushing. He made living a sort of game. So did Oren Hart. At the time of Sate Parmelee Perry's death, Oren Hart was an irascible old tycoon of ninety-four who rode through town in a wheelchair at high speeds shaking his cane at people to get out of his way. Oren was the village's principal businessman, who also built a dam across the river about two hundred yards south of the old iron bridge on Main Street. For many years he used the water power to run a sawmill and a huge grain elevator. As the timber gave out, he converted the sawmill into an electric power plant and Flushing became the first small town in the state to have electric lights. Flushing's blessing was not entirely a godsend. The power plant was not the best in the world. Things were always going wrong with it, especially in the summertime. When the water in the river got low, the dynamos would only turn at quarter or half speed and the light bulbs would glow a faint orange. People always had to keep kerosene lanterns and a large supply of candles in the house. The village might have been able to live with this inconvenience, but Oren Hart himself was a hazard. He was notorious for his inability to get along with people. At one time or another he fought with everyone in Flushing and at the first harsh words he would rush down to the power plant and cut off his antagonist's electric lights. In 1912, when

Flushing voted dry, he made history of a sort by cutting off the electric lights in the Methodist church. He claimed that the ladies of the WCTU were interfering with his private life and so he had every right to interfere with theirs.

Sate Parmelee Perry was something of a character in her own right. For a long time after she died, people used to say, in a joking way, that her ghost was probably stalking the street with all the other ghosts that were rumored to be nearby. It has always seemed to me that the history of a town or locality is interesting in direct proportion to the number of ghosts it sets loose in the community. The village of Flushing is a veritable happy hunting ground. It is situated on the Flint River in the southeastern part of Michigan. The Flint River is not a long stream, being only seventy miles in length, but it is a substantial one. It has cut a deep valley that is green and pleasantly wooded. A part of the Saginaw Valley drainage system, it rises near the eastern border of Genesee County, flows westward across that county, and turns north near the western border to sweep down to Saginaw Bay. Flushing lies at the point where the river makes its great bend to the north.

For many centuries the Saginaw Valley of Michigan was considered the best of all hunting grounds. It teemed with game and was blessed with easily navigable waterways. At one time it belonged to the Sauks, an Algonquin tribe who lived peacefully within its confines. One dark night, toward the end of the seventeenth century, the Chippewa nation invaded it by stealth and massacred the Sauk warriors to a man. This treacherous act set loose several hundred ghosts in the area and they made life pretty hard for the Chippewas. Chippewa hunting parties disappeared without a trace and mysterious plagues and assorted disasters visited the settlements. It was not until the Chippewas sat down in solemn conclave with the departed Sauks that peace descended upon the land. According to legend, the Sauks demanded that the Chippewas keep the land holy. They could live on it in peace and use its resources only if it was kept sacred for all time.

The Chippewas took their vows seriously. During the years of their trust, they never allowed a white man to trade or settle in the Saginaw Valley area. Even the French-speaking *coureurs de bois*—most of whom were half-breeds—were kept out. As late as 1815 United States government survey parties were excluded and only the scantiest information was available. With more than half the Chippewa warriors dead in Tecumseh's wars, the Indians could no longer defend the hunting grounds. Under the terms of a treaty concluded by Lewis Cass in 1819, most of Michigan was thrown open to white settlement. It was not a one-sided treaty, however. With the departed Sauks looking over their shoulders, the Chippewas demanded and received hunting and fishing rights in perpetuity throughout the whole Saginaw Valley area. In addition, they reserved the most beautiful part of the valley for their people. Fifty thousand acres were set aside for a reservation. The present site of the village of Flushing was part of this reservation.

There was a good deal of uncertainty about the temper of the Indians for many years after Lewis Cass's treaty was signed. There was a natural reluctance to disturb the Chippewas in their hunting preserve. Although white settlements were made along the wilderness trail that stretched from Detroit up to Saginaw, pioneers did not venture out of sight of it. It was 1834 before anyone had the courage to explore west of that trail. This was thirty-one years after the state of Ohio was admitted to the Union and only two years before Michigan itself was to become a state—the rest of the territory being well settled. At a fairly late date, therefore, the Saginaw Valley was still a wilderness. It was a beautiful, verdant area with great stands of timber and much natural beauty.

The man who disturbed this quiet scene was a Virginia planter by the name of Thomas L. L. Brent. He had served as minister to

Spain in Jackson's first administration. He brought back a young second wife from Madrid, a Spanish countess forty years younger than himself. Brent's Virginia neighbors ostracized his new wife and, in a gesture of defiance, he decided to set up an estate in the wilderness. He was well known in Washington and among his friends was Lewis Cass, then Secretary of War. Cass suggested that Brent look into the unheld and unexplored land in the Saginaw Valley. In 1834 he came riding up the Detroit-Saginaw trail on horseback, bought a canoe at the tiny settlement of Flint and paddled down the river. Before winter set in he had made his own treaty with the Chippewas and had taken title to 70,000 acres of land, including most of the Chippewa reservation. The ghosts of the Sauk Indians were undoubtedly surprised at this breach of faith on the part of the caretakers of their happy hunting ground. There were stirrings in the forests. Brent proposed to log off the land, then sell it to people who came out from the East. He advertised in eastern newspapers for settlers and then set up his own establishment on the river about five miles below where the village now stands.

Brent's Plantation, as he called it, was nothing short of fantastic. He brought along his slaves and his horses, his carriages, his silver plate, his vintage wines, and his exquisite furniture. He had to build roads to get it all into the area. He erected a great plantation house, put a dam across the river, and constructed a flour mill and a sawmill at either end of the dam. The ghosts of the Sauks calmly watched from a distance and then made a ghost out of Brent. In the spring of 1839 the river flooded far beyond expectations. The dam washed out and several million feet of logs were swept down into Saginaw Bay. Shortly afterwards, the mills mysteriously burned down, one by one. With his funds all tied up in his huge land speculation, Brent was bankrupt. He was more than that. He had a son by his first marriage, who had established a liaison with the Spanish countess. Their love affair had been carried on throughout the three years after the family's arrival in Flushing. The two young people were content to go along as they were while the elder Brent established the empire they would one day inherit, but with the empire destroyed they decided there was nothing to retrieve but their love. On a summer evening in July, 1839, one or the other of them went into Brent's bedroom and murdered the old man in his sleep. The body was stuffed in a trunk and lowered out of a second-story window. A carriage drove up and the trunk was placed on the back. Brent's son and his wife disappeared in the night and were never heard from again. Brent's body was never found. The slaves lingered on for a while and then drifted away. One of them stopped long enough to tell the story of what had happened, but by then it was too late to do anything about it. The house stood, just as it had been left, furniture and all.

Brent's principal legacy to Flushing was his haunted plantation house. It was common knowledge in the village that the old man could be heard stomping through the house at night, bellowing out the names of his wife and son in the empty rooms. On my family's annual Fourth of July picnics, which were always held on the river flats at the plantation, it was part of my father's ritual to go up to the gaping windows toward evening and dare Brent to come out. I always went along to watch this exhibition of courage on my father's part, but I always stood well back behind a tree just in case the old man did answer the taunts.

Brent didn't even leave his name on the village he founded. By the time he died the settlers for whom he had advertised were flocking into the area. The honor of being the first permanent settler went to an Englishman from Devon by the name of John Paton. Brent had applied to the state legislature to have the town named Brent's Mill, but upon hearing of his death Paton asked that the name be changed to Albion. There was already an Albion in Michigan and the chairman of the legislative committee substituted the name of his home town, Flushing, New York. Flushing it stayed.

Brent's ghost had no influence, not even in the legislature, but the Sauks kept things under control. They saw to it that Sate Parmelee Perry took charge in Flushing. She was just the person to keep the happy hunting grounds happy in the spirit of the murdered warriors. She had a passion for flowers and green lawns and tall trees and she patrolled the village streets at all hours of the day and night with one purpose in mind, to keep the town beautiful. She would climb the highest elm tree in town to cut out a dead branch. If a householder wouldn't plant a flower garden, she would plant it for him. If his house needed painting, she was likely to show up one morning with a can of white paint and start in. Her aim was to shame the owner into doing what should be done. It was said that old John Paton stood and stolidly watched her paint his whole house and never even thanked her for it. Most people in Flushing were more appreciative of Sate Perry's efforts. Shortly after she was buried the village council set aside a little plot of land at the end of the old iron bridge on Main Street and named it Sarah Parmelee Perry Park. It bloomed with flowers throughout the summer.

I was four years old when my grandmother died. She had been in Arizona during most of my young life and I never really knew her, but I grew up in the atmosphere she had created and I have always had a great love for green hills and white houses and tall trees. That is always the way I remember Flushing.

CHAPTER TWO

THE NEXT person to get in trouble with the Sauks was Ira T. Sayre. He was a formidable adversary even for a dead Indian. Every morning, when I was a boy, Ira walked from his big house on Mary Street down to his office in the center of town. He was a huge man at that time, tall and getting very fat. He had jowls and his eyes seemed to peer out at a person with suspicion. He always wore a black hat, a black morning coat with a flower in the buttonhole, and a wing collar. He had striped, formal trousers and carried a heavy cane. He rarely acknowledged a greeting. Most certainly he never spoke to anyone first. There was a certain grimness about him and he carried his cane like a bludgeon. He had an air of authority and I think that if he had pointed that cane at the Red Sea it would have rolled back.

Ira Sayre was a lawyer. He had come to Flushing shortly after the Civil War and had married into the Niles family, the most prominent family in town. Using his father-in-law's prestige, he went into politics and was elected to the state legislature. He served there for more than thirty years before moving on to a brief term in the Congress of the United States. For nineteen of those years he was the majority leader of the legislature, and later its speaker. During most of his life he probably wielded as much power as anyone in the state of Michigan.

There was always a rumored taint of corruption about Ira Sayre. His era of power was coincident with the heyday of the lumber industry and the building of most of the state railroads. He was known as the railroads' man. All railroads in Michigan had to secure grants of right-of-way and other privileges from the state legislature. Routes, rates, and other matters of vital concern were constantly matters for public action. Ira Sayre had the final say in all these things. That he took good care of the railroads is attested to by the gold lifetime pass, good for transportation on any railroad in the United States, that he received upon his retirement. He was also paid an extremely generous retainer to handle legal matters for the railroads in Flushing, although it was well known that no legal matters would come up in that remote little village.

Ira Sayre brought the railroad to Flushing. If there was anything better calculated to disturb the serenity of the happy hunting grounds, a Sauk Indian couldn't have found a more disruptive instrument than a steam engine. Flushing's railroad was officially known as the Cincinnati, Saginaw, and Mackinaw (CS&M). It was built in 1888. It never came within three hundred miles of Cincinnati and it stopped two hundred miles short of the straits of Mackinac, but it got to Saginaw.

Saginaw was the most important city in Michigan in the half century after the Civil War. It was the center of the lumber industry, a great lake port, the seat of financial and political power, and a thriving metropolis. The CS&M connected this bustling city with the great Canadian railroad, the Grand Trunk, at the village of Durand. By using the CS&M and the Grand Trunk, shippers could save twenty-four hours between Saginaw, Chicago, and the west. Although the CS&M stretched for only fifty-four miles from end to end, it was alive with trains for twenty-four hours a day.

Flushing was lucky to have the railroad. It had to detour to get there. The official reason given for its coming to the village was to get at the water in the Flint River. It was impossible for the locomotives of that era to make the whole 54-mile run without refilling the water tanks and a stop had to be made some place. The truth of the matter is that the CS&M right-of-way parallels the river for most of its course and crosses at least one other substantial stream. A water stop could have been made at any one of several places along the line, and with less difficulty. The real reason why the railroad came to Flushing was a simple one. Ira T. Sayre raised his cane and said "Come!" The railroad came. The ghosts of the Sauk Indians went to work on the railroad first. They took care of Ira Sayre later.

A look at any map of the state of Michigan will reveal that, if the railroad had been built on a straight line between Saginaw and Durand, the CS&M would have bypassed Flushing by about five miles to the west. Furthermore, if that straight line had been followed, the roadbed would have traversed level ground all the way. It would have been easy to build and easy to operate. When the decision was made to detour into Flushing, the railroad left this level ground and dipped down into the Flint River valley. Having got there, it had to climb out again. This made an uphill and downhill proposition out of an otherwise simple thing. For forty years railroad men cursed the name of Flushing. As it was finally built, the CS&M railroad consists of two long stretches of straight track connected by a curve. The Flushing depot sits at the very deepest part of the curve and, incidentally, at the very lowest point on the line. Everything goes up from there.

The curve was no trouble at all. It was the grade that made railroading what it was on the CS&M. In both directions out of Flushing there is a two-mile, two-percent grade. That means that it rises two feet for every one hundred feet it travels in a horizontal direction. For a fast train on a straight track a two-mile, two-percent grade would not have caused much trouble, but on the CS&M it was a major obstacle. Almost every train that came into Flushing had to stop there. The passenger trains stopped to take on and discharge passengers. The freight trains stopped to take on water. In other words, they stopped just when they should have kept going. A train moving through town at a good speed could have negotiated the grades without difficulty, but all of them had to start from a standing stop and a lot of them didn't make the hills.

The CS&M was not one of Lucius Beebe's railroads. There wasn't a parlor car on it, nor a dining car. Most important of all, there was no such thing as a modern, powerful locomotive. The line was built at a time when the standard American locomotive was the so-called 4-4-0. (A pilot truck of four wheels under the front end of the engine for balance, four large driving wheels, and no following truck to support the cab.) These engines were light and the people who laid down the original rails did not have to construct heavy bridges or use heavy steel. Three years after the CS&M was built it was leased to the Grand Trunk. Rather than go to the expense of rebuilding the entire line with heavier rails and stronger bridges to accommodate bigger locomotives, the Grand Trunk elected to concentrate most of its lighter equipment in the Durand area. Eighty 4-4-0 engines were brought to the Durand roundhouse and served the CS&M. These were the locomotives I grew up with. The railroad men derisively called them "goats," but I thought they were absolutely wonderful.

If the operation of the CS&M was complicated by the grades out of Flushing, it was practically brought to a standstill by the goats. They had no power at all. On the best day they ever had they could not pull more than twenty-five freight cars on a level track—or eight passenger cars. The grades out of Flushing reduced the length of the average freight to fifteen cars and of the average passenger train to three cars. Various practices were adopted to offset these disadvantages. Most through freight trains were pulled by doubleheader engines. Even at that, the longest freight train I ever saw the goats pull through Flushing consisted of thirty-eight cars. Because the trains were so short, we had a lot more trains. There were times during every day when one train was scarcely out of town before another followed it in.

As far as I was concerned, the most interesting result of the complication of diseases from which the CS&M suffered was that every freight train came to Flushing twice. The freights all stopped about a mile out of town—on the downgrade. The engines would unhitch and run into the water tank. The firemen would climb up over the coal in the tender—I always called it the coal car—with their long hooks and reach out for the water spout and pull it over and shove it down into the hole at the very back of the car. When the water overflowed, the spout would be lifted out and swung back from the track. The fireman would drop the lid on the tank with a loud clang. The second engine would then move into position and the process would be repeated. After the engines were both full of water they would back out and hitch onto their train again. When they started they would be going downhill. By the time they hit the Main Street crossing on their second trip into town they would be roaring along at fifty miles an hour. This momentum was just enough to get them over the top of the grades going out of town. One of the most vivid memories of my boyhood is of lying awake at night and hearing those far-off engines laboring up the hills, their exhausts going slower and slower until they were out of earshot.

In spite of all the difficulties they encountered on the CS&M, the railroad men preferred to work that line rather than any of the others that emanated from Durand. This preference was based on the fact that men on the regular runs could do a day's work and still sleep at home and eat most of their meals there. John Reardon, the engineer on the daytime passenger runs, made two round trips to Saginaw each day and was still able to eat all three meals at home. It was said that the southbound evening passenger train was late only five times in twenty years because John Reardon's wife would have killed him if he wasn't home for supper on time. Because the CS&M runs were considered the most desirable and because the senior men in Durand always had the first choice of the runs they would take, the crews on the trains through Flushing rarely changed. Even the firemen and brakemen spurned promotion to engineer and conductor so that they could stay at the top of their respective seniority lists and thus pick the CS&M runs.

All of these veteran railroad men had idiosyncrasies that made the CS&M a little more colorful than it might otherwise have been. John Reardon had his own engine, number 2248. He never allowed any other engineer to touch it and he never touched any other engine if he could help it. When it was necessary for number 2248 to go into the shop for repairs, John Reardon would take a few days off. He had curtains on the windows of his cab and he had carefully painted the sash of those windows Chinese red. He spent the entire layover in Saginaw each afternoon polishing his engine and it always came down the track into Flushing looking as if it had just come out of the factory that built it. When number 2248 finally wore out, John Reardon retired.

Other engineers had their favorite engines, too, although most of them were not as finicky as John Reardon. Burt Emans used number 2315 on the local freight and he incorporated all the comforts of home in the cab. He had a big jug of coffee keeping warm on top of the boiler at all times. He had a clean towel and a razor strop and a mirror hanging from a steam pipe next to his seat. He had a soap tray hooked to another pipe. Quite often he would open a petcock in the cab, draw out a little hot water from the boiler, and shave. Now and then he would do some laundry. He would wash out a pair of gloves, a pair of socks, his towel, or a bandanna handkerchief and hang them out to dry on a clothesline that stretched above the boiler. All the regular engineers had their own whistles and they would tune them just as carefully as the concert master of a symphony orchestra tunes its instruments. When they had to give up an engine they had been driving for years and transfer to another one, they would carefully remove the whistle and install it on the new engine.

I was not aware that Ira Sayre had been instrumental in bringing the railroad to Flushing. Had I been, I most certainly would have felt more kindly toward him, for the railroad was the greatest single thing in my life. I do not know when I first became interested in it, nor do I know how old I was when the facts of its operation straightened themselves out in my mind. By the time I was four, however, I was so completely enthralled that I was playing train with everything I could get my hands on. I must have been five when I started visiting the depot regularly, and it couldn't have been much later than that when I began knowing one engine from another. When I was six years old I already knew enough about most of the engines to imitate their various whistles and draw pictures of them. I kept a list of them as soon as I was able to write. Flushing may have been a paradise set down in the loveliest part of Michigan to the grownups, but to me it was interesting because of those trains.

CHAPTER THREE

WHEN I WAS in the third grade, our teacher asked the twelve boys in my class what we were going to do when we grew up. Nine of the twelve said they were going to be locomotive engineers. The other boys may or may not have meant what they said, but I did. I loved the railroad and everything on it with a passion that has seldom been equaled.

I went to the West Side school. Flushing had two schools, one on each end of town, but the new school building (built in 1878) had room for only the kindergarten and ten of the twelve grades. The other two grades went across the river to the West Side school and from the time I entered the first grade, at the age of five, my grade was one of the two that were relegated to that place of exile.

The West Side school was the original school in Flushing township. It had been built before the Civil War. It was a one-story building of red brick and had two rooms. The larger of these rooms had two blocks of seats separated by a big open space in the center. The teachers' desks occupied this open space, one facing in each direction. The smaller of the two rooms, at the back of the building, was a recitation room. One grade would march in there while the other studied, then come back into the big room while the other grade went out to do its reciting.

The West Side school was a primitive building. It had no running water and no sanitary facilities. Electric lights and a furnace to replace the old potbellied stove had been added only a year before I started going there. Drinking water came from an ancient pump in the front yard. If a student wanted a drink of water he raised his hand with one finger extended. When recognized he would go out and hold one hand over the spigot while pumping with the other. When his hand was holding back enough water for his needs, he would bend over and drink from his cupped hand. If a student had to go to the bathroom, he held up two fingers and skittered out the back door. Two outhouses were perched on the very back of the school property and getting to them involved a walk—or a run—of half a block. Going to these outhouses in the wintertime involved some physical courage.

The best thing about the West Side school, as far as I was concerned, was the fact that it was located close to the railroad. The outhouses sat on a bluff that overhung the tracks at the very point where they made their turn southwest to Durand. From most of the windows of the school I could look up the tracks toward Durand for a mile or more. I could hear the northbound trains whistle for the crossing three miles away. I couldn't hear the southbound trains until they whistled for Henry Chatters's crossing just north of town, but that was still five minutes away. Even if I had been content to just sit and watch the trains out the windows, I couldn't have picked a better place to go to school. But I wasn't content to do just that.

The West Side school was just a half mile south of the depot. I could run out the back door of the school, duck down the bluff behind the two outhouses and be right on the tracks. From there I could run along the ties to the depot in less than five minutes. (It took me a little longer the other way because it was uphill.) School started at nine o'clock in the morning. It let out at quarter of twelve for dinner. It reconvened at 1:15 for the afternoon session, and dismissed for the day at four o'clock. This fitted exactly with the way the trains ran. The southbound morning passenger train was due at the depot at quarter of nine, just fifteen minutes before school began. The northbound morning passenger train was due at 11:56, just eleven minutes after we were dismissed for the noon recess.

In Flushing the depot was a good half mile from the post office in the middle of town so Charlie Thompson, a round little retired farmer had been hired to carry the mail back and forth to the depot. Every morning at exactly 8:30 he would carry the mailbags out of the post office and put them in his buggy. Once the mail was loaded into the buggy, he would unhitch his horse, climb into the seat, and start off at a slow trot across the old iron bridge and up the west Main Street hill. He would arrive at the depot, hitch his horse to a post around at the back, load the mail on the baggage wagon, then wheel it out beside the tracks.

My life was coordinated with Charlie Thompson's journey to the depot. It was my custom to rush out the front door of our house in the morning, dash across the street, and climb the wire fence around J. B. French's farm equipment yard. I would streak down the alley that ran through the yard, let myself in the back door of Mr. French's hardware store, race down the aisles and out the front door into Main Street. I would arrive at the post office and climb into Charlie Thompson's buggy just as he clucked to his horse. I never missed this connection, although I suppose Charlie *did* wait for me a few times. When we got to the depot I would help Charlie drag the mailbags out of the buggy and load them on the baggage wagon. Then, while he was wheeling it out to the tracks, I would duck into the waiting room, shinny up the wall, and reach around through the ticket window and release the lock on the door into the station agent's office. Once inside there I would rush over to the telegrapher's desk and look through the train passage book to see what engines had gone through town during the night. When anyone had forgotten to put down an engine number, as they sometimes did on the midnight Flyer, I reprimanded him. This didn't happen often after my first year of going to the depot, I can tell you.

By the time I had finished checking the operation of the railroad, John Reardon would be rumbling across the Main Street crossing. I would go out and talk to him while he oiled his engine. He seemed to like me because I never failed to inquire after the health of number 2248. He would crawl back up into the cab and sit down. In a moment Beans McAuslin, his fireman, would get the signal from Mr. Blades, the conductor, and reach up and pull the bell rope. John Reardon would pull on his throttle and number 2248 would chug slowly up the hill toward Durand. I would run along the tracks after it as fast as I could go, scramble up the bluff behind the school, and usually settle into my seat just as the last bell stopped ringing. On a snowy day when the drifts were deep I was often slowed down, but I managed to keep from being marked tardy by stopping in the outhouse and taking off my mackinaw. The teacher always assumed that I had been to school on time and had taken a little detour.

During the morning session of school, the only train to come to Flushing was the northbound local freight. This usually waited for John Reardon in Lennon, the next town to the south, and then came on north. I knew number 2315 almost as well as Burt Emans, the engineer, did, so I never felt it necessary to check closely on this train. I preferred to save my emergency procedures for the afternoon. However, if number 2315 had been turned into the shop for repairs and there was a substitute engine, I felt justified in taking the necessary steps. I could tell a strange engine as far away as I could hear it. The minute Burt Emans blew the whistle on one of these strangers for Morrish's crossing, three miles away, I had my hand in the air with two fingers up. When the teacher noticed me and nodded, I would let myself out the back door and run for the outhouse. Instead of entering it, however, I would duck around behind it and slide down the bank to the railroad tracks. I would usually arrive there just as Burt Emans came panting up to the switch at the south end of town. While the brakeman was unhitching the engine from the train, I would be talking up to Burt in the cab, finding out all I could about the new engine. When he moved on into town to start switching, I would scramble back up the bank and return to school.

When we were dismissed at quarter of twelve, I was out the back door and running. I usually made it to the depot just as the northbound passenger train came around the bend at the south of town. I would check with John Reardon to find out how number 2248 had survived the thirty-mile round trip to Durand, talk a little to Mr. O'Brien, the railway mail clerk, and then, as the train chugged up the north grade out of town, I would help Charlie Thompson load the mailbags into his buggy. Upon arrival at the post office I would help drag the mail in and wait until Frank Perkins, the postmaster, opened the first-class bag. If there was a special delivery letter in it, and there usually was one, Frank would get down the clipboard with the delivery sheet, hand the letter and the board to me, and I would go off at a run to deliver it. I got eight cents for delivering each special delivery letter and I think I delivered every one that came to Flushing from the time I was six years old. I made as much as ninety-six cents in some weeks and that was a lot of money for a boy my age. Most of the time I considered myself independently wealthy. I've since come to believe that I may have been the youngest employee the United States Post Office Department ever had.

By the time I'd delivered the mail and got home for the noon-time meal, the rest of the family was just sitting down. Although we all sat around the dining-room table for dinner, as we called it, there was no real formality about it and there were no penalties for being late. I would rush through the food put before me and run most of the way back to school, stopping off in the post office to drop the delivery sheet and collect my eight cents. The afternoon was always busier for me than the forenoon because there was a steady stream of trains. By that time the local freight would have finished most of its switching at the towns along the CS&M and the main line would be clear so that the chief dispatcher could release a flood of through trains. The northbound afternoon manifest—a fast freight with cars for Saginaw only—arrived first. The two engines unhitched for their trip to the water tank in full view of the West Side school. This train was usually pulled by number 2300 and number 2258. I knew both of those engines well and I never bothered to do anything more than look out the window at them. (The second engine of a doubleheader never whistled, so I had to look to make sure that a stranger didn't slip by. Even if there was a new engine, I didn't do any more than look because I knew it would be back in town on the southbound manifest late in the afternoon.)

The afternoon extras were the trains that played hob with my schooling. Sometimes two or three of them would go by in the course of an afternoon and they were always pulled by engines that I knew little about. The minute I heard a whistle my hand would go up and I would duck for the back door. The funny thing about all these visits to the outhouse was the fact that my teachers never seemed to realize exactly what was going on. For five of the seven years I attended the West Side school one of the two teachers was my aunt Esther and she finally got so worried about my frequent trips to the outhouse that she told my mother my kidneys ought to be checked. My mother put me in the family car and drove me over to Flint to see Dr. McKenna, our family physician. When I got into the room alone with the doctor and he started asking me questions, I had to tell him the truth. He sat down in his chair and laughed. Still laughing, he rolled up the top on his desk and wrote a note for me to take to my teacher. It said simply that I should be allowed to drink as much water as I wanted to and that I should be allowed to go to the bathroom as often as I wanted to, until further notice. This was an unexpected boon to me because it turned out that I could go and watch trains on either one or two fingers. Dr. McKenna died in 1960 at the age of ninety-six, and for all the rest of his long life he never failed to inquire gravely about my kidneys.

The minute school was over in the afternoon, I headed straight for the depot again. I usually got there about the time the southbound way train pulled in to take water. (The way train went north early in the morning and concerned itself only with seasonal chores. It hauled livestock on Monday, sugar beets in the fall, and sand and gravel in the summer.) The way train was followed closely by the southbound afternoon manifest, and finally by the southbound local freight.

Of all the trains on the line, my favorite one was that local freight. Although it switched around Flushing for two hours each morning, I rarely saw it close up during the week until it arrived on its return trip to Durand in the afternoon. Burt Emans usually brought his whole train right on down to the water tank at that time because he only pulled a few empty cars southbound. While Burt was oiling number 2315 and the fireman was taking water, I crawled up into the cab for the ride out to the south end of town. When the brief business of afternoon switching was done and number 2315 pulled up the hill toward Durand, my railroading was usually concluded for the day. I rarely hung around the depot until the evening passenger train came south. It arrived too close to suppertime, besides which fact I already knew that it would be pulled by number 2248 and that it would be right on time. Occasionally, when John Reardon took a day off and I heard a strange whistle, I would rush over and meet the train. Of course, by the time the trains began rushing through town in the late evening—there were a great many of them after the evening passenger train went north—I was already in bed. All I could do was lie there and listen to the whistles and wonder what I was missing.

Saturdays and other days when there was no school were always my happiest times. I was at the depot bright and early. The minute Burt Emans brought number 2315 into town and parked the less-than-carload freight car at the freight depot I climbed up in the cab and took my seat on the fireman's box. When the brakemen signaled that they were ready to start the day's switching I reached up and pulled the bell rope, then leaned out the window on my elbows like all enginemen did. As time passed I learned everything about an engine. I could read the various gauges. I knew what each valve wheel was for, and I knew the difference between the train brake and the engine brake. I stoked the firebox and I helped take water. I blew the whistle. I could couple and uncouple the cars on the train and I was taught how to bleed an air line. I knew all the hand signals. I talked the language that the trainmen used. I called a caboose a way car, the semaphore a red board. I knew what a brakeman meant when he set out a car or lined up a switch. I referred to the different kinds of engines as the railroad men did, as goats, jacks, uprights, stokers, Panamas, or pigs, not as 4-4-0's or 2-8-2's. I did errands for all the trainmen. I took Burt Emans's jug over to the hotel and had it filled with coffee. I bought sandwiches for Pete Ronald, one of the brakemen, and cigars for Mac Durfee, the other brakeman. I even helped Mr. O'Brien, the railway mail clerk, identify names when he couldn't make out the handwriting on the envelopes.

My complete absorption with the CS&M railroad had numerous benefits. There was the matter of prestige. I was never the best baseball player or football player in the village, but I always managed to get chosen first on all the teams because I controlled certain privileges. No other boy could get a ride in the cab of number 2315 without my approval and once they crawled up the iron steps of the engine they were under my complete control. When I took a boy to Burt Emans to get him a ride, Burt would consider the matter thoughtfully and then nod. "All right. You do just what George tells you." (All the railroad men called me George, for what reason I do not know unless it was because they called all small boys George.) Under such a blanket endorsement I could naturally let one of my friends ring the bell at the proper time or even throw a shovelful of coal into the firebox occasionally.

My life on the railroad had drawbacks, too. I am always surprised that I ever got an education at all. I was not content just to sneak out the back door of the West Side school. I spent a lot of my time in school drawing pictures when I should have been doing arithmetic or practicing penmanship. I think I must have drawn a picture of every engine that showed up in Flushing. All of them, from 2242 to 2321, were supposed to be the same, but I saw differences in them. When I drew number 2254, I made it swaybacked. That's the way it looked to me. The front springs on number 2283 were weak so that it looked like a hound dog sniffing along the rails. I drew it that way.

I suppose all this had some influence on my later life. Whether it came from my preoccupation with engine numbers or not, I have always had a phenomenal memory for numbers of all kinds. I can remember telephone numbers, license numbers, street numbers, and statistics. I never get on a bus, subway car, or train without automatically noticing the number of the car. But there is more to it than that. When I look back at my early life I find myself inclined to relate everything to the railroad.

CHAPTER FOUR

PEOPLE HAVE a tendency to write things into their childhood that were never actually there. Any child's memory is fragmentary at best. It's only precocious boys and girls who understand what is going on around them. They certainly have no sense of the significance of things. I was five years old when the United States entered World War I. I was six and a half when the war ended. The war was certainly the most important thing that happened in the world during the first twelve years of my life, but if I was to say that it touched me deeply I would be telling an untruth. I recall, vaguely, that I had a soldier's suit of some kind. And at some time during the war—I think I was in the first grade—we pulled pieces of cloth apart to make something for the soldiers. I have no idea what we were doing, but I can remember those little pieces of thread lying in a heap on my desk. Later in that same period we went through a month of wearing masks across our mouths so that we wouldn't get influenza. There were gasless Sundays and German spies who supposedly put glass in bread.

I've never been able to sort out all these things and put them in their proper places.

I can remember standing on a hill on a dark November afternoon and hearing the old steam fire whistle. I could see the waterworks from where I was standing and the plume of white steam from the whistle was the only bright thing in the landscape. I ran down the hill and across the old iron bridge and up to my house. I asked my mother why the whistle was blowing. She said the war was over. That was the false armistice. I don't know why, but I always associate that afternoon with the Turks. Somewhere I had just heard that the Turks had surrendered. I didn't know much about the Turks except that they were on the other side. When the real Armistice came shortly after that day, my father put us all in the family car and we went over to Flint to see the celebration. It was a sunny morning and the weather was warm. The crowds were large and there was a lot of noise and I saw some French flags, which I thought were very beautiful. A streetcar went by us with men riding on the roof of it. So much for Armistice Day.

All during World War I my friends and I played at war without knowing very much about it. There was a big peach orchard adjacent to the school. It had ceased to bear fruit and the trees stood in long rows, dead and uncared for. The soil was sandy in the peach orchard and it was easy to dig. By the end of the war we had dug a trench system that would have served the American Expeditionary Force. We spent a lot of our time in those trenches. We would go over the top and in the wintertime we would pelt the enemy with snowballs. Even the girls got in the game, serving as Red Cross nurses. Everyone wanted to be Americans, of course. We had a hard time finding Germans and for quite a long time we just pretended there were Germans. We finally persuaded one boy in my grade to be a German. He was Bill Layman, a hulking bruiser of a boy who had performed the incredible feat of failing both the first and second grades so that he was two years older than the rest of us. He was possessed of dark, bushy eyebrows which made him look like some of the Huns on the posters. Bill was a good-natured fellow and didn't want to be a German, but someone's uncle sent back a souvenir from the war. It was one of those shiny, black spiked helmets that the Germans wore. We agreed to let Bill wear the German helmet if he would be the German army. It was a big temptation and he accepted the deal. He began wearing the helmet all over town, everywhere he went, in school and out of school, in the peach orchard and out of the peach orchard. All of us got to calling him Kaiser Bill and for as long as I knew him—a good many years after the war—he was always Kaiser Bill. Bill had no trouble recruiting soldiers for the German army. His first recruit was his brother Oscar, who was also in our grade and had to do what Bill told him or get beat up. Oscar brought along his best friend, Art Ailing, the village tough. Art introduced the equivalent of the atom bomb into our war. He dipped his snowballs in water and froze them and the American army was soon beset by desertions. By the end of the war the German army was bigger than the American army. We just managed to hang on until the Armistice.

Here and there in this floating dream of related and unplaced incidents that was my early boyhood, a series of events took place that are still vivid and which I can pinpoint exactly. The first day that I can really remember from beginning to end was my sixth birthday, which came on the 14th of February, 1918. It had nothing to do with the war. It had to do with the railroad and the West Side school, the two most important things in my life at that moment.

The winter of 1917-18 was one of the bitterest winters that Michigan ever had. It started to snow in October and it snowed regularly every few days; by the first of February there were eight or ten feet of snow on the ground. The temperature was at zero or below for several months.

February is always a bitter month in Michigan, and that year it brought the worst weather in an already unprecedented winter. There were two heavy blizzards in quick succession during the first ten days and the temperature dropped to forty below zero at one point. Then, on the morning of February 11, when people were beginning to get back to normal, a third blizzard drove in from the north and proved to be the worst storm of all. It lasted for two full days and when it was done Flushing was isolated from the rest of the world. The roads were blocked and the telephone wires were down. For the first time since it was built, the railroad was forced to suspend operations. The last train through town was the morning southbound passenger on February 11. It didn't arrive until after noon and just barely made it that last few miles to Durand and safety. The only contact the village had with the outside world was that one thin telegraph line that stretched along the snow-covered tracks from Durand up to Saginaw.

Through the two days of the raging storm, Flushing functioned as normally as it could. Nothing like a blizzard ever stopped a Michigander completely. The schools stayed open and the stores on Main Street conducted business. My father wore his high-top boots, his mackinaw, and his fur hat to work instead of his business suit, but he went to his office.

The snow stopped falling and the wind stopped howling about noon on February 13. At dinnertime my father shoveled a path out to the barn and cleared away the snow in front of the doors so that he could get his car out. During the afternoon session of school the clouds drifted away and the sun came out. When I looked out the windows at the countryside, the snow was so bright that it dazzled me. Although the temperature was ten below zero, it never occurred to me or any of my schoolmates to stay inside and keep warm. After I plodded home through the snowdrifts that afternoon, I put on a few extra clothes, dug my sled out from under the back porch, and waded over to the Cherry Street hill to help build a new coasting run. I was still there on the hill at 5:30, even though it had got dark. It was just about that time that I heard a train whistle far in the distance.

I was well aware that there had been no trains for two days. I ran through a back yard to my own house and shoved my sled under the porch. The snow was much too deep to try cutting through Mr. French's farm equipment yard, so I ran down the middle of Elm Street, turned the corner on Maple, and headed for the old iron bridge across the river. I arrived at the corner of Main Street just in time to see Owen Mulcahy coming toward me in his cutter. He was sitting there in the seat all wrapped up in his huge bearskin coat and fur hat. His horse was blowing out jets of steam as he plodded along. There was no one else in sight on all of Main Street.

I got out on the edge of the roadway and Owen Mulcahy saw me and grinned. He flicked his whip over the horse's head and the animal broke into a trot with a jangle of sleigh bells. I turned and set myself and, as the horse went by, ran a few quick steps and reached out to grab the back of the cutter seat. I was almost yanked off my feet, but I hung on and nimbly jumped onto the runner. Owen Mulcahy looked over his shoulder to see if I was on and gave another flick of his whip. The horse moved along at a good fast trot now. We skimmed along, down over the bridge and out West Main Street with the snow flying. I wasn't frightened. I knew that the horse wouldn't hold that pace very long in the deep snow, especially when he started to climb the hill toward the depot. I was right. By the time we reached the railroad tracks the cutter had slowed down to a walk and all I had to do was step off the runner. I waved to Owen as he turned his horse for home.

The depot was almost completely dark as I waded across Main Street and approached it. The only light showing came from the bright bulb that hung down on the long cord over the telegrapher's desk. I let myself into the waiting room, shinnied up and reached through the ticket window to release the lock on the door to the station agent's office. I found Percy Benjamin, the telegrapher, standing beside the red-hot stove, his hands behind his back, looking somberly out the window to the south. I dragged the high stool over from the freight agent's desk and put it in place behind Percy, then climbed up on it so I could look out, too. I had only been perched there for a moment when a brilliant white light came edging around the curve at the south end of town. It came toward us very slowly and it was not until it got opposite the depot that I made out that the light was high up on the front end of a snowplow that was being pushed by two engines. Behind the second of the two engines trailed a caboose. The plow and the two engines and the caboose were completely caked with ice and snow. They didn't stop at the depot. They kept chugging on across Main Street and came to a halt at the water tank. A moment later the back door of the caboose opened and two trainmen climbed cautiously down the icy steps of the back platform and waded across Main Street, their lanterns swinging from their arms. They entered the waiting room with a great stomping of feet and came into the station agent's office.

Ordinarily the firemen scrambled back over the coal in the coal car when it was time to take water, but that night they didn't. Both of them climbed down out of the engine cabs carrying huge torches and axes. They chippd big chunks of ice off the steps of their respective engines, then both of them went to the back of the coal car of the first engine and chipped the ice off the ladder that led up the back of it. When they had the way cleared they climbed up and chopped away the ice around the tank cover. They reached over with their long hooks for the water spout, but it was frozen in place so they shouted something and threw one of the torches to the ground. The engineers, who had now crawled down out of the cabs, picked up the torch and held it up against the water spout. In a moment the spout swung free and the two firemen carefully pushed it down into the hole on the coal car.

The two trainmen inside the depot waited until the water started to flow, then told Percy Benjamin they wanted to send a telegram back to the dispatcher in Durand, notifying him they had got as far as Flushing. When Percy sat down at his telegraph key, the two trainmen went over to the stove, took off their big mittens, and held out their hands. The lanterns still hung from the crooks of their arms by the big hoops, giving off the faint smell of kerosene. I watched the engines through the window. Two engineers were probing into every little nook and cranny of the locomotive with torches and oilcans. The firemen finally lifted the water spout and shoved it back from the coal car of the first engine, then crawled to the ground. Each of them climbed up into the cab of his respective engine and slid back the windows on the engineer's side and looked out. Each gave a short warning blast on the whistle and the two engines moved slowly forward so that the second engine would be in position to take water. The firemen slid the windows shut and climbed down to the ground again to repeat the chipping process on the coal car of the second engine and the engineers resumed their probing with torch and oilcan.

Percy Benjamin was still sitting in front of his telegraph key waiting for an answer to his message when the water taking was finished. Each engine gave a short whistle warning and then backed across Main Street slowly and came to a stop directly in front of the depot. The big numbers on the side of the coal cars were barely visible through the ice, but I could make them out. One engine was number 2310. The other was number 2279. I remembered this very well because I called them off to Percy Benjamin and he wrote them in the train passage book. For the rest of my life in Flushing I used to get that particular train passage book down off the shelf in the baggage room and look at those two numbers and try to remember what they looked like that night.

The engines stood there in the dark, steam and smoke swirling down around them occasionally, red spots from the roaring fireboxes glowing in the night. The cab windows were tightly closed against the cold, of course, and huge canvas curtains hung down from the roof of the cabs to close the open passageway between engines and coal cars. While the two panting engines stood out there in the darkness, the telegraph key began to click. Percy Benjamin took the pencil from behind his ear and began to write in that clear, beautiful hand of his. When the clicking ceased, he tore off the sheet of paper and handed it to one of the trainmen. They looked at it and muttered something about having to stop in Montrose to send another telegram and then one of them asked Percy about the cut north of town.

"Snow's drifted twenty feet or more in back of Henry Chatters's barn," Percy said.

One of the trainmen whistled and shook his head.

"We'll never get through there with this rig," he said.

The cut to which the men had referred was a deep excavation about a mile north of the depot. In order to keep the tracks of a railroad from going up and down like a roller-coaster, construction men dig through a hill or build causeways across ravines. When they dig through a hill it is known as a cut. When they build a causeway, it is known as a fill. The cut north of Flushing, behind Henry Chatters's barn, was the deepest on the whole CS&M, the tracks lying twenty feet below the brow of the hill. From either side of the rails the ground sloped up steeply and evenly. A person standing behind Henry Chatters's barn looked down on the trains as they passed by. In a blizzard the winds filled the cut with snow.

The two trainmen were plainly skeptical about being able to push the snow out of the cut. They pulled on their mittens, turned up their lanterns, and walked out of the office into the darkness. They went to stand beneath the engine cabs and the windows slid back and heads leaned out to talk down to them. One of the firemen handed down an ax and the two trainmen spent several minutes chipping ice off the steps of the caboose, then handed the ax back up to the cab window. The windows slid shut and the two trainmen climbed up onto the platform of the caboose and went inside. The whistle on the first engine gave two short blasts and the second engine answered it. The bright headlight on the front of the snowplow flashed on and the train chugged slowly off into the snow to the north.

I was still watching the twin red lights on the back of the caboose when the telephone rang. Percy Benjamin picked it up and answered it, then turned to me.

"Your mother wants you to come home to supper," he said. My mother always knew where to find me.

I trudged down the Main Street hill in the deep snow and across the bridge and up to my house. As I went in the door I could still hear the engines chugging slowly in the distance.

After supper that night I was allowed to go coasting until bedtime, but I never got over to the Cherry Street hill. As I let myself out the back door I heard a train whistle out south of town. It wasn't a familiar whistle and I knew it was nowhere near time for the evening passenger train to go north. I ran for the depot. There weren't any cutters to ride on this time and the snow slowed me down as I climbed the Main Street hill. I found Percy Benjamin locking up the door of the depot. He told me there would be no more trains that night. The snowplow hadn't been able to get through the cut back of Henry Chatters's barn and had gone back to Durand to pick up an extra engine. They would try again the next morning. That was the situation on the night before my sixth birthday.

I had certain small chores assigned to me at that time. They involved getting up very early in the morning. We had a hired girl by the name of Mrs. Parks. She came from over near Brent Creek and she wasn't any girl at all. She was a dour, hatchet-faced widow and was a Seventh-Day Adventist. She usually sat up half of every night with her feet in the oven of the kitchen range, reading the Bible. She disapproved of almost everything that went on in our family and I think she blamed the coming end of the world on the way we lived. Most of the time she wasn't even on speaking terms with my parents, but she got the work done and she put up with me because I brought in her firewood and water.

Mrs. Parks's alarm clock went off promptly at six o'clock on the morning of my birthday and the first thing she did was to stumble into my room and shake me awake. I climbed sleepily out of my nice warm bed, grabbed up my clothes, and groped my way down the back stairs to the kitchen. By the time I got there, Mrs. Parks was already standing in front of the range in her long, white flannel nightgown. She was grouchily poking up the embers of the fire and had put new wood in. The teakettle was already warming on the open back hole. Upon my arrival Mrs. Parks turned abruptly and gave her attention to getting me dressed. My mother had been putting up with my efforts to dress myself for some time, no matter how misguided those efforts were, but Mrs. Parks was having none of that nonsense. When she dressed me the whole operation took about five minutes from long underwear to earmuffs. She plunked me down on a chair to pull on my stockings, yanked me to my feet to pull on my pants, spun me around to button up my shirt, stood-me-still to pull the sweater over my head, then pushed me back down again to lace and buckle my high-top boots. It was a flurry of action in which no one said a word. When I was completely accoutered, Mrs. Parks stood me up and aimed me in the direction of the back door. By the time I put my hand on the knob, she was already on her broomstick, flying up the back stairs to get her own clothes on.

My first chore was to bring in the firewood for the kitchen range. On that morning, as I stumbled out the back door, still rubbing the sleep out of my eyes, I was brought to attention by the sound of a train whistle. This was not a remote whistle. The train was right in town and it was whistling for the Main Street crossing. What was more, it was moving fast, like one of the manifests that had already taken water and was getting up speed for the run up the grade out of town. I stopped to listen. My first reaction was one of rage. I was quite put out that the CS&M had sneaked a snowplow through town in the middle of the night after Percy Benjamin had promised me that it wasn't coming until morning. I had been counting on getting up to the depot before school to watch it go through. Not only had the snowplow gone through, but here was a fast freight on its way. I knew that by the time I got to the depot there would be two or three more and that I would miss them all.

I didn't know it but the train whistle I heard *was* the snowplow's engine. The engines pushing the plow had come into town and had taken water. They had then pushed forward to the cut behind Henry Chatters's barn and had run into the drift that had stopped them the night before. Even with three engines the plow had stalled, but it had pushed well into the drift by this time and it seemed as though it might break through with one more effort. The engines backed up into town and through it to the grade on the southern outskirts, almost three miles from the drift. Then, after getting a good start, they came roaring down through Flushing. By the time they reached Henry Chatters's crossing they were doing close to fifty miles an hour. When I stepped out the back door that morning the engines were in the middle of their headlong rush.

I listened to the roar of the locomotive exhausts for a moment, then walked down off the back porch to the woodpile. Grabbing an armful of firewood, I went angrily back into the house. I was in the kitchen for perhaps two minutes. When I came out onto the back porch again there was no noise at all. In that short space of time, Flushing's only train wreck had occurred. The snowplow was a caboose-type car made of wood. When it hit the drift, instead of knifing through it, the plow crumpled into kindling wood. The first engine behind it ran right through it and slammed into the drift which was packed solid now, like a wall of ice. The second engine climbed right up on top of the first engine, hung there for a moment, and then toppled over. The third engine went straight up in the air and stayed there, its cow-catcher pointing up to heaven.

Henry Chatters's hired man was in the barn milking cows when the accident occurred. The barn abutted on the tracks, only a few yards from the crumpled engines. The hired man ran out to see what had happened. He pulled one of the injured engine-men out of a snowbank and carried him up to the house, but it was a good fifteen minutes before Henry Chatters put in a phone call to my grandfather Love, who was then president of the village, and notified him. It was to be ten minutes after that before most people in Flushing knew. My grandfather told Addie Badger, the telephone operator, to start calling doctors and others who would be needed, but it all took time.

While all these things were taking place, I was busy carrying wood into the house, first for the kitchen range and then for the fireplace. When I had finished, Mrs. Parks was back in the kitchen. My second chore of the morning was to go up to Mrs. Niles's pump on the corner and bring back a pail of water. Mrs. Parks took the dipper out of the pail, put the leftover water into the big copper kettle on the back of the stove, and handed the empty pail to me. She also took the steaming teakettle off the back hole and handed it to me. The boiling water was for me to pour down Mrs. Niles's pump, which was usually frozen at that time of the morning. I got the little box sled out from under the porch, put the pail and the teakettle in it and plodded out our driveway and down the unplowed sidewalk to the pump.

By the time I started out for the water, my grandfather was organizing. His first thought was to get the doctors out to the wreck. To that end he had routed my cousin Durward out of bed with orders to go out to the barn and hitch up the mare to the cutter. Because of the prolonged snowfall the roads out of town were impassable to automobiles. The doctors would get up to the depot as soon as possible and the cutter would be waiting for them there.

It was still dark and before I even reached the pump that

morning I was aware that something unusual was happening. Lights began to go on in all the houses around me. As I filled my pail, Dr. Blakesly's car came roaring down Maple Street and disappeared around the Main Street corner onto the bridge. When I approached our house I found all the lights on, even those in the front parlor. This never happened in the night unless someone was sick or unless there was a fire in the town—the only two emergencies I could think of. I hurried around to the back and nervously lifted the water pail out of the box sled and carried it up the back steps. Mrs. Parks was waiting for me and she grabbed the pail out of my hand before I got to the back door, then snapped at me to hurry up and get the teakettle. I went back and brought the teakettle up to the kitchen door and she grabbed that, ran to the stove with it, and filled it full of boiling water from the pan she had simmering on the stove. As she did so, my father came out through the pantry door and grabbed it. He was dressed in his big hunting boots, his fur hat, and his mackinaw. He brushed by me with the kettle of water and ran down the back steps and out along the path he had cleared to the barn. He slid back the barn doors and went in to pour the hot water down the radiator of the car. In a few moments I heard the agonized grind of the self-starter and, after what seemed a long time, the roar of the motor.

My father was a reckless driver under any circumstances, but that morning he was more reckless than usual. He backed out of the barn so fast that he almost knocked down Dunn's woodshed. He turned his wheels, shifted gears with a grind, and stepped on the accelerator. The tire chains dug into the deep snow and spun as the car inched forward. I ran down the back steps and went to stand on the hitching block beside the driveway as the car fought its way toward the street. My father saw me standing there and stopped as he came abreast of me, leaned over, and spoke to me through the little flap on the side curtain. He told me to go get the teakettle and to close the barn doors. I asked him where he was going.

"Over to Grandfather's house to get his cutter. There's been a train wreck," he said.

A train wreck? *A TRAIN WRECK!!!*

"I want to see the train wreck," I yelled.

"It's no place for little boys," he said, and put the car in gear again and roared out of the driveway, slewed into the street, and disappeared.

I think I hated my father at that moment. It's a wonder I didn't tear the barn door off its track. I stormed into the kitchen in a fine pout and almost threw the teakettle onto the stove. I got no sympathy at all from Mrs. Parks. She had work to do and she was doing it. She had already reached her midmorning speed and was bustling about the kitchen at a dog trot, lifting things here, putting them down there, slamming the cupboard doors, and talking to herself. Nothing short of the coming of the Lord would have slowed her down. As I followed her back and forth across the kitchen, the telephone rang in the pantry. My mother came through the swinging door from the dining room to answer it. Mrs. Parks thought that the telephone was one of the Devil's own instruments and wouldn't touch it. My mother was always annoyed at this and on this particular morning she was almost cross. She told whoever it was on the other end of the line that she already knew about the train wreck and that my father had gone to take the doctors out to it. By the time she finished saying this my two brothers had pushed through the swinging door and were standing beside her, pulling at her old blue bathrobe. She had been dressing Walter in front of the fireplace when the phone rang and he was still in his long underwear and bare feet. My youngest brother, John, was wearing his long nightgown. After she'd hung up the receiver my mother picked John up and shooed Walter ahead of her back through the door. I followed along behind and went to stand in front of the fireplace. There ensued a long dialogue during which I let my mother know that I wanted to go to the train wreck. My mother said very little, but I *do* remember that she said train wrecks were no places for little boys—this was becoming almost a litany—and that I had to go to school. My brother Walter interrupted this conversation from time to time by squirming down off my mother's lap and by insisting that *he* wanted to go both to the train wreck and to school. I reminded him that he was not yet four years old and that when he got to be as old as I was he would *hate* school. I also felt it necessary to tell John to shut up. He was jumping up and down and clapping his hands and saying "Me, too" to everything.

The telephone rang again and my mother sighed, got up, and went to answer it. Yes, she said, she'd heard about the train wreck. After she'd hung up, she turned the crank on the side of the phone and lifted up the receiver again. She told Addie Badger that if anyone else wanted to tell her about the train wreck to tell them that she already knew about it.

To the accompaniment of my pleading, which had become a whine by now, my mother finally got Walter dressed and put John in his high chair. Then she bustled about the kitchen, dodging Mrs. Parks, and got some breakfast ready. I sat at my place at the dining-room table eating my oatmeal and still muttering about not being allowed to go to the train wreck. My mother had no time to pay any attention to me. She was spooning food into John's mouth and keeping a wary eye on Walter, who had a tendency to throw his breakfast around the room. Just at the end of the meal, Mrs. Parks stuck her head through the pantry doorway.

"Do you want me to make the c-a-k-e, or do you want to do it?" she asked my mother.

"I'll do it," my mother said.

I sat there, screwing up my face and mulling c-a-k-e over for several minutes. I'd heard that word before someplace. I suddenly sat bolt upright in my chair.

"Cake!" I said. "Why can't I go to the train wreck on my birthday?"

I don't think my mother had considered *this* argument at all. She stared at me for a long moment and it was about that time that the phone rang. I knew from the way my mother talked that my father was on the other end of the line, so I stuck my head into the pantry and asked again that I be allowed to go to the train wreck on my birthday.

I had made a point with my mother. She shooed me back out of the pantry and closed the door tight, but I listened at the crack. She reminded my father that it was my birthday and that I was crazy about the railroad. She didn't think there would be another train wreck in Flushing in my lifetime and she thought I ought to see this one. My father invoked all the old arguments about small boys only getting in the way, and about my missing school, but my mother was a strong advocate. When she came back from the pantry she told me that Mrs. Gage was going out to Henry Chatters's farm to cook a meal for the men who were working on the wreckage and that Joe Gage was going to take her and a load of groceries out in my grandfather Love's cutter. He would pick me up.

My mother devoted the next half hour to getting me properly dressed for a morning out of doors in zero weather. She put so many sweaters on me that I could hardly move and she finished by wrapping a scarf around my face as though I were a mummy. When she was all done, she stood me up in the front hall for a final inspection. She then added one more touch. She got the old lap robe out of the closet, folded it carefully, and draped it across my arm.

Having made certain that I couldn't possibly freeze to death, she now took the time to give me a meticulous set of instructions. I was to go down to the corner of Main Street by the bridge, next to Fred Graves's barbershop, and stand there. Joe Gage would load the groceries into the cutter and then drive past the corner to get me. I wasn't to leave the corner because, if I did, Joe Gage might miss me and I wouldn't get to see the train wreck.

"Now, remember," my mother said as I turned to go out the door, "you're to stay on that corner. You are *not* to go into the barbershop."

My mother felt this last sentence to be absolutely necessary. She had been having a feud with Fred Graves for more than a year. My brother Walter had beautiful black curly hair and it was my mother's pride and joy. Fred Graves had been itching to get his hands on that hair. He thought it made Walter into a sissy. One day Walter decided he was grown up and he stalked into Fred Graves's barbershop as he had seen the men do and asked for a shave and a haircut. Fred Graves wasn't going to miss an opportunity like *that.* He put Walter in the chair and cut off the curls. When her shorn son came into the house that night, my mother wept. She went down and told Fred Graves what she thought of him. Not more than a month after that *I* went into the barbershop for some reason or other and Fred Graves told me a dirty story. I was only five and I didn't know a dirty joke from any other kind, so I went home and told it to my mother, four-letter word and all. That was the end of Fred Graves in our family. When my mother went to see him *that* time she took my father's shaving mug off his wall, and my grandpa Perry's too. All of us knew better than to go into Fred Graves's barbershop again. I wouldn't have gone in it that morning if I was freezing to death.

I let myself out the door and trudged through the snow down to Main Street. I was so heavily bundled that I couldn't turn my head. I arrived at the corner without incident and planted my feet on the sidewalk. Fortunately, I was out of the wind so it wasn't too cold. From where I stood I could see everything that went on in the business block. Only one automobile was abroad that morning, but I could look up the street and see my grandfather's horse tied to the rail in front of the grocery store. I even saw Joe Gage come out once and put an armload of groceries in the cutter, then go back inside.

Fred Graves's barbershop was the center of every piece of news and gossip in Flushing. If you stood near the door you could hear people discuss everything that was going on in town. All the men stopped on the corner every morning on the way in and out for their morning shave to pass on the latest information to the people they met. Shortly after I arrived at the corner that morning, a train came rolling into town from the south. I soon learned, by eavesdropping, that this was a rescue train. Flushing had no hospital, being a small town, but Durand had one. Shortly after the wreck had occurred, Tom Bulger, the station agent, had telegraphed Durand and had told the chief dispatcher that several men had been injured and needed hospital care. The dispatcher immediately sent out an engine and baggage car to bring the men back to Durand. This was the train I heard going through town. It was to pick up the trainmen at Henry Chatters's house, where they were being cared for. As soon as it got back to Lennon, a wrecking train would come to Flushing to clean up the mess.

I must have arrived at the corner about quarter of nine. Fifteen minutes after I got there I heard the school bells tolling in the distance. I hadn't given much thought to school until I heard the bells. I suddenly felt very triumphant. I imagined Mrs. Crosspatch (her name was really Mrs. Leroy) standing in front of the class and looking down at my empty seat with a frown. If there was anything Mrs. Crosspatch didn't like it was for one of us to miss a day of school, and here I was going to the train wreck and she wouldn't be able to do anything about it.

I was still gloating when the fire whistle started to blow. Art Phillips, the school janitor, had come back in from ringing the bell to find the whole basement in flames. In his absence coal gas had exploded and had blown the furnace door open. Flames had leapt out and quickly kindled the tinder-dry old wood of the basement ceiling. Art had turned in the alarm at once.

Flushing had a volunteer fire department and in 1918 the

equipment was very primitive. It consisted of a two-wheel hose cart and a rickety old ladder wagon. The fire chief was the same Joe Gage who was supposed to pick me up and take me out to see the train wreck. When the fire whistle blew, the various volunteer firemen were supposed to drive to the village firehouse. The hose cart and ladder wagon would be hitched to whatever cars arrived first. Because Fred Graves's barbershop was close to the village firehouse, Fred was the key to most of the fire fighting in town. He kept his fireman's hat and raincoat hanging next to his barber chair and when the fire whistle blew it was his job to run around the corner, open the firehouse doors, and trundle out the two carts to hitch onto the first car that arrived. (Fred lived above the shop and every night when he went upstairs he would hang the hat and coat beside his bed.) On the morning I was standing on the corner, Fred put down his razor, grabbed his coat and hat, and rushed out the door. He brushed by me, whirled around the corner, and got the firehouse open. A car came slewing down Maple Street in the snow, stopped briefly to pick up the hose cart, and sped away. Before it was out of sight across the bridge, the ladder wagon had been hitched to the second car and was following it. All I had to do to see this was to sidle around the corner away from Main Street. People came pouring by me from every direction. I knew, almost at once, that the fire was at the West Side school because I heard someone shout the news as he passed. On any other day of any other year, I would have been overjoyed at this, but on that morning I was so preoccupied by a much more fascinating disaster—the train wreck—that I was hardly excited.

I have no idea how long the initial excitement lasted. People were running by me and across the bridge. Now and then a car or a cutter skidded past. Then, just as suddenly as it had all started, everything was quiet. The stores were empty. The streets were deserted. If anyone had been able to get into the village of Flushing that morning, he could have stolen the whole town.

There *had* been a complication, but that was quickly solved. Most of the able-bodied men in town were out at Henry Chatters's farm looking at the train wreck and among their numbers was seventy percent of the fire department. They had got out to the wreck by wading through the deep drifts for more than a mile and if they had tried to get back the same way it would have taken them more than an hour. Fortunately, the crew of the rescue train never hesitated. They signaled all the men to climb aboard the baggage car or the engine and within five minutes the train was backing rapidly into town to deposit everyone at the bottom of the bluff behind the outhouses that overlooked the track, less than a block from the school. They arrived even before the hydrant was thawed out.

While all the noise and excitement was swirling around me, I stood on the corner in some bewilderment. While I was around the corner, briefly, watching the activity at the firehouse, Joe Gage disappeared. At the first sound of the fire whistle, he had put down an armload of groceries and cranked up the telephone to find out from Addie Badger where the fire was. Then he rushed out the door, jumped in the cutter, clucked at the horse, and stormed down the street in a wild jangle of sleigh bells and a cloud of snow. He went past my corner while I was still watching the hitching of the fire carts. It wasn't until I moved back *around* the corner and looked up Main Street that I discovered he was gone. I knew he was the fire chief and I was pretty sure he had gone to the fire, but I hadn't seen him go and I couldn't be too certain.

I was vastly pleased that the West Side school was burning down. It was the one fire I wanted to see above all others, but there was that train wreck. I wanted to see that more than I wanted to see the fire. If I left the corner and went to the fire it might not be a very big one. I might get there after it was out and all the firemen would be gone—including Joe Gage. He would come to the corner, find out I wasn't there, and go to the wreck without me. I had something else to think about, too. If I actually went up to see the fire, the chances were that Mrs. Crosspatch would see me and shoo me right back into the school with the others when it was all over. *That* way I would miss the train wreck, too. I decided I had better stay where I was.

I stood on the corner at Fred Graves's barbershop in the cold in the middle of a town that was practically deserted. I can't describe, to this day, the agony I went through. At 9:45 I heard the rescue train back through town for the second time with its cargo of injured men. I squatted on the sidewalk and peered up the hill in an effort to get a glimpse of it. Just twice on that morning I weakened. Shortly before 10:30 I looked up toward the school and saw a column of dense black smoke rising in the air and I started across the bridge, determined to see the fire. Just as I reached the west end of the bridge I heard the whistle of the wrecking train as it moved slowly through town. I changed my direction and started toward the depot. I was halfway out Main Street, opposite the lumber yard, when I heard sleigh bells. I turned and saw a cutter crossing the bridge to the east. It looked like my grandfather's cutter, and it was, but Joe Gage wasn't driving it. My cousin Durward was taking the perishables back to the store so they wouldn't be frozen. I didn't know that, but I turned and hurried back to the corner and stood waiting. Nothing happened. Durward took the groceries into the store and then led the horse and cutter around the corner to the livery stable and left them there. He went back to the fire by taking a short cut across the railroad bridge and missed me completely. At shortly after eleven o'clock I heard the wrecking train come into town from Henry Chatters's farm to deposit the first wrecked engine on the siding by the depot. I started across the bridge again and this time I almost got to the depot. I was walking half frontwards and half backwards and I saw my father's car go slewing around the corner from Emily Street and across the bridge. He was on his way to the firehouse to pick up some more hose. I hesitated just long enough so that I missed him when he came back across the bridge. I had learned my lesson. I decided that I would stand on that corner until someone came for me. I did, too, all alone, with the blanket still over my arm. At 12:15 the wrecking train brought the second wrecked engine into town. At one o'clock people started to come back from the fire. At two o'clock the wrecking train came into town for the third time. It hitched the last of the three wrecked engines to the other two twisted hulks and pulled them off to Durand and the junk heap. Fred Graves came across the bridge in a car pulling the ladder wagon and helped push it and the hose cart back into the firehouse. Then he closed the doors and came around the corner and went into his shop, hung up his hat and coat, and began stropping his razor. At quarter of three there was another train whistle to the south. An engine came pushing a huge rotary plow across Main Street and kept right on going past the water tank. It came to the famous drift behind Henry Chatters's barn and waded through it with no trouble at all.

It was twenty minutes after three before my grandfather Love came walking across the bridge and up to the front of Fred Graves's barbershop to put an end to my vigil, the saddest birthday I ever had. He listened to my story and took me into Darby's poolroom for a sandwich and a piece of pie. Afterwards we went to the livery stable and got the horse and cutter and drove out to Henry Chatters's, but there wasn't anything left of the train wreck by that time, not even a scrap of kindling or a snowdrift. Nor was there anything to see at the school except broken windows and charred wood and a river of ice coming out the front and back doors.

There wasn't much anyone could do to console me for a long time after that. My mother had a big party for me with hot dogs and whipped-cream cake—my two favorite dishes—but I didn't care much for the whole business. I had missed the only two important things that had ever happened in Flushing.

CHAPTER FIVE

THE PEOPLE of Flushing had a curious attitude toward the West Side school. They were always talking about replacing it with a new building, but they had never quite got around to doing it. Now, when it was gutted by fire, they had a good excuse to build a new one. They didn't. They also had a good excuse to modernize the old building. They didn't. It was rebuilt exactly as it had been before, outhouses and all.

I have never been sure who was responsible for this, but I have always suspected that it may have been my grandfather Love. As president of the village council he ran the affairs of the village with an iron hand and it was just the kind of thing that was typical of him. He was a frugal man of Scottish descent, and he did not take kindly to change, especially if it involved the expenditure of money.

George Love's total schooling took him through the second grade. He learned to read and write and do simple figures. That was about all. I don't recall that he ever read a book in his whole life and he always exhibited a hearty contempt for education and educators. When I finally went to the University, he characterized it as a "waste of your God-damned time." He was brought up to the backbreaking work of a farm. He was one of eleven children, brought up in the central part of Michigan, and had helped his father clear a section of land before he was twelve. He left home to make his own way in the world at the age of fifteen.

Grandfather chose the lumber woods for a career. In 1871 the state of Michigan was in the midst of its great lumbering boom. Strong, sturdy men were in demand in the woods and my grandfather certainly fitted that description. He had grown up to be a bull of a youth, weighing over two hundred twenty pounds and standing six feet two inches. He was hot-tempered, quick with his fists, and possessed of prodigious strength. In these respects he never changed until the day he died. When he was seventy-two years old he was attending a baseball game in Flushing one Sunday afternoon and was standing near the edge of a chicken-wire backstop behind home plate. This backstop was supported by four-by-four fir posts. He had inadvertently taken up a position so that one shoulder stuck out from behind this backstop and during the course of the game he turned his head to look behind him for a moment. As he did so, the batter fouled a ball backwards which caught him squarely in the exposed shoulder. He hadn't seen where the blow came from, but his reaction was automatic. Without thinking or looking he doubled up his fist and swung. He delivered a right cross that caught the four-by-four at jaw level. The four-by-four snapped off like a toothpick and the whole backstop settled down around Grandfather's head. That was the kind of thing Grandfather did all his life.

The rules of the lumber woods were simple. The only way to settle an argument was to fight with fists. The man who could whip every other man in his camp or gang was the boss. For twenty years George Love was the king of the woods. Among the muscle men who cut down the timber of Michigan he was famous from one end of the state to the other. He held every job in the woods and he excelled at all of them, working the forests from the Saginaw Valley to the Upper Peninsula, always out of doors in all kinds of weather and always doing the hardest kind of physical work.

Grandfather was not the original Paul Bunyan, but he was a

legend in his own lifetime. He once upheld the honor of the lumbermen against John L. Sullivan. In the 1880's Sullivan made several barnstorming trips through the country. It was his practice to stop wherever anyone could be found to fight him. A purse would be put up by the townspeople and the local challenger would climb into the ring. If Sullivan could knock him down within four three-minute rounds he would take the purse. If the local man managed to stay on his feet, Sullivan would return the purse. If Sullivan was knocked down, he would match the purse and give the money to the local backers. In the course of one of his tours Sullivan invaded the iron-mining and lumbering country around Lake Superior. My grandfather was engaged in a logging operation near Big Manistique at the time and, after some persuasion, agreed to challenge the champion. The fight was held in Duluth on a bitter winter night and people were still talking about it in the Upper Peninsula in 1934. Grandfather knocked Sullivan down, all right, but Sullivan knocked him down, too, in what must have been one of the bloodiest short fights in history. At the end of it Sullivan returned the purse to the lumbermen who had backed it, but his pride was hurt. For the next five years he kept trying to get Grandfather back into the ring with him.

Grandfather was married to Ida Currens of Alma, Michigan, in 1881 and the first eight years of their married life were spent in the lumber camps where Grandfather did the bossing and Grandmother did the cooking—for fifty men. Somehow, during that eight years, Grandmother managed to bear two children. The older, a girl, was born in 1882. The younger, a boy, was born three years later. The boy was to be my father.

My aunt Edith was an adorable little girl with a light in her eyes and a smile of entrancing beauty. She was the greatest softening influence in my grandfather's life and the one person he loved above all others. It was because of my grandmother's gentle insistence that a lumber camp full of brutes who communicated in four-letter words was no place to bring up a little girl that

Grandfather gave up the life in the woods, at which he had always been such a success, when Edith was eight years old.

For five years thereafter Grandfather did a variety of things. He owned a saloon, he worked for the railroad, and he bought a lumber yard. His first two enterprises were hardly more edifying than working in the woods. He made money in the saloon, but his customers were all the same lumbermen with whom he had worked for twenty years. He spent most of his time throwing them into the street when they became obstreperous. And while he was ostensibly a brakeman on the railroad he was really a bouncer and had been hired to handle the roughnecks who rode back and forth on the trains to the north woods.

Grandfather's lumber yard was in the little Michigan town of Fowlerville. He moved his family there in the spring of 1894. At that time his daughter Edith had seemed to be in ruddy good health, but shortly after the move she began to ail. As she steadily grew worse, the disease was diagnosed as diabetes. There was no hope whatsoever for her. She lived into the spring of 1895 and then died. It was a devastating blow for Grandfather and, for the rest of his life, he seemed deliberately to hold back from giving his affection to anyone. On the day of her death, he is reputed to have taken a quart of whiskey, climbed into a horse and buggy, and disappeared for a week. He told my grandmother that he would never live for another day in Fowlerville, and he never did. He came driving into Flushing in his horse and buggy one day in 1895, walked into the lumber yard there, asked if it was for sale, and bought it on the spot with cash he was carrying in his pocket. Before summer was over he had bought a house and had moved his family into it. He lived in Flushing for the rest of his life. An interesting sequel to this story is that shortly after my grandmother moved into the house—within a day or two—she discovered she was pregnant with my aunt Esther. My grandfather always seemed to think this was a good omen.

The next ten years of Grandfather's life were just short of

incredible. He was a man with hardly any education, who had worked with his hands at hard physical labor for most of his life. He had little, if any, real charm or selling ability, yet he managed to build up a business empire that was worth well over a million dollars. He ran one of the first chain operations in the United States. Chains were not exactly new in 1895, but they were rare and the principles which have made them such a success in later years were practically unknown. Grandfather eventually came to own thirty-two lumber yards in Central Michigan, all of them moneymakers and all of them models of efficient management. Grandfather seems to have stumbled on the idea after he bought the Flushing yard and realized that he still owned the Fowlerville one and was making money out of it. The absentee management had not made any appreciable difference. He tried buying a third yard and it also made money. He was probably lucky, but he also realized that the real secret in an operation of this kind was in getting the right managers. He was one of the shrewdest judges of men in his area and he knew all the men in the lumber business. He had his pick of good men and he selected the best ones, and flourished.

It was shortly after Grandfather came to Flushing that he met Ira Sayre. In order to expand his holdings as rapidly as he did, he had to have outside capital. Ira Sayre furnished a good part of it and became a partner in the business. It was an uneasy partnership from the first and soon collapsed in a spectacular fashion.

Ira had come back to Flushing in retirement. He had built himself an imposing home on Mary Street and seemed content to practice law and engage in various business deals. Actually, he held tight to the reins of Republican party machinery in the county, and through it still exerted tremendous influence in the state. In the village, politics were conducted along party lines and Ira ran the village and used the party machinery there as the instrument of his control.

The operation of the lumber chain was a two-headed affair.

Offices had been set up in the county seat at Flint and Ira Sayre occupied them for several days a week, looking after the fiscal and administrative side of the business. My grandfather Love spent most of *his* time traveling around to the various yards. One May morning in 1905 Grandfather got off a train at the Flint depot and stalked up Saginaw Street to the Dryden Building where the offices were located. Without a word, he stepped in the door and yanked Ira Sayre to his feet. The first time he hit Ira, he knocked him right through a wooden partition into a doctor's office next door. Grandfather walked out into the hall, entered the doctor's office, picked Ira up, got him straightened out, then hit him again and knocked him through the wall into the dressmaker's next door. Big as he was, Ira Sayre was no match for my grandfather. Before that morning was over, Grandfather almost killed him. Ira was left lying unconscious in the wreckage of one whole floor of the Dryden Building. Having finished what he came to do, Grandfather walked back down to the depot and caught the first train to Durand, where there was a connection to Flushing.

Ira Sayre took six months to get over that beating. And, although he was a lawyer, he never instituted any kind of proceedings against Grandfather. What is more, *he* paid the damages to the Dryden Building out of his own pocket and they ran to $5,000, a considerable sum for those days. As for Grandfather, he never went near the lumber company or any of its yards again. The day after the fight he walked into the law office of Frank Sayre—Ira's brother, who scarcely spoke to Ira himself—and deeded the entire company over to Ira, thus divesting himself of one million dollars with a scratch of a pen. Neither Ira Sayre nor Grandfather ever said one word to anyone about this affair—why it happened or what had preceded it. Many years later, after Grandfather's death, my father asked Grandma Love why Grandfather had signed the company over like that. She said that Ira had already stolen it—and that succinct statement was all any of us ever found out about the whole business. Fortunately for Grandfather, the yards in Flushing and Fowlerville had never been included in the chain, so he continued to run them and make money out of them for many years.

The fight at the Dryden Building may have settled the affairs of the lumber company, but it only marked the beginning of a feud that was to last for eighteen years—until Ira Sayre died. The hardheaded Scottish stubbornness that was the basic trait of Grandfather's character would never let him forget what had happened. The utter defeat of his former partner came to be the only thing that he lived for.

Grandfather attacked Ira Sayre on his own ground—the political field. He joined the Democratic party. Up till then no Democrat had ever held office in the village of Flushing. By 1910, five years after Grandfather went to work, there were three Democrats on the village council. In 1912, with the help of Woodrow Wilson, all eleven seats on the council were taken by Democrats and my grandfather was elected president of that body. He ran the village with only one thing in mind—the ruin of Ira T. Sayre. He snatched all the choicest plums out of Ira's hands, one by one. By delivering the village's vote in the Democratic column, year after year, he thoroughly discredited Ira with the county Republican committee, and through that with the state committee. Grandfather did such a complete job that by the time Ira died he was scarcely remembered in the state of Michigan. It was almost incidental that the village of Flushing had the best municipal government in the area during those years. Grandfather was a conservative, frugal man and had little sense of progress, yet the only real advances ever made in the town were accomplished under his administration. New wells were drilled and the water system was improved. The new bridge was built across the river and Main Street was paved. The Fire Department was modernized and protection was extended to the whole township.

As a boy, I was only vaguely aware that my grandfather and Ira Sayre did not like each other. I knew nothing about their long-standing feud. If anyone had told me of it, I would undoubtedly have assumed that Grandfather was automatically right. I heard a great many stories about Grandfather and I can never remember a day when I was not impressed by him. I knew exactly what he believed in from the time I was very small. He believed in honesty, hard work, in fighting for the things in which he believed, and in thrift. He observed me with interest, but with very little affection, and he never lost an opportunity to impress upon me what it would take to gain his regard.

My grandfather was a rough-spoken man who didn't care how he looked. He lumbered about town in a purposeful way, a black cigar clenched between his teeth, the ashes forever dropping down his front. He preferred the company of men at all times and cared little about the social life of the town. Although he had practically given away a million dollars, he was still reasonably well off. He had made shrewd investments all his life. In 1915, when he reached the age of fifty-nine, he sold his Flushing lumber yard to my father and lived the life of a retired man. The Fowlerville lumber yard and the houses he owned provided him with an income. And at various times while he was lumbering he had bought tracts of logged off land. Now and then he sold some of this at a nice profit. He spent part of every day in Frawley's poolroom playing cards, and Frawley's had the roughest group of habitués in town. As he grew older he became more stubborn and grumpier and his black temper got him into all kinds of episodes.

There was the case of Sime Bresnahan. Sime was the one man in Flushing who approached Grandfather in physical strength. He was a huge Irish farmer who lived west of town and who dropped in at Frawley's several times a week to play rummy. For a long time people had conjectured what would happen if Sime and Grandfather ever had a fight, but because they were both

Democrats and rummy players, no one ever really thought it would come about. One day, about a year after he retired, my grandfather got out his old Mitchell car and started for Flint. The road was still a sandy trail in those days and once a car got out of the wheel tracks it was more than likely to get stuck. About halfway to Flint, Grandfather overtook a horse and buggy plodding leisurely along the trail. Sime Bresnahan was driving it. Grandpa blew his horn for Sime to get out of the way, but Sime chose to ignore it. Grandfather blew again and Sime still ignored it. Grandfather blew a third time and was again ignored. He then drove up behind the buggy and, after gently nudging against it, pulled down hard on the gas lever. The buggy toppled over in the ditch and Sime went sprawling. Grandfather stopped his car, got out, and went over to the upside-down buggy and helped the horse get back on its feet. By that time Sime had picked himself up and was ready for action. The fight that ensued lasted for half an hour. All through this time the two men took turns knocking each other down. There were no witnesses, but one man said later that it would have been worth a hundred dollars to have seen it. At the end of it both combatants were battered and torn and muddy. They finally sat down on the edge of a ditch, exhausted, and lit up cigars. After they had finished smoking, Grandfather helped Sime get the buggy back on its wheels, watched while he climbed into the seat, and then gave some instructions.

"You drive up the road," he told Sime, as Sime reported later. "In a few minutes I'm going to come up behind you and blow my horn, and by Jesus this time you'd better get out of the way." Sime did. The next day they were playing cards together, black eyes, bruises, and all, as though nothing had happened. Both Grandfather and Sime Bresnahan were sixty years old at the time this happened.

Grandfather had nothing to do after he sold the lumber yard except run the town. He wandered around the village, looking in on everything that was going on. Most of the time he just observed, but now and then he decided that people needed prodding. One summer my father was having a new roof put on one of his lumber sheds and Grandfather stopped by to watch. The longer he stood there the harder he chewed on his cigar and the blacker his scowl became. The roof boards were sixteen-foot shiplap and the carpenters would come down a long ladder from the roof, pick up two boards from the pile, put them on their shoulders, and climb back up to the roof. Grandpa spat and became fidgety and finally called my father over.

"These men are beating you out of a lot of money," he said.

My father asked how.

"Because they're only carrying two boards at a time up that ladder. I can carry more boards than that and I'm an old man and have a wooden leg."

An argument ensued with my father taking the part of the carpenters. No one was going to change Grandfather's mind and he irritated my father enough so that my father bet him $100 that he couldn't carry more than two boards up the ladder. Grandfather took off his coat, rolled up his sleeves, and went over to the nearest pile, which consisted of sixteen boards, hoisted them all to his shoulder, and started up the ladder. He got up as far as the fifth rung and the ladder gave way. The rung he was standing on broke and he fell to the next below, which also broke. He went right on down to the ground and when he hit the bottom his wooden leg shattered into pieces. We had to carry Grandfather off on a stretcher, but before he left he glowered at my father and told him that there'd better be a stronger ladder there that afternoon. He was taken to the hospital in Flint, where the stub of his leg was inspected for splinters. It was found to be all right and he bought a new artificial leg on the spot, paying an extra hundred dollars to get it adjusted and fitted by that afternoon. He was back at the lumber yard by four o'clock. He counted out sixteen boards, hoisted them to his shoulder, and carried them up the new heavy ladder. When he came down and had collected his hundred dollars, he said nothing at all to the workmen. He just glowered at them for several minutes, then left. After he'd gone they all started carrying six boards up the ladder at a time.

Grandfather's wooden leg is a story in itself. He was found to be suffering from diabetes. When he was advised by the doctors to observe a strict diet, he announced that he didn't *want* to live if he couldn't have the things he wanted to eat. He kept right on with his visits to Frawley's poolroom every day, where part of his ritual was the downing of four shots of whiskey in the back room. At home, he defiantly ate everything that was put in front of him.

One spring, while doing some carpenter work on one of his houses, he stepped on a rusty nail. Gangrene set in and for once there was nothing Grandfather could do to whip it. On a hot day he checked in at the hospital in Flint carrying a small black bag. He undressed, took a flannel nightgown out of the bag, put it on over his long underwear, and got into bed. Almost at once he was at war with everyone in the hospital. It started over the long underwear. The doctors and the nurses wanted it off, but Grandfather insisted that he had never gone to bed without it in his life and he was damned if he was going to start now. In the end it came off, of course. The actual operation took place at nine o'clock the next morning. Around noon that day, my father enquired by telephone to see if everything was all right. A nervous doctor assured him that the operation was successful, but suggested that my father come right over. When he entered the hospital room at one'clock, just four hours after the operation, he found Grandfather sitting up in bed, propped up by pillows, and in one of his blackest moods. My father didn't even have time to ask how Grandfather felt before Grandfather pointed at the little black bag which had been placed on a chair in the corner.

"Earl," he said, "open that bag and get me a cigar out of there.

The God-damned nurses tell me I can't have one, but I'm God-damned if I'm going to let any woman tell me what to do."

When my father looked in the bag, he found only a box of cigars. My grandfather hadn't even brought a razor. While my father was thinking about the implications of this, Grandfather sat there in bed puffing on his cigar in a very relieved fashion. When he finished, he looked at the stub and heaved a sigh.

"I feel better," he said. He put the butt in the ashtray, threw back the covers, and swung his legs, including the heavily bandaged stump, to the side. "Now let's get the hell out of here."

It took an awful lot of doing to keep Grandfather in the hospital for the required number of days. My father finally had to take Grandma over and get her a bed next door to him. Even then, he went through one of the most hectic periods of convalescence in medical history. He insulted the doctors and swore at the nurses and the whole staff of the hospital was more than glad to see him go home. The minute he got into the house he began insisting that he be fitted for an artificial leg. When he was finally convinced that this was impossible, he had himself taken down to Frawley's poolroom in a wheelchair. It was less than a week since the operation, and there he sat at the card table, banging the cards on the table with such force that the glasses jumped. He was in such a nasty mood during that first month he was home that no one in town dared cross him. Certainly the regulars at Frawley's didn't dare do anything so rash as to win a game of rummy from him.

The truth of the matter was that Grandfather had suffered the first real defeat of his life, and I suppose he did just what other people do under similar circumstances. He took his frustration out on others. He seemed to feel that he still might win out if he persevered. The people of Flushing soon learned that they were not to make any slighting remarks about his leg, but now and then someone would forget and the fireworks would start. One night someone at Frawley's had a drink too many and taunted Grandfather about it. He threw the man bodily into the street and then, just for good measure, he threw everyone else out the front door, too. That was one of the few times my grandmother ever became really angry at him. She reminded him that it was unseemly for a sixty-four-year-old man to brawl in public places. She didn't speak to him for a week until he promised that it wouldn't happen again.

Although Grandfather's proneness to fight anything or anyone at any time was the mark of his long years in the lumber camps, he was in most respects a typical small-town resident of his time. The house he lived in on West Main Street was a large, substantial one. Behind it stood a big barn. Like most people of his generation, he was not entirely sold on the automobile. He kept a horse, and in the wintertime he depended entirely upon his cutter. His car would be put up on blocks in the fall and left there until the snow melted in the spring. He was never a good driver and he always treated a car as though it was a balky horse. Whenever he was behind the steering wheel, one could see him fighting it. If anything happened on the road, he always blamed it on the car, not on himself. He had a long history of trouble with cars. His first car, a Mitchell, he bought in 1915 and it was the only one he ever liked. After it wore out, he was never satisfied with any other. During the last thirteen years of his life he had twenty cars. It would take him three months before he started swearing at a car and another three months before he got rid of it. He bought a Buick. One day he parked it on a hill and didn't set the brake firmly. It started to roll and ended up in a creek. Grandfather would never buy another Buick because "the brakes are no damned good." The radiator on a Marmon he owned boiled over, a common occurrence in those days. He called Marmons "God-damned teakettles" and would never buy another.

One of the first cars Grandfather bought after the Mitchell died of old age was a Ford roadster. Grandfather was almost as big as the Ford and when he was riding around in it he always looked as if he was going to overpower it. His head bumped against the top and his hand seemed ready to crush the steering wheel if he squeezed it. It was quite a sight to see him crank that Ford. He would step up to the front of the car and spin the crank so fast that one expected the roadster to flip right over on its side. One day he was spinning it and the car sputtered and backfired. The crank kicked back and broke his thumb. It would have broken anyone else's arm. Grandfather looked down at his thumb in some surprise, then at the crank. He reached down, yanked it out of the front of the car, reared back, and threw it through the windshield. Then he walked around to the side, bent down and grabbed the running board and lifted. The Ford flipped over into the ditch like a toy. Grandfather then walked to the nearest telephone and called Bill Frawley, the Ford dealer. "Come and get your God-damned tin lizzie," he said. He never owned another Ford and wouldn't even ride in one.

After he got his wooden leg he began having real trouble with his driving. His foot kept getting tangled up in the pedals and there was a long series of minor accidents. Everyone knew better than to try to get him to stop driving, so the whole family joined in to do it subtly. When the signal went out, someone always showed up on some pretext or other. They wanted to try out the new car or they thought they needed some fresh air. By one means and another Grandpa was kept out of the driver's seat a lot of the time. Nothing serious happened for several years. Then the Flushing High School organized an orchestra and entered a county contest in Flint. Grandfather volunteered to help out with the transportation. No one trusted him with the students, but he was allowed to take a carload of instruments. He had just bought a brand-new Studebaker and wasn't quite used to it. About halfway to Flint his wooden leg got tangled up in the accelerator and he couldn't get it loose. While he was bending over, trying to disentangle the leg, the car ran head on into a tree and they dug Grandfather out of the wreckage with a bass viol smashed over his head. Miraculously, he received only minor injuries in this accident, but it so happened that a state trooper was a witness to it and Grandfather's driver's license was revoked. He fought this action for the last years of his life the same way he had fought Ira Sayre. He lived long enough to see Franklin D. Roosevelt elected as President of the United States and to see a Democrat elected governor of Michigan. He took the position that it served the Republicans right for revoking his license.

For all of his willfulness, Grandfather Love was a powerful and commanding figure. He could have prevailed in any age and against any adversity for he had courage and inner strength to go with his physical strength. His view of life was simple and uncomplicated. There was right and there was wrong. There was black and there was white. There was no such thing as compromise. He did not bestow his respect freely. A person could earn it only after a long hard trial. One of the few people who enjoyed Grandfather's high regard was the other man who had played a prominent part in the February train wreck and fire, Joe Gage.

Until 1912 Flushing had had no Negroes; for eight straight federal censuses, the population of the village is listed as "all white." Then, in the year I was born, Joe Gage came to town. He arrived there by chance. He was born in Wilkes Barre, Pennsylvania, in 1867, the son of a slave couple who had been freed during the Civil War. He was orphaned at the age of eight and by the time he was twelve he was a full-fledged coal miner. Joe wandered the United States until he was twenty-two, holding almost every type of job that was open to Negroes, but always ending up back in the coal mines. Then he gravitated to the St. Charles mines, near Saginaw, married, and settled down. He picked up extra money as a professional boxer. He was a welterweight, weighing about 145 pounds.

For many years, just before and after the turn of the century, boxing was illegal in Michigan, but so-called exhibitions were held in barns hidden in the woods, in the back rooms of saloons, or at the bottoms of quarries. Joe took part in about a hundred of these matches and once remarked that he spent more time running across fields to get away from deputy sheriffs than he did in the ring. He was not the best fighter in Michigan, but he was far from the worst, and he built up a solid local reputation in the Saginaw area.

When the restrictions against prizefighting were removed, the young men of Flushing decided to hold a boxing match. My father was well known in Detroit sporting circles and he took on the task of finding the fighters. He was a good friend of Ad Wolgast, then the lightweight champion of the world. Wolgast was training for his fight with Willie Ritchie. He felt that a four-round exhibition would sharpen him a little and as a favor to my father he agreed to come up to Flushing for a fee of $500, provided an opponent could be found who would not cause him too much trouble. Joe Gage was recommended by a friend in Saginaw.

The match was held on a Saturday night, early in the summer of 1912. I have never been able to find any record of it, but Wolgast won the fight handily, under an assumed name. After it was over he was driven to Flint, where he caught an interurban back to Detroit. Joe Gage was not so lucky. The fight ended after the last train had left for Saginaw and there wasn't another one until Monday morning. No one had thought to provide Joe with accommodations for the night and he went up to the depot, stretched out on the baggage wagon, and tried to sleep. He couldn't get comfortable, so he started to walk. By morning he had covered every street in town. It was a small village with heavily shaded streets and white houses sitting back on wide lawns. It was quiet and peaceful and cool and Joe liked it much better than the dirty mining towns in which he had lived for most of his life. The next morning he walked to my father's house and knocked on the door. My father was in the kitchen preparing the usual Sunday morning breakfast of pancakes and sausages. He talked about that visit many times in later years. He invited Joe to come in and eat. He brought a dish to the dining-room table with about thirty pancakes on it. My mother took three, my father took six, and Joe took all the rest. My father went out to the kitchen and cooked up another batch of thirty and the same thing happened. The third time he looked at Joe.

"This time, *you* cook," he said.

Joe got to laughing so hard he never ate another pancake.

Joe Gage wanted to live in Flushing. Before he left for Saginaw on the Monday morning train, my father and most of the other young men in the village had subscribed $25 each to finance a Flushing Health Club. Imbued with enthusiasm for the newly legalized sport of boxing, all of them wanted to be prize-fighters. Joe would teach them. He would give everyone in town lessons. In return for the money the original subscribers put up, he would give each of them five free lessons.

Joe Gage was forty-five years old when he opened the Flushing Health Club. He was a perfect physical specimen with lightning-like reflexes who could hit an ordinary man five times before taking a blow himself. He never learned to pull a punch and that was his undoing. Within four months of the time he opened his establishment he had knocked every young man in town through the ropes of his ring. It was very discouraging; the young men quit coming, and Flushing's first venture into physical fitness passed into limbo with startling rapidity. But by the time it disappeared Joe was already a bona fide resident of the community. He had rented a house up by the high school and had brought his wife Elsie to live in it. The house had a big lawn with lilacs and the flowers in the front yard and a sizable vegetable garden at the back. Joe kept it painted a pristine white and the lawn and the flowers were always beautiful. The thing he liked best was the long porch. He told my father that it was the first porch he ever sat on and he did not intend to give it up.

When the Health Club went out of business, Joe Gage used his remaining savings to buy a barber chair. He rented a small store on the main business block and opened a shop. For the rest of his life, no matter what else he became involved in, he was essentially a barber. It took some courage for him to open a barbershop, for there were already two in the village and both were well entrenched. The biggest one, at the west end of the main business block, next to the bridge, was owned by Fred Graves. Virtually every man in the village dropped in there every morning for a shave and the walls of the shop were lined with the personally inscribed shaving mugs of the whole male population. There was not much chance that they would desert Fred Graves.

Fred Goyer, whose shop graced the other end of the business block, was the "economy" barber. He charged ten cents for a haircut and the waiting line was long and active. Fred had only one barber chair, but he had fifteen other chairs ranged along the wall and they were always filled with farmers and the youth of the village. Whenever a customer got out of the barber chair, everyone would get up and move along one chair. Fred Goyer wasn't much of a barber. A patron would usually walk out of his shop with bristles on the top of his head where the hair had been, but at ten cents no one had any right to complain about the quality of the work.

Neither Fred Graves nor Fred Goyer had the women of Flushing on his side. Most wives and mothers abhorred the looks of men who came out of Fred Goyer's shop. And most of them didn't even like to walk by Fred Graves's shop. A certain air of ribaldry hung over that corner by the bridge and there was a distinct feeling that each woman's anatomy was being discussed as she walked by. Neither barber went out of his way to make the women feel better. Fred Graves seemed to delight in making them angry. My mother's troubles with him had been experienced in one way or another by every matron in town.

It was the women who made Joe Gage a success as a barber. It wasn't easy. Joe was never a cheap barber. He charged fifty cents for a haircut, an astronomical sum in those days. But people paid it. Mothers knew their children would be properly groomed and that they themselves could go into Joe's shop without hearing any profanity. Later, after the women started bobbing their hair in the early 1920's, Joe got *all* their business and he really prospered.

I do not think that Joe Gage overcharged for his haircuts. A boy certainly got his money's worth. He was the first barber I ever knew who gave away lollypops to his customers. He also gave balloons, tops, kites, and baseballs. He entertained his customers as he cut their hair. He would stop in the middle of whatever he was doing and put on the boxing gloves and go a quick round with a boy. He would Indian-wrestle, play mumblety-peg, or teach a boy how to whittle. He would repair a coaster wagon or paint a name on a sled. He was a talented man in many ways. He was the best whistler who ever came to Flushing. He could imitate birds or whistle a song. He could sing. He could tell stories. Sometimes in the middle of a haircut he would get so engrossed in one of his own stories that he would draw up a stool and sit down. When my brother Walter stalked into *his* shop and asked for a shave, a shave was forthcoming. Joe lathered Walter's face, used the back of a comb to shave off the lather, applied a hot towel, and finished off with a generous application of witch hazel and lilac water.

There is one point that should be made about Joe Gage. He was a genial, pleasant person, but he kowtowed to no one. Shortly after he opened his barbershop he came marching into Fred Graves's place one morning and shook his fist under Fred's nose.

"It's all right for you to say that I don't give people good haircuts, Fred, and it's all right if you tell them I charge too much money, but don't you ever tell people, again, not to come to me because I'm a nigger or I'll be down here and break you in two."

Fred never mentioned Joe's color again.

Joe's wife, Elsie, was as well liked in Flushing as Joe was, but no one ever called her Elsie. She was always Mrs. Gage. She was an excellent businesswoman and made a success of her own. In her first years she confined herself to cooking, but as time passed she proved to be as excellent a manager as she was a cook. She could cook for a gathering of a hundred and fifty people as easily as for five people. She cooked for all the large fraternal gatherings and for the weekly chicken dinners given by both churches. In addition she cooked for the hotel dining room. Then she went into the catering business. She had her own staff—all of them white—and she was soon managing all the public affairs in town.

The Gages prospered. They bought the house they lived in and furnished it attractively, but Joe's prosperity and the quiet dignity with which he lived were only part of his story. He was not a common man in any way. One morning he was sweeping the floor of his barbership as Ray Budd passed by. Ray was what might be called the gayest young blade in town. He was the chief organizer of the entertainment at various village affairs and usually acted out the leading role. He had been trying to organize a quartet for some little time and as he passed by Joe's shop he thought he heard Joe singing. He went back and coaxed Joe into repeating. Ray knew a good bass voice when he heard one and he soon talked Joe into becoming a member of the quartet. From that time on, not one social event was ever held in Flushing without some contribution from Joe Gage. His voice was too good to stay buried in a quartet, however. He always sang a solo as a part of every program on which he appeared. Sometimes he sang a duet with my aunt Esther.

My aunt Esther was my father's younger sister. She had suffered from glandular trouble from early childhood. By the time she was a young woman her weight had soared to almost four hundred pounds. She was to carry this great bulk all her life, but she had one compensation. She had a glorious contralto voice. She completed four years of training at a conservatory of music and auditioned for Giulio Gatti-Casazza of the New York Metropolitan Opera. She was offered a contract provided she could lose some of her weight. She was never able to lose the weight and she never sang at the Metropolitan. She came back to Flushing in 1915 and for the rest of her life taught in the public schools. Quite early after her return to the village someone asked her to play the role of Aunt Jemima in the annual minstrel show and in the course of it she sang a duet with Joe Gage. There was never anything like the reaction to that number in the history of Flushing. Forever after, whenever a few people would gather together shouts would go up asking for a duet. Whenever they sang together I was moved to rapture, as was everyone else in town.

People were always digging out new information about Joe's talents. He was a good dancer. At one time in his life he had been a porter in a hotel that catered to theatrical people and he had learned a creditable soft-shoe, a tap dance, and a clog. But the thing that enthralled all the boys of the village was the bones. The bones were two flat sticks that were held between the fingers of one hand and clacked together, in case anyone has forgotten. They made a sound not unlike castinets, but a good man on the bones could make a louder and more tuneful noise. Joe was good. He could make those bones sing. This particular talent was discovered the first year he was end man at the annual minstrel show. From then on he carried his bones in his hip pocket at all times and a concert went along with every haircut. All the boys in town made their own bones under his guidance and all the boys learned to play them. There was a long period when playing the bones was considered the ultimate in musical accomplishment in Flushing.

Joe became a member of the volunteer fire department shortly after he arrived in Flushing and soon showed that he knew more about fire fighting than anyone the town had ever known.

At that time it was the custom for all the firemen to run to the village firehouse as soon as the fire whistle blew. They would then push and pull the hose cart and the ladder wagon to the scene of the fire. There were only five automobiles in the whole town, but Joe suggested that the owners of them be taken into the department and that trailer hitches of some sort be put on the backs of the cars. When the fire whistle blew, the cars would go to the firehouse and pick up the equipment. All the other firemen would run directly to the fire. No one had ever thought of this before and when it was first tried out it was discovered that it saved almost ten minutes. This kept many blazes from getting a big start. As time went on and the number of autos increased, the Flushing Fire Department became surprisingly mobile despite its primitive equipment.

Joe suggested and carried through other improvements. In winter weather he would close up his shop each morning and wander up and down the streets with a huge torch, thawing out the hydrants. He caused a big silo to be built behind the village council chambers and after each fire he hung the hose there to dry. Each month he would go down to the council meeting and ask the council to let him buy a modern pumper fire truck so that he could extend fire protection to the farmers out in the township. He even designed the truck he wanted.

When Claude Wood, the chief of the fire department, enlisted in the army in 1917, Joe Gage was unanimously elected to take his place. In later years he served as president of the Board of Commerce, acted as president of the village council, and was held in considerable esteem, but it was as chief of the fire department that most people in Flushing always remembered him best. In 1918 it was Joe Gage who saved the town from destruction.

CHAPTER SIX

WHEN I STOOD on the corner by Fred Graves's barber shop on that bitter cold February day, I didn't know that I would stand on that same corner less than two months later and watch an even bigger catastrophe than the one I had missed. I would see almost all of the second one. After it was over, Flushing would never be the same town again. The central fixtures involved in the disaster of April, 1918, were the railroad bridge and the buildings of the Hart Milling and Power Company which stood on the river flats about a block south of Main Street and behind the stores of the business block. The principal actors in the drama, besides Joe Gage, were Bob Hart and my cousin Durward.

Although the railroad had come to Flushing, it hadn't been built all the way into town. In order to keep from constructing an even steeper grade than they already had, the railroad men laid the right-of-way along a series of ridges on the edge of the valley. The depot, at the time it was built, was the westernmost building in town and stood at the top of a long hill at the very end of Main Street, a good half mile from the old iron bridge and the business district. Because the CS&M derived most of its revenue from the stores and other enterprises gathered in the center of town, it was deemed desirable to provide some easier access to the railroad for the shippers and receivers of freight. To that end a long spur track was built from the main line down onto the floor of the river valley. This spur switched off the main line about a half mile north of the depot and descended along the side of the valley ridges until it reached Main Street, then curved to the east. Upon reaching the river it was carried across the stream on a long trestle supported by concrete piers. Once it reached the east side of the river, it branched out into a sizable railroad yard with tracks fanning out in several directions to serve the various customers located in the center of town. Among those customers was a flour mill, the old steam water-pumping station, and the various buildings that made up the Hart Milling and Power Company. Every morning the local freight spent more than an hour switching on the east side of the river and each day a car was placed at the freight warehouse that had been built back of the stores. This car was loaded with less-than-carload freight. Flushing was the only town outside of Saginaw with enough business to warrant a whole car of this kind of merchandise all to itself.

The railroad bridge across the river was Flushing's most impressive structure, but it was only one of three man-made works which crossed the river in the village. An old bridge which carried Main Street over the stream had been built in the 1860's. It was a landmark and was the only vehicular bridge across the Flint River for a distance of sixteen miles, but it was not as long as the railroad bridge. It sat about a hundred yards downstream, north, of the trestle. About fifty yards *above* the trestle stood Hart's dam. It was made of stone and concrete and was about fifteen feet high and ten feet thick, a massive structure.

The power plant and the elevator which stood beside the dam were wooden buildings, about five stories high and topped with cupolas. A high walkway connected them about three stories above the ground. Originally it carried the belts from the water wheels to the machinery in the elevator, but after Oren Hart converted his sawmill to an electric power plant the belts were taken out. There were other buildings in the Hart Milling and Power Company complex, including several sheds for the loading and storage of fruit, and there were some stock pens.

By 1918, although Oren Hart was still alive, most of the management of the Hart Milling and Power Company had been taken over by Young Bob Hart, as he was called despite the fact that he was nearing seventy. Bob Hart was one of the most remarkable men that Flushing ever produced. He was a tall, well-built man with ferocious black mustaches and flashing eyes. He was always ready to fight against what he considered to be injustice and much of the time he was at war on several fronts. He was the lifelong enemy of Ira Sayre, he defended himself ably against the big public utilities who wanted his franchise. He baited pipsqueaks and jumped on do-gooders. He believed in progress. He was the first person in the village to use the long-distance telephone and he used it often. If he didn't like the way a car was spotted on one of his sidings he would call Montreal and complain to the president of the Grand Trunk Railroad in person. If he didn't like the way Woodrow Wilson was running the country, he would call the White House. He did a lot of things for Flushing. When the new wells for the water system were drilled east of town, he provided modern electric pumps for them. He put street lights on every corner at his own expense. He was one of the first electric magnates to stretch his power lines into the country so that farmers could have lights.

Physically, Bob Hart was a vigorous, exuberant man. When he pushed his father through the business district in the wheelchair, Main Street always looked a little like a chicken yard invaded by a Model T Ford. Old Oren would be waving his cane at people and Bob would be moving at a fast lope. Clucking pedestrians would scatter in all directions. Bob Hart did most of the work at the Hart Milling and Power Company. He read the meters, kept the books, made out the monthly bills, wired the houses, made electrical repairs, and helped the farmers unload their grain at the elevator. If he wasn't at the power plant he was running about to the various Hart farms. He had a red Marmon roadster and he always drove it at high speed with the top down. He liked to put on the boxing gloves and go a few rounds. He liked to go skiing in Canada. He liked to swim. He liked to hunt. During the last big snowstorm in February, 1918, he broke his leg while sliding down the Cherry Street hill on a Flexible Flyer sled. (Shortly after this accident, Bob's son Oren came home from the war with a leg wound and every morning three generations of Harts would come rampaging down Main Street in their wheelchairs, one after the other. Later in the spring, at the annual Board of Commerce minstrel show, the whole cast performed in wheelchairs.)

The winter of 1918 ended with Bob Hart still hobbling around on a cane. Spring came abruptly and the first week of April was unseasonably warm. The mountains of snow that had blanketed Michigan melted and the water poured into the rivers. The Flint River rose rapidly toward the high-water mark. The water flowed over the sturdy dam at Flushing with a steady roar and by the first Friday in April it had risen to within five feet of the tops of the piers on the railroad bridge.

Fishing was a favorite occupation for many of the men in Flushing in the springtime. Several varieties of fish came swimming up the river in the floods and they milled about below the dam, trying to fight their way up over the chutes. Large dip nets, about eight feet square, were lowered into the water for short periods, and when they were raised there was almost always a fish in them. Most of the fishing was done from the banks of the streams, the nets being tied to the ends of long cedar poles that stuck out over the water. A few of the older men fished from the railroad bridge, however. The piers stuck out for ten feet on either side of the tracks and the tops of these piers provided ideal platforms on which to stand. Windlasses were carried out and used to lower and raise the nets. It was a profitable enterprise while it lasted. The fish could be sold to housewives for twenty-five cents apiece and there was practically no expense as the nets were used year after year.

My cousin Durward earned extra money by tending the nets when the fishermen wanted a little time off. He was a helpful, gifted, and industrious boy of sixteen who was well liked in the village. He was the orphaned son of my grandfather Love's younger brother and had come to live at my grandfather's house in 1910. By the time he was fourteen he had already built a house with his own hands from foundation to roof peak. He held down a job in Grant Reid's garage after school and on Saturdays. Durward also had a streak of the daredevil in him. He once had the whole town holding its breath when he climbed up the outside of Henry Chatters's store and back down again in emulation of a human fly who had visited Flushing a few weeks before. Durward was better than the human fly. In the spring of 1917 he had rescued a boy from drowning by diving into the river below the dam during the flood.

On that first Saturday night in April, 1918, Durward had agreed to tend six different nets, three of them out along the railroad bridge. This was quite a job and it promised to keep him running back and forth between the various locations all night. He had eaten an early supper and had gone down to the river just before dark. At about nine o'clock that evening he came running up to my grandfather Love's house to get his raincoat, rain hat, and boots because it had started to sprinkle. The rain became increasingly heavy as the evening progressed. About eleven o'clock the lightning began to flash and the thunder began to rumble in the west. The electrical storm that arrived around midnight was one of the heaviest ever experienced in Flushing. Bolt after bolt of lightning streaked down out of the sky, accompanied by almost instantaneous crashes of thunder. I was asleep when the storm began, but I woke when a lightning bolt struck the big elm tree on the corner by Mrs. Niles's pump. I looked out the bedroom window at the dazzling display of streaks crisscrossing the sky, and I was afraid. I walked down the stairs in the dark and found my mother sitting in her nightgown in the parlor watching the storm out the front windows. I went to sit beside her and she put her arm around me. I had no sooner sat down than there came what I always remember as the brightest flash of lightning and the loudest crack of thunder I ever heard. It seemed to me, then, and it still does, that two lightning bolts struck simultaneously from different directions. This may not be possible, but the flash and the thunder shook the house and the ground under it. I didn't learn for some time that this bolt, or these bolts, had struck the railroad bridge. The lightning struck with such force that it shook three of the fishermen off the piers and into the swirling river, now only a foot below them. All three were swept away in the angry waters. They were heavily bundled in oilskins and rubber boots and had no way of saving themselves. All three were drowned. Another casualty of that same lightning bolt was the huge electric light pole which stood in the river at about the middle of the bridge. This pole carried the main power lines to the part of the village on the west side of the river. It was split from top to bottom and all the wires at the top of it burned and crackled and smoked. Some of them broke and dropped off into the river. There was no electricity on the west side of town until the next day. The drowning of the three fishermen caused a considerable stir. Many men of the town, including my father, went down to the river to search along the banks for the bodies in the dark of the storm. There was a great deal of excitement at the railroad bridge itself and as a small crowd milled around on the east end of it, a man noticed what appeared to be a bundle of clothes lying between the rails. When he investigated it, he found that it was my cousin Durward. Durward was dead. In his hands were two fish, also dead. Evidently just before the big bolt struck the bridge he had pulled up a net and had taken the two fish from it. He had climbed up from the pier and had started to run along the tracks to put his catch in one of the submerged boxes along the riverbank. He had one foot on the steel rail at the moment the lightning hit. The charge had run along the rail in both directions and Durward had died instantly, electrocuted. The finding of Durward's body sent the gathering crowd out along the bridge in search of other victims and the body of another man was found lying at the opposite end of the trestle. He had also been electrocuted, probably by the same charge that had killed Durward.

In a village the size of Flushing an accident that takes the lives of five men is a catastrophe. By two o'clock in the morning the whole town was awake. I sat there in the window beside my mother and brothers and watched the men running toward the river in the storm. The lightning flashes still seemed to be following each other as rapidly as ever. High up on the hill at the southwest corner of town a lightning bolt struck a huge oak tree at the corner of Percy Benjamin's front yard. The tree split from top to bottom and half of it fell over on Percy's porch. Not more than ten minutes after that, another bolt struck a barn about a mile south of Percy's and it began to burn. Soon the whole sky was red with the glow of the fire and I could see the flames leaping high into the air.

Flushing was a sober town when that Sunday morning dawned. By that time half the people in the village were down by the river. The bodies of the three drowned fishermen were found, one by one, and carried up to the old iron bridge and laid out. There was a large crowd gathered at the railroad bridge trying to reconstruct the events of the night. No one knew exactly where the big lightning bolt had struck and several men were snooping around the piers to see if they could find out. One of these investigators suddenly uttered a shout and called for Tom Bulger, the station agent. He came running and looked at one of the piers. Huge I beams of cast iron carried the ties and rails between the piers and one of these I beams had been moved a good two feet by the force of the bolt and was resting on its concrete base by a bare fraction of an inch. Tom Bulger immediately went up to the depot and telegraphed the news to the chief dispatcher in Durand. Even though it was Sunday, an engine was sent out and a maintenance crew came with it to look over the damage and try to repair it. These men poked around the bridge all afternoon and finally built a barrier across the west end of it so that no freight cars would run out on it. The construction foreman told Tom Bulger that it would be several days before the men and equipment could be collected to make adequate repairs.

On the Monday morning after the electrical storm, Bob Hart came over to look at the bridge himself. He had already repaired the damage to his electric lines and had arranged for a new pole to take the place of the one that had been shattered. He couldn't understand why it was going to take so long to reseat an I beam and he expressed himself rather vehemently to Fred Graves about it during his regular morning shave. He intimated that he was going to call the president of the Grand Trunk in Montreal and complain. Before noon he wheeled his father up to the bank and then put him in the Marmon for the run out to the farm for dinner. After Bob came in from the farm he spent about an hour reading electric meters in various parts of town and then went down to the power plant. He climbed to his office on the second floor and lifted the telephone and told Addie Badger to put through the call to Montreal. While he was waiting for Addie to call him back, he began making out the bills for the meters he had just finished reading. He was sitting there at his desk, all alone, when the fire alarm came in.

The fire alarm system in Flushing was a simple one. A series of twenty red pull boxes had been placed in the various parts of town. When the lever was pulled on any of them, a bell would ring in the electric power plant and holes would be punched out on a tape in the office. At the time the old sawmill had been converted to an electric power plant a siren was installed on top of the firehouse as a village fire whistle. The switch to this fire whistle had been placed on the third floor of the power plant so that anyone working in the elevator could run through the high walkway and pull it. If the person who was to pull the switch happened to be working in the power plant office, as Bob Hart was that afternoon, all he had to do was run up one flight of stairs. Usually the procedure was to run up and pull the switch and then run back down and look at how many holes had been punched out and then tell Addie Badger which box had been pulled so she could tell the firemen when they called in.

At about 3:30 on that Monday afternoon Tom Bulger was on his way back to the depot from the bank. As he walked across the old iron bridge on Main Street, he looked upstream at the railroad bridge and his eyes swept along it from east to west, again trying to pick out the spot where the lightning had struck. The corner of his eye happened to catch the big white power plant and he jumped. Little tongues of flame were licking the shingles on the roof of the cupola. He turned and ran back across the bridge and pulled the lever on the fire alarm box outside of Fred Graves's barbershop.

When the alarm came in, Bob Hart jumped to his feet, grabbed his cane, and hobbled up the stairs. When he reached the third floor he was hit in the face by a puff of heavy smoke and very intense heat. He managed to reach the fire whistle switch and pull it, and then had to run for his life. On his way down to the ground floor he stopped long enough to yell into the phone to Addie Badger and then, for some reason, he gathered up the sheaf of bills he had been making out and ran. It was the only thing he saved. No one ever knew exactly what started the fire, but it was always Bob Hart's theory that the same lightning bolt that caused all the damage had burned off the insulation on some of the wiring in the mill and that it had been smoldering for a day and a half.

If anyone were to ask me the one single thing that I remember best about my boyhood, I would answer unhesitatingly that it was the sound of that fire whistle in April, 1918. It blew for eighteen hours. Once Bob Hart had pulled the switch, there was no way of turning it off. The tone of it kept getting lower and lower until it settled into a slow, ghostly moan. It didn't die out until the next morning. The sound of it disturbed my dreams for months afterwards.

School had just been dismissed for the day when the fire whistle started to blow. Because of the earlier fire at the West Side school, my grade was attending classes in the old Presbyterian church building on Main Street. As usual, I had started running for the depot that afternoon and was in the middle of the main business block when the whistle started. I arrived at the corner by Fred Graves's barbershop before the hose cart and the ladder wagon were trundled across Main Street and down the hill to the power plant. From my familiar corner I could see everything that was going on. My first glimpse of the mill that day was a startling one. The flames had burst through the sides of the cupola in force and the top of the building looked like a giant torch. Smoke was beginning to billow from the lower windows of the structure. Because I didn't have to get any closer to watch the drama unfold, I stood there for hours. From time to time, as the fire burned, I turned around and looked up at the fire whistle and wished someone would turn it off.

It was obvious when the blaze started that the most serious initial handicap was the lack of long ladders. Nothing on the rickety old ladder cart would reach above the second floor of the mill. When the longest ladder was placed up against the building and the firemen climbed to the top of it and pointed the hose upward the stream nowhere near reached the cupola where the fire was. The only thing the firemen could do was to wait until the fire burned down to where the water could reach it. Unfortunately, the source of power for the electric pumps was in the very building that was burning. Just as the fire burned down within reach the power began to fail and the streams from the hoses began to arch and dribble. In later years I could never understand why the pumps failed and at the same time the fire whistle blew as though nothing affected it.

Long before the water failed Joe Gage had anticipated what would happen. After a hurried consultation with my grandfather Love, Joe sent a crew of men over to the old steam waterworks that had been out of service for more than a year. Fires were to be built under the boilers and a head of steam built up, but even under the best conditions it would be a long time before water would begin coming through the hydrants again. Coal had to be hauled for the fires and several hasty excavations had to be dug to reconnect the old pumps with the system of water mains. It would turn out to be four hours before pressure was available again. In the meantime Joe Gage began organizing bucket brigades. Within an hour after the alarm was turned in, every man in Flushing was a member of the fire department and under Joe's command.

The danger to the whole village had been evident to Joe Gage from the moment the fire broke through the cupola. The power plant was doomed and the fire there became a raging furnace within a half hour. Attention was turned to saving the elevator. Smoke had begun seeping out around the edges of the windows of that structure quite early. As the fire in the power plant burned downwards, it began to creep out along the high walkway that connected the two buildings at the third-floor level. It was out of reach from the ground and firemen were sent into the elevator with buckets of water. They climbed up the stairs and even got out onto the walkway, but they were soon driven out by the intense heat and the dense smoke.

About an hour after the fire started, a new menace presented itself. The fire in the old wooden power plant was blazing high in the air. Burning embers and flaming shingles floated upward and were caught by the strong April wind. At about 4:30 one of these embers landed on the roof of the hotel and Joe Gage dispatched an eight-man squad there under the command of Tom

Bulger. Each man was equipped with a bucket of water and a broom. They climbed to the roof through a skylight and beat out the small blaze that had started. Within an hour after that fifteen more fires were started by the wind-blown torches. Tom Bulger and his men and another squad under the command of Fred Graves put them all out without serious damage. This success couldn't last forever. At a little after six an ember fell in the haystack at the back of the livery stable and that building was soon afire from end to end. The horses were led out with difficulty, but there wasn't a chance to save the building.

At about 4:15 that afternoon, before any of the other fires had started, and about the time the water pressure began to fail, Joe Gage had instructed Addie Badger to call on the neighboring communities for help. He was especially anxious for the city of Flint to send some of their equipment. Flint had motorized pumpers that could suck water out of the river and put a stream on a blaze, and that city also had an aerial ladder. The Flint Fire Department dispatched two of the pumpers and the ladder truck as soon as the call came in, but the ladder truck broke down on the way and never did reach Flushing. The two pumpers, with sirens blowing, made the ten-mile trip over the bumpy roads in forty-five minutes. They had just strung hose lines and were starting to throw water on the elevator when the livery stable caught fire. One of the hose lines was shifted to the new blaze, but it was soon evident that the fire was out of control. Joe Gage directed that the hose be used to prevent other buildings in that neighborhood from catching. Meanwhile, hose carts and ladder wagons from other villages began arriving. These visiting firemen, for the most part, were organized into broom-and-bucket patrols to watch over the rest of the town. They would put out a hundred small blazes before the day was done.

At six o'clock on that April Monday it began to get dark. By that time the electric power plant was burned to the ground, but it was still a burning pyre with tongues of flame leaping high into the air. It gave off enough heat to scorch the clothing of anyone who ventured too close. The elevator was now a spectacular torch, the whole upper third of it ablaze. The firemen had ceased pouring water on it and were giving their attention to saving the fruit-loading sheds and the livestock pens. They played water from one of the Flint hoses on these structures. The livery stable was ablaze from end to end. This building was nestled in behind the stores on the south side of Main Street and was almost up against the freight warehouse. None of the nearby structures was considered safe.

As darkness settled in, the sky became a brilliant red. People from as far away as Lennon, Montrose, and Flint could see it. Word had gone out to the towns by telephone and telegraph and many of the townspeople had already started for Flushing to help. As the glow in the sky further advertised the village's desperate plight, farmers and other people who had not yet heard of the fire became aware of it. People streamed along the roads toward Flushing in cars and on horseback and in buggies. The evening passenger train from Saginaw was held at Montrose for fifteen minutes while citizens of that village clambered aboard with fire extinguishers, axes, shovels, brooms, and pails. At Brent Creek another fifty fire fighters got aboard from the surrounding countryside. Later that evening the northbound train from Durand and Lennon brought a hundred fire fighters. The streets of Flushing were filled with running, shouting, grim-faced people. Long lines of men passed buckets up from the riverbank to put out smaller fires. Some of those lines were two blocks long.

At about quarter of seven a flaming ember landed on the top of Grant Reid's garage, a three-story wooden building with a flat roof that nestled against the steep riverbank where the old iron bridge struck out across the stream. The entrance to the garage was at the back and was reached by a small roadway that had been built along the riverbank. The two pumpers from the Flint

Fire Department had been located on this roadway when they first began sucking the water out of the river.

The roof of Grant Reid's garage had a false façade. When the flaming ember fell on the flat roof it was not immediately discovered. The fire spread rapidly over the tar-paper roofing and by the time the flames were first seen it was obvious that the garage was doomed. Everyone turned his attention to getting the cars out while a bucket brigade was formed. There were at least eighteen automobiles in the building when the fire started and many of them were in various stages of disassembly. These had to be pushed out by hand. (One had to be lifted up and carried out because there were no wheels on it.) The only way to get the cars out along the roadway was to move the two fire trucks. The hoses were hastily pulled out of the river and the two pumpers pulled out of the way while the cars were pushed out of danger. The minute the streams from the hoses were taken off the buildings next to the livery stable and the elevator they began to smolder. Despite the heroic efforts of long lines of men with pails of water to get near these buildings in the intense heat, they burst into flames. Worse than that, Grant Reid's garage with its oil-soaked floors and highly inflammable stock was soon enveloped in flames. Joe Gage ordered the pumpers back into position immediately, but just as the first one was backing down into the roadway, the gasoline tank in Grant Reid's basement exploded with a roar. Almost all of the windows on Main Street were blown out in this explosion and other windows, all over town, were broken. Worst of all, flaming boards and sparks were thrown high into the air and some of them landed three blocks away. The old wooden building on the corner across the street caught fire in a dozen places and all the nearest buildings, including Fred Graves's barbershop, had small fires in them. I didn't know it at the time, but my own house was set on fire by the falling debris from Grant Reid's garage, as was every house in our block. The broom-and-bucket patrols were on all these fires as soon as they started. At our house a hole was burned in the roof, but it was only about a foot square.

It was now 7:30 in the evening and Flushing had reached its moment of crisis. There was a good chance that the whole village was doomed unless a miracle occurred—and just about then the miracle did occur. Hoses had been attached to hydrants all over the area and suddenly water began to trickle from some of them and then it began to gush forth in streams. The steam power plant was finally in operation. The fire in the wooden building across from Grant Reid's garage was put out at once and then all the hoses were turned on the flour mill near the livery stable. It was saved.

I had watched all this from the corner by Fred Graves's barbershop. I had left that corner only twice during the afternoon and evening. The first time was when the Flint pumpers arrived. I went down to make myself acquainted with the firemen who ran them and to find out how they worked. They were something entirely new in my life. The second time I left the corner was when the freight warehouse next to the livery stable caught fire. It was a good thing I picked that time to go because if I had been on Fred Graves's corner when Grant Reid's garage blew up I might have been set on fire myself.

The fires continued to burn for many more hours, even after the water came on. None of the buildings that were blazing fiercely could be saved. The fruit-loading sheds and the stock pens and the freight warehouse burned to the ground. One other structure suffered serious damage that night. All afternoon and all evening embers kept dropping on the railroad bridge and in several places fires got a good start before they were quenched. Enough ties were burned through so that an extensive rebuilding job would be necessary if the bridge was to be used again.

I have no idea how long I stayed to watch the fire that evening. I was only six years old and I began to get a little confused with all I had seen. My mother came looking for me at a little after eight o'clock and found me sitting on the steps of Fred Graves's barbershop. I was so tired I wasn't even trying to see around or under people any more. My mother brought a thermos bottle full of milk and some sandwiches in a paper bag and sat down beside me while I ate. I must have gone to sleep while sitting there for I woke up at home in my own bed and it was morning. The fires were all burned out. That next day I didn't have to go to school because of Durward's funeral and after we came back from the cemetery my father took me by the hand and we went down to the power plant. It was still warm and little wisps of smoke were creeping out of various parts of the wreckage. The thing I remember best about it was looking down into that tangled mess to see that the water wheel was still turning as though nothing had happened.

Most of the buildings destroyed by the fire were never rebuilt. The old railroad bridge was never repaired because its principal customer, the Hart Milling and Power Company, had been burned out. Planks were laid over the burned-out ties and during all the rest of my boyhood we used it only as a foot bridge. Bob Hart rebuilt his power plant, but he did not rebuild the elevator.

As a result of the fire Joe Gage got the motorized fire equipment he wanted. And as a result of the fire Flushing's power plant was new and modern. It could do things that the old one couldn't do. While it was being built, old Oren Hart died and in his memory Bob Hart offered to install new street-lighting equipment that the new plant made possible. Boulevard lights were to be put in along Main Street. In order to install them the old hitching rails would have to come down. When they had been dismantled, Flushing woke up to the fact that the day of the horse and buggy was gone. If I were asked to put my finger on the exact moment that the village of Flushing changed from a traditional, rural American community to a modern town, I would have to say that it was on the afternoon that Bob Hart pulled the switch on the fire whistle.

CHAPTER SEVEN

THE CHANGE in Flushing was not quite as abrupt as I have made it seem. . . . The fire caused the change, but it delayed it, too. For a year and a half, while Bob Hart rebuilt his power plant, people were forced to wait for the improvements they might otherwise have made. It was a long period of kerosene lamps and candles when life reverted to pre-electrical days. I was six when the period began and almost eight when it ended, so that my first meaningful memories are of the time when the village and its people were frozen into the old way of life. For my family, the fire had the added effect of further incapacitating a house which had never worked very well to begin with.

We lived in a house that my grandpa Perry had built in 1906. It was on Elm Street, only a block behind the business district. It was the most modern house that could be built at that time. Grandpa lived in it for only two years before Sate Parmelee Perry was found to be suffering from "weak lungs." He sold his prosperous business and gave the house to his only daughter, my mother, and moved to Arizona. After Sate Parmelee Perry's funeral, Grandpa came to live with us. He took over the management of the house as though he had never been away. My father's eyes were on wider horizons and he had never been much interested in the day-to-day household chores, so Grandpa fired the furnace, tended the garden, did the odd jobs, and enjoyed his grandchildren. Grandpa set the pace of our everyday living. He was a man of the nineteenth century and, although he had seen the advent of many inventions and had installed them in his house, he was used to the fact that many of them didn't work as advertised and he could get along without them. Consequently, we lived placidly, half in and half out of a world that was rapidly ceasing to exist.

Our house was the first one in Flushing to have *built-in* electric lights. Most of the houses had electricity, but the wiring had been added long after the houses were built. On almost every ceiling in town double wires ran out from the wall to a central light socket. In our house the wires were out of sight, inside the walls. We had the first push-button light switches in town. Everyone else had round ones with spring knobs that were hard for little boys to turn. The light fixtures themselves consisted of bare bulbs that stuck out of that light socket in the ceiling. Now and then one would find a bulb hanging down on a long cord. Adults could reach up and turn a knob to make a light come on, but I always had to move a stool over under the cord and climb up to reach a switch. It was not until very much later that someone found a way of tying a cord on those hanging lights so that a boy could reach up and pull it. No house in the Flushing of my boyhood had any such thing as a floor plug. Other so-called modern conveniences were primitive, too.

The water system in our house didn't work very well. Water was always an interesting subject in Flushing. The village had installed a system of water mains in about 1895. A big steam-pumping station was built down by the river. Fire hydrants were installed on every corner and householders laid pipes into their homes. When our house was being built this work was nearing completion. The very latest plumbing fixtures were installed. One thing that was missing was a hand pump. Nearly every house in Flushing had one of these perched on the kitchen sink.

If the pump wasn't in the kitchen, it was just outside the back door. In expectation of the running water to come, our house simply had faucets in the kitchen. This proved to be mighty embarrassing to us.

The original plan, at the time Flushing's water system was installed, was to use the water from the river. A purification plant was built next to the pumping station and, at the inception of service, it seemed adequate. Unfortunately, in the ten years or more between the time the first pipe was laid and the completion of the system, the city of Flint, just ten miles upstream, began to grow by leaps and bounds. The city fathers of Flint made no provision at all for growth. They simply dumped the sewage and an increasing amount of industrial waste into the river. By the time Flushing was to run its first water through the new pipes the river was hopelessly polluted. More and more purifying agents were dumped into the village's water supply and it became more and more unusable. One man whose house caught on fire during this period even tried to stop the fire department from pouring hydrant water onto the blaze. No one drank the water from the pipes and it was considered generally unfit for anything unless it was boiled first.

The village of Flushing sued the city of Flint to stop the pollution, and as the filth spread downstream other villages joined in. When the federal government finally stepped in to stop the pollution of Saginaw Bay, Flushing was awarded substantial damages and all of this money was used to drill new wells east of town. In the meantime, many years had gone by and the old water had been in the mains so long that it was deemed advisable to wait until the pipes had been cleansed for several months before anyone started drinking from the village supply. Then one day Flushing had a flushing day. Everyone was supposed to turn on his faucets for half an hour and let the new water course through the pipes. This promptly caused the whole system to break down and the village was dry for a week. To the older residents even time was not enough to make the water safe for drinking. There were many families in Flushing who would still not drink water out of a faucet as late as 1940.

The failure of the faucets to deliver drinking water had a lasting effect on the way many people lived. In most homes I visited, all anyone had to do was to pump out a glass full of water at the kitchen sink when he wanted a drink, but in houses like ours that had put too much faith in the new system, the water had to be carried from a neighbor's pump. From the time I was old enough to carry a pailful of water, it was my chore to go up to Mrs. Niles's pump on the corner and bring back three pails a day. The drinking water was kept in a pail on a small table in one corner of the kitchen. A dipper floated on the surface of it. If any of the family wanted a drink, he just went over and drank out of the dipper. As a concession to sanitation, it was usually the custom to pour a guest's water into a glass.

Just as we kept lamps and candles around for those times when the power plant wasn't working, so did we cling to the old institutions for those moments when the plumbing broke down. Every home, including ours, had an outhouse. We all had inside toilets, but they were not perfected yet. They clogged up, backed up, overflowed at the back, and leaked at the bottom. A year never went by when we didn't have to go out back for periods of a week or two at a time. During these periods my father and Grandpa Perry would range through the house in a bad temper, carrying wrenches, plungers, mops, and long coils of wire, trying to find out what was the matter. It was much the same in every household and frequently, during visits to the homes of friends, I would be advised that I had to go out back.

Running water in a house was one thing. Running hot water was something else. Although there were hot-water faucets, no water ever came out of them during the first five years of my life. A huge copper kettle was kept on the back of the stove and if we needed hot water we dipped it out of the kettle. About the time the village switched over from river water to well water, my father tried something new. He ran water pipes around the inside of the firebox of the furnace and then up through the kitchen floor to a long, slender, cylindrical tank that stood on end beside the stove. From the tank, pipes ran to the various hot-water faucets. The system never worked out quite the way my father thought it would. In the summertime, when there was no fire in the furnace, we would always go back to dipping water out of the kettle. In the wintertime, when the weather was cold, we were in trouble, and it was cold most of the time. Cold weather meant a hot fire in the furnace and a continual hot fire in the furnace meant that the water kept getting hotter and hotter. Eventually it would start to boil. The tank in the kitchen would start to shake. Then it would begin to rumble ominously. Dishes in the pantry would rattle and pans on the stove would start slopping liquid. For some reason, no one in our family ever seemed to anticipate this so that when it happened we had to rush to general quarters. Some adult in the family would run into the kitchen and open a valve at the bottom of the tank. Immediately a jet of white steam would whoosh out with blinding force, blocking the pantry door. Meanwhile, someone else would have rushed through my mother's sewing room and into the bathroom to open the hot-water faucets there. Steam would rush from these, too. A third member of the family would run out the front door and around to the back of the house, entering through the back door to turn on the hot-water faucet in the kitchen. (We were never a well-enough coordinated family to get the kitchen faucet man past the water tank before the valve was turned on.) Within a few minutes the whole back part of the house would be so full of steam that we couldn't see across a room. Each spring, after a winter of this kind of thing, the plaster would fall from the ceiling of the kitchen in great chunks and long strips of paper would peel off the bathroom wall. There *was* one hard-and-fast rule about this. I had strict orders to stay away from that valve on the kitchen tank. Whenever I saw steam it always reminded me of an engine on the railroad and I liked to make believe I was an engineer turning it on and off. One winter I got so interested in this that I almost let the whole house blow up.

We had one modern thing in our house that *did* work. We had a system of hot-air registers connected by long ducts to the furnace. It was a considerable improvement over most other heating devices then in use in the village. Most homes had huge anthracite-burning stoves that sat in the middle of the living room. These heated two rooms on the ground floor at best. In winter the upper rooms of such a house were quite likely to be icy cold. I stayed all night at my grandfather Love's house or a friend's quite often and I soon noticed that in most of these families standard night wear during the winter was a long flannel nightgown worn over a suit of heavy underwear. Grandfather Love never went to bed in his life without his underwear on, at least not in the wintertime. Furthermore, he slept between blankets. I don't think anyone would have dared crawl in bed between linen sheets in most of the houses in Flushing. Our hot-air registers could be adjusted to bring warmth into any room. In the midst of cold spells, the registers in the upper part of the house would be closed during the day, thus directing all the warm air into the rooms that were being used the most, but about a half hour before bedtime my mother would go upstairs and open all the registers so that the bedrooms would be warm and pleasant. We never went to bed in *our* heavy underwear and we *always* slept between sheets. There was quite a difference in the way we smelled, if nothing else. (Of course, Grandpa Perry didn't change. After fifty-five years of sleeping in *his* underwear, the habit was so deeply ingrained in him that he kept right on with it, central heat or no central heat.)

No comment on heating devices would be complete without mention of the kitchen range. I cannot remember a house in the village that didn't have one, and I cannot remember when there was not a fire in our own. I strongly suspect that the kitchen range had a lot to do with shaping our habits. Major use of it was made in the morning hours and the fires were allowed to die down in the afternoon, especially in the summertime, so that the women could get out of that heat. Because of this custom, in our part of the world, the midday meal was always the biggest and most substantial one. My father and Grandpa Perry always came home for this meal and we sat down at the dining-room table, *en famille,* as did most of our neighbors. This midday meal was called dinner and it consisted of heavy, hearty food. A dessert was always served. The evening meal, or supper, was much lighter. Quite often it consisted of warmed-up leftovers or such conglomerations as hash that could be prepared quickly.

My mother never seems to have had any trouble cooking on her range even though there was no way to regulate the heat or tell what the temperature of the oven was. She was a taster, a sticker, and a mover. She never went near the stove without dipping a spoon into something and tasting it. She was forever moving pans from one part of the stove to another as they needed more or less heat and she kept a broom by the oven. From time to time she would grab a straw from it and jab it into something in the oven.

Almost every other modern piece of equipment was missing from our kitchen. There was no electrical refrigerator, of course. We had an old wooden icebox that sat on the back porch. It was out there rather than in the house so that it wouldn't drip on the floor. Every second day in warm weather I would take my coaster wagon and go down to the village icehouse, pick up a piece of ice, stop at Mrs. Niles's pump on the way home to wash the sawdust off, and watch while Grandpa Perry put it in the box. My grandfather Love didn't put much faith in ice or iceboxes. He had sunk a deep shaft in the ground beside his well and had installed a little dumbwaiter in it. He called it a "safe." The butter, eggs, cheese, and a big metal can of milk were kept down there. Almost every time I went over to his house, my grandmother would send me out to bring in a crock of butter or an egg. I would go out and lift the wooden cover off the shaft and start pulling on the rope. After a long time the platform would come into view and I would take what was needed, then slowly let the platform down again. I learned very early in life not to drop that dumbwaiter back down the shaft and not to forget to put the cover back on. My grandfather gave me a whipping for each of these offenses and he had to whip you only once to make you remember something forever. The butter was always hard when it came out of that hole, and the milk was always cool. But both my mother and my grandmother felt that cooling or refrigeration had certain limitations. For the long pull, the only sure way to keep a thing was to can it. There was scarcely a day in either household when a big kettle of something was not stewing on the back of the range with the Ball Mason jars and their rubber rings all laid out ready for use. It wasn't any wonder that life centered around that old kitchen range.

My grandmother Love canned quite a lot of meat as well as vegetables. During the summer months, at her house, one rarely got fresh meat. There were meat markets in Flushing, but during most of my boyhood nearly every family still bought its meat on the hoof. My father bought a pig, a steer, and a sheep each summer. The farmer from whom he bought the animal would fatten it until the first cold weather arrived, then butcher it and deliver the dressed meat to our house. My father and Grandpa Perry would cut it up and hang it on huge hooks out on the second floor of the barn where it would usually freeze. There was a big pit out near the barn and all summer long we would collect hickory wood for it. My father smoked his own hams and bacon and made his own sausage and headcheese. My mother made her own lard. For several weeks each winter she would be boiling fat on the stove and when I would come home from school she would fish several chitlings out of the pot and hand them to me while they were still hot. I would toss them back and forth from hand to hand until they cooled and then eat them. Lard cracklings, as I called them, were almost as good as candy.

Baking was another of my mother's major preoccupations. Every noon when I came home from school there would be fresh cookies, cakes, and pies cooling on top of the stove and each Saturday morning there would be fresh doughnuts. My mother made her own bread, too. Twice a week there would be a big bowl of dough sitting on the kitchen table. It would keep rising and rising all afternoon and all night. On the second morning it would be popped into the oven and we'd have hot bread for dinner. The next day we could make toast by holding a piece of bread in a wire grill over an open hole in the stove.

My mother ironed with triangular-shaped pieces of metal called sadirons that sat heating on top of the stove. Whenever the one she was using got cold, she would detach the handle and hook it onto a new one. All of our laundry was done on the back porch on a washboard. Aside from a broom and a dust mop, a Bissell carpet sweeper was our only cleaning device. I think I should add that we weren't forced into this way of life by the burning of the power plant. We simply never had had any modern electrical appliances up until that time. Everyone considered it a normal thing.

The outside of our house was as important as the inside. We had a barn and a chicken coop and a vegetable garden that took up about an acre of ground. All the other families in town had the same things. Every family had a few chickens and each family had its preferences. My grandfather Love was partial to Plymouth Rocks and my aunt Alice always had Rhode Island Reds. Grandpa Perry liked White Leghorns. Each spring people would send away and get fifty or a hundred baby chicks and for a week or two the post office would be full of cheeping boxes. Mr. O'Brien, the railway mail clerk on the passenger trains, usually had to put on an extra mail car for a week to handle all those chickens that were delivered along the line.

I was somewhat identified with chickens in Flushing from the time I was three years old. Grandpa Perry was painting one of his houses green at the time and each evening he would bring the half-used cans of paint home and line them up inside the barn. I found them there early one morning and decided to do a little painting myself. I started out on the barn door, leaving a wide swath of green abstract doodlings across the front of it. Barns don't move, however, and it isn't much fun to paint a stationary target. I headed for the chicken coop. At that time of my life I could move almost as quickly as the chickens could and I dipped my brush in my green pail and started running. By the time anyone discovered me I had made Green Leghorns out of all Grandpa's White Leghorns and for good measure I had painted all the eggs in the henhouse green, too. This created quite a sensation in the village. For several days afterwards the townspeople came up to stand in our back yard and look at the green chickens. They would stand there laughing and then go and bring back their friends. For all the rest of my boyhood, there was one stock question that I was asked every day, "Have you painted any more chickens lately?"

I always liked the chickens. Life was something of a perpetual Easter egg hunt when I was small. Each morning I would go out to the chicken coop and let myself into the henhouse to look for eggs. I knew which hens belonged on which nests and which ones were laying. I would collect the day's production and bring it into the kitchen for my mother. I stayed away from the chicken coop, though, when Grandpa went out with his ax to get a hen for the weekend. I never got over being frightened at the sight of a headless chicken flopping around the back yard. It was the most jarring thing in that whole world I lived in. The rest of it was pretty stable and all I had to do was grow up.

CHAPTER EIGHT

If my grandpa Perry represented the old Flushing, the town that had always been there, my father represented the forces that were to bring about its change. My father was never at home in the world that his own father and the others of the older generation found so comfortable and so reassuring. It was strange, in a way, because his background seemed to indicate that he was even more rustic than his elders.

My father had arrived in Flushing as a country bumpkin in a red suit in 1895. He was ten years old and in the sixth grade, a year behind my mother. He had been brought up more by his grandparents than by his own mother and father. There were no schools in the lumber camps and he had been left behind on the family farm to get what education he could. He had grown to love the country passionately, and when his family gave up the lumber camps for a more civilized existence he ran away from home three different times and found his way back to his grandfather's, so he was allowed to stay there until his grandfather died, an event that occurred the summer Grandfather Love moved to Flushing.

The average midwestern boy of the 1890's dropped out of school at the end of the eighth grade. Had it not been for the fact that my father met my mother and fell in love with her at an early age, he would have had only an eighth-grade education, too, but he plodded along through the eleventh grade, an educational high-water mark for Loves until that time. When my mother graduated from high school, my father saw no reason for hanging around the school building any longer and quit. He wasn't noted as a scholar, but he made quite a mark for himself as an athlete and soon decided to become a professional baseball player. He joined the Niles team of the old Central Michigan League and in his first season won the batting championship. He was sold to Peoria of the Three-I League the next year and won the batting championship in that league. In his third year he was with New Orleans of the Southern Association, and at the beginning of the 1904 season spent one month with the Cleveland Indians of the American League. He was built along the same lines as Babe Ruth with powerful arms and shoulders and long, slender legs. He had great natural ability. He probably could have gone on to become a regular, perhaps a star, in baseball, either as a batter or as a pitcher. When the Cleveland management decided he was a pitcher and sent him to the Pacific Coast League for another year's experience, he quit. He never reported to Portland and he never played another game of professional baseball.

My father had two good reasons for not continuing a baseball career. While he was at New Orleans he had become acquainted with the owner of the Fordyce Lumber Company, one of the largest lumber manufacturers in the South. He was given the wholesale selling territory for the state of Michigan in the off season. He was a natural salesman and in the few months he was on the road that winter he made as much money as he could have made in three years of minor league baseball. When he was faced with another year in the minors he saw no use in it.

Another thing had happened. He had been in love with my mother since the first day he had seen her. In the spring of 1904 they had eloped to Bowling Green, Ohio. My mother was a senior in college—she was the first woman from Flushing who had ever gone to college—and she couldn't reveal her marriage without resigning from school and she felt obliged to finish her education. My father couldn't stand the thought of being out in Portland, Oregon, away from his bride for one whole summer. This helped him make up his mind to quit baseball.

My father was a lumber salesman for eleven years and traveled the length and breadth of the state of Michigan. At least once each year he visited New Orleans, and he made an annual trip to the West Coast, for he represented several firms there. He also was an officer of the National Wholesale Lumber Dealers' Association and often spent time in other major American cities. By the time he was thirty years old my father was by far the most cosmopolitan man in the village of Flushing. He had made famous friends. Ring Lardner had been at Niles when my father was there and they were always close. Many of the baseball players with whom he had played in the minors had gone on to be major league stars and my father was popular with all of them. Many of them visited our house each year during the hunting season. It was a heady atmosphere for a boy like me to grow up in.

My father was probably the man who brought the twentieth century to Flushing. He was the first man in the village to own a car, buying a Ford roadster in the summer of 1904. He never did own a horse. Although the roads were not good enough in Michigan to allow him to use his automobile extensively until 1911, he was aware of its potentiality and placed his dependence in his car long before anyone else in the town did. By 1912, when most people considered the safe cruising range of a car to be about ten miles, my father was putting 20,000 miles a year on his. Other people took the train to Detroit. My father drove his car. Most people in Flushing spent two weeks at Mud Lake, about ten miles away, each summer. My father blithely piled all of us into the car and drove 135 miles across the state to Grand Haven and rented a cottage on Lake Michigan. We would get up at dawn and drive sixteen long hours to make it, but we never failed to come out on the sand dunes just as the sun was setting over the lake. There was no question about it, because of my father our family simply had more mobility than anyone else in town. Most of the boys and girls in my grade at school had never even seen Detroit or Lake Michigan or a steamer. I had a tremendous advantage over them.

The automobile was not the only manifestation of my father's modernity. He put different values on things. At a time when almost every householder in town spent an hour or two in the garden each evening, my father scorned it as a waste of time. He didn't mind if Grandpa Perry got out and "puttered around," as he called it, but he felt his own time was too valuable for that. In that hour or two he could drive over to Flint and sell a bill of lumber for a house and stop on the way home and buy all the vegetables he needed. He gave up buying his meat on the hoof because of the time he wasted in preparing it.

My father had more informal social ideas than anyone else in town. Like most houses in the village, our house had a formal parlor. My father hated the parlor. It was situated at the front of the house and was usually shut off from the living room by sliding doors. The furniture was ornate and uncomfortable. The main piece was an upright piano that no one in our family could play (my mother had it tuned once every year, anyway). The parlor was saved for formal occasions. Two or three times a year my mother would open up the doors and pull back the heavy draperies and dust off the furniture. Guests would arrive and sit stiffly on the edges of their chairs for an hour, then disappear. My mother would close the draperies, slide the doors shut, and that would be that.

On one of his trips somewhere my father bought a new Victrola and some records. My mother thought that the Victrola was a fairly good piece of furniture and should go in the parlor, so it was put there, but my father insisted that we slide back the doors so that he could play the records he had bought. That ended the parlor as a formal room. Nothing could ever be formal again after that. As I remember them, one of the records was called "Oh, Gee, Say, Gee, You Ought to See My GiGi from the Fiji Isles." Another was "Around Her Neck She Wore a Yaller Ribbon." There were others, equally raucous. It wasn't long before my mother got into the spirit of things and left the doors open all the time. People like Pat Frawley, who played the piano like a barroom entertainer, got access to the upright and it wasn't long before people actually began enjoying themselves in the parlor.

Most people in Flushing went to the Chautauqua in the summertime or devoted themselves to lodge work in the winter. My father had very little patience for this kind of thing. He was the only person in town that I knew about who ever saw a Broadway musical comedy. Quite often he would take my mother to Detroit to see a show, or to Chicago for a week's vacation. They were always going somewhere and seeing things that other people in Flushing thought were frivolous. I grew up with the conviction that my father and mother didn't laugh at the same things that other people laughed at. As far as lodges were concerned, my father was almost an iconoclast. He joined the Masons, but he never pursued his studies. The Elks were more his speed. Although he was a widely known and respected member of various lumbermen's associations, the one thing that he enjoyed was something called the Royal and Concacitated Order of the Hoo Hoos in which he held the office of Grand Snark. This gave him the privilege of wearing a black dunce's hat and a long, flowing black robe with a hunched and spitting black cat on it. When the Ku Klux Klan burned a fiery cross on Bill Frawley's lawn one night (Flushing was full of Frawleys), my father got on his Snark's robe and went up there. He scared the members of the Klan half to death and there were no more fiery crosses in Flushing.

After being on the road as a traveling salesman for eleven years, my father finally bought the Flushing lumber yard from Grandfather Love in 1915 and, for the first time became what might be called a bona fide, full-time resident of the village. After he'd settled down and looked around, his first reaction was that the town needed pepping up. He immediately organized the Flushing Board of Commerce and it became his personal instrument of influence in the town. He enlisted all the young men as members and kept them stirred up a good deal of the time. The annual minstrel show and the annual street fair, the village baseball team, and the monthly dinners that usually turned into poker sessions were continuing projects. They gave Flushing the aura of a town that was always busy doing something. Most of the advances that came in the village resulted from the suggestions made by the Board of Commerce. Although my father never evinced any interest at all in village politics, he really ran the town. He simply used the Board of Commerce instead of the village council.

Flushing had always been a quiet village with its own personality and its own way of doing things. Just ten miles away was the city of Flint. It might just as well have been a hundred miles away. Big things were happening in Flint all during this period. In 1900 it was a busy county seat with several small manufacturing plants. It had been a lumbering town until the lumber gave out and had passed on to building fine carriages. Its population was 10,000. In 1904 the manufacture of the Buick automobile was begun there and in that same year the General Motors Corporation was organized there. By 1910 Flint had grown to 30,000 people. In the following decade Chevrolet began manufacturing there and the population would rise to 90,000. In this same period Flushing grew from 971 to 1,169 people. Flint was the comet that swept across the night sky. Flushing was the little star that twinkled at it as it went by.

The spectacle of the small town that remained just as it was while the world was being turned over just ten miles away was not an unusual one in America. In all the Flushings, the interests of the villagers turned inward. With communications and transportation still largely undeveloped, each community maintained a certain insularity. But my father knew what was going on in Flint and he was the type of man who couldn't sit by and watch it without doing something about it. He wasn't content to be just a small-town lumber dealer who now and again sold a house or a barn. People were pouring into Flint and houses were being built there and he intended to get some of the business. He did, and was soon selling much more lumber in Flint than in Flushing. Hardly a day went by when he didn't get into his car and go over to Flint to talk business with someone. Within a year after he bought the yard he bought a truck to haul the lumber over to Flint, then two trucks. He was an energetic young man in the prime of life and he understood the world that was unfolding before him better than anyone else in Flushing. He made the most of it. It had a profound effect on the village because my father was popular and admired. When the people of Flushing saw that he was going to Flint and back in his automobile once or twice every day, they began to realize that it could be done. It didn't happen overnight, but it happened. In Flushing, at least, my father was the apostle of change.

I lived in my mother's world, not my father's. This is a normal state of affairs in almost any house, but in ours it was accentuated simply because my father was on the go so much of the time. My mother fed me, clothed me, taught me, and entertained me. She made the rules and set the tenor of the household. Her ideas, not my father's, became my ideas. My father served as sort of a chief magistrate. He had neither the time nor the inclination to teach me anything. He did not know what subjects I studied in school or what grades I made. Whenever I had a mark on my report card that I didn't think my mother should see, I would take it over to my father's office and get him to sign it. He would study the card impatiently for a moment, frown at it, then turn it over and write his name, I knew I was perfectly safe. My father didn't know a good mark from a bad one. He never even knew what I ate. If my mother was having trouble getting me to try something, he would point his finger at me and say "Eat it!" Five minutes later he might push his plate back with the same item untouched. I had the audacity to call his attention to this one day and he looked at the plate rather sheepishly, then ate what he'd made me eat.

My father did not believe in doing things with his boys. There was none of this buddy-buddy business in our house. He could have taught me quite a lot about playing baseball, but he never did. About once a year we would be playing ball in the street and he would hitch up his trousers and come down off the front porch. He would pick up a bat, spit on his hands, and say, "Pitch to me." I would throw a ball at him and he would knock it clear out of sight over Mrs. Niles's house. "Well, you're not a baseball player yet," he would say, and go back to the porch and sit down. That would end *that* for another year. Once in a while he would roughhouse with the three of us at once and he always seemed to enjoy it, but most of the time we ever went anywhere with him or did anything with him, it was because my mother insisted on it.

Like most fathers of his generation, my father believed in stern discipline. He had a variety of weapons he used on me and my brothers, but the one I remember best was his razor strop. Now and then it would develop that he had saved a hickory switch. Occasionally he resorted to a hairbrush. I got a whipping about once a week, which was about on a par with other boys my age. There were certain hard-and-fast rules that were always good for a licking when violated. Back talk, disobedience in any form, long and continued procrastination in carrying out duties, or the commission of a cardinal sin were grounds for action. Lying, stealing, and unmanliness were the cardinal sins in our house. Most of the time when the world was about to come down around my ears, my mother would be the judge. She would wait until my father came home in the evening and would hold a quiet consultation with him at the conclusion of which he would approach me and majestically point to the bathroom without a word. If I had been especially bad, he would just pick me up and carry me in by the seat of the britches. Now and then, however, he would overhear something himself and jump up from a chair and take action without consulting anyone. Shortly before my fifth birthday I started stealing small change from my mother's purse. The day my father found out about it is one I shall never forget as long as I live. I was soundly whipped, stripped of all my privileges, and threatened with fifteen years in the county jail. It was a terrifying few hours, I can tell you. The punishment worked. I may not be the most honest man since Abraham Lincoln, but I don't think I've stolen anything from women's purses since I was five years old.

While my father rushed about the surrounding countryside in a continuing expenditure of energy, my mother stayed at home and ran the house and looked after the family. Although she always had a hired girl, there was enough work to keep her busy. Except for Mrs. Parks, who came and went every year or so, most of my mother's hired girls were young daughters of immigrant families. Sometimes they went to high school. Sometimes they just worked. My mother taught them to cook and how to dress and corrected their English. They sat at the dining-room table along with the rest of us and were treated like one of the family. During the morning hours our house was always bustling with activity. My mother usually walked three or four miles back and forth across the kitchen. Almost every morning someone would drop by and sit at the kitchen table drinking coffee while my mother swirled about at her work. As a rule, the morning visitors were always men who happened to be in the neighborhood. Joe Gage or Pick Parsell, the butcher, or Bill Adams, the coal wagon driver, and even Ira Sayre would sit there and talk and laugh. There was always a lot of laughter in that kitchen. It was a happy place.

In the afternoons, after dinner, the hired girl would go up the back stairs to her room. She wasn't expected to do any work until it was time to get supper and she could get dressed up and go downtown or sleep or anything else she wanted to do. My mother would go to her sewing room. That sewing room was just behind the living room and it was my mother's favorite room. She used it for everything. There was a sewing machine and a dressmaker's dummy and a pattern board and a cabinet full of thread. Sometimes my mother would move her bed down there and use it for a bedroom. (All her babies were born there.) It was the traditional sickroom. Most of the time she used it to entertain her friends. Every afternoon women would start dropping in about 1:30. Sometimes there would be five or six of them. They would sit around the sewing room on chairs, knitting or mending from the baskets they had brought with them. Now and then one of them would get up and use the sewing machine or drape a piece of cloth on the dummy. They would talk away and laugh and never drop a stitch. About four o'clock they would all get up, put their paraphernalia in their baskets, and go home to get supper. Once every year Alice Smith, the village dressmaker, would come to our house and work in the sewing room making dresses for my mother. These were "good" dresses. My mother made all her own housedresses.

We had one ritual every week. It started late on Saturday afternoon and rarely varied. My father would come home from his office about 5:30. One by one, beginning with the youngest, he would put his three sons in the bathtub and scrub them. Scrub is not an idle word. He used a stiff-bristled brush and he started at the top of our heads and burnished every square inch of us all the way down to the tips of our toes. On those rare occasions when my father was not able to be home at those Saturday-night bath hours, I always heaved a sigh of relief because my mother and Grandpa Perry, the substitute scrubbers, always used a washcloth, a much softer and gentler cleaning device. Upon emerging from the tub we were immediately dressed in our best clothes and were expected to sit primly in the living room until supper was ready. There was no crawling around the floor or romping in the back yard. We were clean and we were expected to stay clean until after Sunday school the next morning. About the only other stress placed on cleanliness in our house was before regular meals. Upon reporting into the dining room we were expected to march over to our father at the head of the table and thrust out our hands to him. He would inspect them and if they passed minimum standards we were allowed to sit down. If they were dirty, my father would grab us and drag us into the bathroom and apply the scrub brush, after which he would give us a lick or two with the razor strop.

Supper on Saturday night was always a gala occasion. It was a big meal with a roast or a chicken. More often than not we had company. Upon conclusion of the meal (my brothers and I never had to wait for the grownups to finish), we would present ourselves at the head of the table with outstretched hands. My father would put some money in them and we would turn and rush out the front door and run as fast as we could go to the Ideal Theater. When we emerged from the movie at a little after nine we would find either my parents or Grandpa Perry waiting for us. If the weather was good, we would be escorted solemnly across Main Street to Frank DeRose's ice-cream parlor for a treat. If the weather was bad, we would ride home in the family car and find that my mother had prepared fudge or taffy or popcorn balls. Sometimes we roasted marshmallows in the fireplace. We always had a good time on Saturday night—after the bath.

My father had one hard-and-fast rule about Sunday. He believed that it should be a complete day of rest for my mother. She was never allowed to do any housework on that day from the time she got up in the morning until she went to bed. There was nothing in the way of a religious observance about this. It was simply based on my father's regard for my mother. This day of rest accounted for the big festive suppers on Saturday night. There were always plenty of leftovers and whenever anyone wanted anything to eat on Sunday, after breakfast, he was supposed to go out and help himself to a slice of cold meat or a drumstick.

Sunday breakfast was my father's meal. He prepared it and served it and it was always my favorite meal of the week. He loaded the table with huge stacks of pancakes and platters of sausage. Sometimes he served an alternate breakfast of lamb chops and johnnycake. I liked that almost as much as I did pancakes. After Sunday breakfast my father would dress us in our best clothes again and we would set out up Elm Street to Sunday school. The ritual was over for the week.

I have always had a feeling that my mother indulged us a little too much, especially me. There was a reason for it. I was not the first child born to my parents. I had an older sister, Susan Elinor, who was born in 1909. She lived for nine months and her death was a tragedy. My mother had a young girl from one of the nearby farms working for her at the time. One morning this girl was given the task of bathing the baby. She heated the water on the stove until it reached the boiling point, then poured it into a small tub. At that moment she was called away for some reason and when she came back she forgot that she hadn't added any cold water to the tub. She picked the baby up and put her down in the boiling water. In effect, Susan Elinor was scalded to death. She died in convulsions within a few minutes. Some measure of the kind of woman my mother was can be seen by her reaction to this accident. She was as heartbroken over the girl's remorse as she was over the loss of her own child. As long as the girl lived my mother drove out into the country each week to reassure her and comfort her. When the girl died in the influenza epidemic of 1918, my mother bought a headstone for her grave and each year after that went out to the little country cemetery to put flowers on her grave.

I was born two years after Susan Elinor's death and I did not make life very easy for my mother. A few seconds after I was born the doctor held me up by the heels.

"This child is deformed," he told my mother. "He's going to be hunchbacked. What do you think?"

My mother's answer, reputedly, was pretty emphatic, so the doctor shrugged his shoulders and beat me until I yelled. As an afterthought he gave me a good sound whack on the neck which seems to have knocked that part of me into place. As far as I know, I've never been hunchbacked since. I just get a little round-shouldered from lack of money, now and then.

In rapid succession, during my first months, I suffered through whooping cough, measles, mumps, chicken pox, diphtheria, scarlet fever, typhoid, and, as sort of a grand finale, pneumonia. At the age of five months and three days, during the pneumonia, I was given up for dead. I don't know *how* I got out of that one.

My mother had lost one baby and she did not intend to lose another one. When the pneumonia was over she began fattening me up for the next siege. I never got sick again, but I got so fat they could have put me in a circus. My mother continued to pamper me until I was four years old. By that time she had borne two other sons, and it was obvious that I was going to live. A process of deflation set in, but it took me quite a long time to get over all that coddling. It was pretty hard, but a boy couldn't remain a crybaby very long with a grandfather like my grandfather Love or a father like my father or the two wild Indians I had for brothers. In fact, I don't think it was possible for a boy to remain a crybaby in Flushing. By the time I was six I was about normal.

CHAPTER NINE

IN THE first several months after the fire at Hart's Mill I was scarcely aware of its effect on the village. It was summer and I was indoors only a fraction of the time. On those rare occasions when the weather or family demands forced me into the house the lack of electricity did not bother me. I was already used to the vagaries of Oren Hart and his inefficient power-generating equipment and I rather expected to have to read by kerosene lamps in July and August.

I had no pressing duties as a boy. There were a few small chores assigned to me, such as bringing the water from Mrs. Niles's pump. None of them were onerous. My main job was going to school and as long as I took care of *that* no one paid much attention to the other things I did. My mother didn't have to worry about me. There were only one or two dangerous places in the town and I knew enough to stay away from them. There were very few automobiles on the streets. Those that did make their way around the village traveled slowly. There was little danger of being run over. There were 231 houses in Flushing and almost every boy was known to the householders. My mother could find me simply by lifting the telephone and calling a few selected people. (Most mothers had a distinctive call that couldn't be mistaken by anyone. My aunt Alice used to stick her head out her back door and yell at the top of her high soprano voice, "Aaaaaaaaaaaaaaaaaarrrrrrrrrrrrrrttttttttttttttteeeeeeeeee-eeeeeeee. Aaaaaaaaaaaaaaaarrrrrrrrrrrrrrrrrttttttttttttttteeeeeeee-eeeeeeeeee!" It sounded like a Kansas football chant. Fat Calkins's mother, who lived up on the top of the Cherry Street hill, used to step out *her* back door and blow a bugle. Fat could hear it clear over at the depot a half mile away.)

Our life was outdoors from one end of the year to the other. There was no gymnasium in the town so we spent our winters coasting. The only basketball game I ever saw was played by girls on an open-air court out back of the school. Outside of coasting, our main preoccupations were baseball and football and in that summer after the fire I was just beginning to fit into the pattern of the village. We played baseball wherever we happened to be when the fancy took us, in the street, in an empty lot, or in a back yard. It was too much trouble to go all the way up to school where there was a playing field.

We had only one equipment problem in our games. That was getting a ball to play with. We used a ball until there wasn't any ball left. When the cover came off, we wrapped it in black friction tape. When it got lop-sided, we stopped the game and pounded it back into shape. When it started unraveling, we re-wound it. Finally, when it got so small we could hardly see it, we would combine it with another ball to make a new one. There was no such thing as a soft ball in Flushing. I never saw one until my family moved to Flint. Even then, for a long time, we called it an "indoor" ball and used it only in a gymnasium.

Bats were never a problem. We all had bats, but very few of them were whole bats. At one time or another all of them had been broken, but as long as we could put them back together and tape them we used them. Most of us had gloves, and those gloves had a tremendous influence on us. It usually shaped our whole career. My father gave my brother Walter a catcher's mitt on his fifth birthday. It was just one of those happenstance things, but it made a catcher out of Walter and he has remained a catcher all his life. Lyle Cuddeback was a right-handed pitcher until the fourth grade and then someone gave him a left-hander's first baseman's mitt. For the rest of his career he was a left-handed first baseman. Of course, no one had any spiked shoes, uniforms, catcher's masks, or chest protectors. We just never worried about them.

Football replaced baseball in the fall. There was none of this touch football business with us. There was not even much passing in our game. We played straight-ahead, bone-crushing football, or around the end, zigzag football. In choosing up sides we always picked the biggest boys first. There was only one football helmet in town and that belonged to Gaylord Gibbons, the quarterback on the high school team. Naturally, we didn't get to use it. Nor did we have shoulder pads, boned pants, or nose guards. I broke my collarbone twice before I was twelve years old. My brother broke his arm. My cousin Artie broke his leg. I don't think there was a boy in Flushing who hadn't broken something. I don't know how many shirts and sweaters I had ripped off my back or how many pairs of pants were torn at the knees. My mother and father never complained about the clothes or the doctor's bills.

Winter in Flushing lasted from the last week in November until late in March. The ground was always covered with a deep blanket of snow. Although there was some ice skating, coasting was the big thing. Topographically, the village was ideally suited for this sport. The heart of the town lay on the floor of the river valley and the streets all ran up out of it so that there were a good many steep hills. We built the coasting runs after each fresh snowfall and all the boys and girls in each neighborhood took part in making the one nearest their own homes. Deep tracks would be traced out with sleds and bobs and then the run would be iced down with water carried from the pumps. The hills would be lightning fast and sleds would streak down them at speeds of up to thirty miles per hour and travel for distances of three quarters of a mile out onto the river flats. There was always a great deal of rivalry between the different neighborhoods to see who could build the best runs. Many of the adults had bobsleds and late at night they would go to whichever hill was supposed to be best and spend hours coasting.

We had one other winter sport. We indulged in it on Saturdays when the farmers came to town in their sleighs and cutters. We called it "bob-hopping." The idea was to catch rides on the runners of sleighs. The most fun and the biggest challenge to our agility was the cutter. A cutter usually moved much faster than a team-drawn box sleigh and it took speed and expert timing to jump on or off. Getting off a fast-moving cutter was an exercise in courage. A boy's legs simply would not go fast enough when he hit the ground and ordinarily he would go end over end in a somersault. I learned quite early to wait until I came to a big snowdrift before jumping off. I always ended up buried in one of these deep drifts, head first. After a whole day of wading and rolling around in the snow at this pastime, our clothes would be wet through and our faces would be a deep red with the cold. But no one ever thought of going indoors until darkness fell and the last sleighs were leaving town.

There were other outdoor sports, both winter and summer, but they were never as popular. Flushing was never a great swimming town. The only place with clear, unpolluted water was the Clay Pit, an old abandoned quarry about a mile north of town. It was dangerous. It was about eighty feet deep, a half mile in circumference, and filled with icy-cold spring water. The banks were steep and went straight down to the bottom. Several village youths had been drowned there before my time and it was off limits to me and to most other boys. The traditional old swimming hole, about a mile south of town on Cold Creek, was too shallow and too dirty for any real fun.

I became involved in one enterprise that summer after the fire that had nothing to do with baseball or sports, or even the railroad. It had to do with my grandpa Perry's garden. In addition to the sizable plot he kept in our back yard, he also started one on the river flats back of the lumber yard. In the one at home he planted long neat rows of radishes, onions, beets, and things like that. In the garden by the river he put corn and potatoes. He also planted pumpkins and squash between the rows of corn, but I didn't know that. At the head of each row of vegetables he nailed the seed package to the stake and any investigator could tell exactly what was growing there simply by looking at the pictures. Because he had planted the pumpkins and squash haphazardly, he did not bother to put the pictures on the stakes. I inspected the pictures that summer, as I always did. I was extraordinarily fond of pumpkin pie and I was naturally concerned that we have enough pumpkins to see us through the next winter. I couldn't find any rows of pumpkins and I began to worry.

Boys never take regular routes to get anywhere. They take short cuts. I had been doing that since I was old enough to walk. My favorite route to the downtown district led me through J. B. French's farm equipment yard and through the back door of his store out onto Main Street. I could have run through the aisles of other stores, and sometimes did, but French's hardware was always my preferred route. It was the only store in town with an elevator. It was a rather primitive one that was raised and lowered by pulling on ropes, but I was fascinated by it. It was at the back of the store. If Alf Hand was getting ready to pull on the ropes to lift it to the second or third floor, I could get on and ride with him. Quite often he would even let me pull the ropes. If Alf Hand wasn't around, I could always stop and talk with Mr. J. B. French himself. Mr. French was a tall, dignified-looking man who always said good morning to me and asked me about all the projects I had going around town. We had already discussed many possible business deals at the time I was six, but none of them had come to fruition. I was quite interested in a Flexible Flyer sled, and he had several very fine baseball gloves on the second floor that could have been useful to me. At the time I became worried about the pumpkins, we had only recently begun discussing the possibility that I might buy the steam threshing machine that sat out in the farm implement yard. It had been there quite a while and I knew he wanted to get rid of it. I was definitely interested.

I also knew that Mr. French sold pumpkin seeds and one day before I went through his store I counted the money in my savings bank and found two dollars there. I took the money with me and told Alf Hand that I wanted two dollars' worth of pumpkin seeds. He scratched his head and brought me forty packages of seeds, took my two dollars, and told me to wait for a receipt. He then disappeared into the office. A moment later Mr. French came bustling out smiling and firmly shook my hand. He told me that he was pleased to do business with me and asked me if I was going into the pumpkin business. I told him that I was worried because my grandpa Perry hadn't planted any pumpkins. He considered this for a moment and then told me that I was absolutely right to be worried and that he was willing to help me. Inasmuch as I had established my credit by paying cash for forty packs of pumpkin seeds, he was prepared to sell me one hundred more packs. He would sell them to me at the wholesale price of one penny a package, and would give me a year to pay. He had only one stipulation. I was not to tell anyone about the transaction because other people would be angry about the favoritism he had shown. This deal seemed like one I couldn't possibly turn down. I shook hands with Mr. French and he personally escorted me to the back door with my hundred and forty packages. As he let me out into the alley, he informed me that I had some very special seeds and that it might be a good idea if he showed me exactly how to plant them. I watched very carefully while he demonstrated.

I planted pumpkin seeds somewhere in Flushing every day for the next two weeks. I planted them in the garden behind our house, but I ran out of space there after the twenty-fifth package. I planted them in my mother's flower beds around the house. I planted them in Sarah Parmelee Perry Park at the end of the bridge on Main Street. After all, it was named after my grandmother. I planted them in my grandfather Love's garden. I planted them in my aunt Alice's garden. I planted them in Ed McKenzie's garden. I think that everyone in Flushing had at least one pack of my pumpkin seeds before I finished that year. I even had two packs in the flower boxes that Tom Bulger kept outside the depot. Naturally, I never told anyone I was planting them because I had promised Mr. French not to tell anyone I had them. I just wandered around in people's gardens as unobtrusively as I could, planting seeds.

I don't think I lost a pumpkin. No one ever saw as many pumpkins as Flushing grew that year. Mr. J. B. French used to walk around town smiling at first. Then he would stop in the middle of a block and start to laugh. At the end he was laughing so hard he couldn't stand up straight. People began to think he was going crazy or had taken to drink or something, but after a while, as the pumpkins kept growing, all the others in town would meet each other on the street and start laughing, too. It got to be a rule not to touch a pumpkin so everybody could find out just how many there were. Someone eventually told who planted all those pumpkins and I am pretty sure I know who it was. My father gave me a little talk about being careful of Mr. French, after that, but I didn't take it seriously. I couldn't very well stay away from him because he had that threshing machine I wanted.

When the baseball season was over and the pumpkins had been harvested and it began to get dark early, I turned more and more of my attention to the railroad. This was the very highest peak of the CS&M railroad. It was still wartime and the trains literally clogged the tracks for twenty-four hours a day. Even after the Armistice was signed that November there seemed to be no appreciable slacking off. That summer and fall and winter Percy Benjamin was still working at the depot. To me, Percy was the railroad.

Percy Benjamin's official title was night trick telegraph operator. He was a little man with large owlish eyes, a long sharp nose, and a shiny bald head who always wore a green eyeshade and sheets of paper wrapped around his shirt sleeves. He was fidgety and tended to move in jerks and jumps. Most of the time he wore a bewildered expression on his face. He had a peculiar reputation in Flushing. People liked him and he was generally considered quite harmless, but he had a great name for being a practical joker and most of the time his jokes were pretty horrendous. He didn't care who his victims were, either. It didn't make much difference that some people, including my father, thought that some of his jokes were the result of accidents. If they could they gave Percy a wide berth at all times. They had good reason to do so.

Percy Benjamin was a local boy, a contemporary of my mother and father, who was in his middle thirties at the time of the war. He had been six years old when the railroad was built and had developed as great a love for it as I did. His interest was in telegraphy, however, instead of engines. While he was still a boy he had bought a telegraph key and had practiced at home until he was an expert. Although he didn't go to work at the depot until 1915, he soon became known as the best telegrapher not only on the CS&M but on the whole Grand Trunk. He had a sure hand and often sent messages so fast that the chief dispatcher, who was no slouch himself, had to ask him to slow down. Unfortunately, telegraphy may have been Percy Benjamin's only talent. In Flushing he had a long record of failure.

At one time or another, before he went to work for the railroad, Percy had tried a wide variety of jobs in the village. He hung wallpaper for Frank Haskell, but he only hung it for a few weeks. He kept putting two different kinds of wallpaper side by side on the same wall. He stepped in pails of liquid paste and tracked it around on people's rugs. He got tangled up with the long sheets when he tried to paste them on a ceiling and ended up with them wrapped around himself. When Frank Haskell fired him it was generally conceded he would never make a paperhanger even if he turned into a centipede.

For a time Percy tried to learn the butcher trade in Ed Letts's meat market. One day he sawed off the tip of the little finger of his left hand. He ran up the street to Doc Wheeler's office and had the hand bandaged and then went back to work. Somehow, in the hullabaloo over the mishap, Percy forgot to reclaim the finger and later in the day he inadvertently wrapped it up in a pound of hamburger he sent up to Frank Niles's house. That night, at supper, Frank fished it out of the pile of meat on his plate and held it up for his wife to see and asked, "What's this?" Mrs. Niles fainted dead away and that ended Percy's career as a butcher.

At one period Percy drove a team of horses in my grandfather Love's lumber yard. One day he loaded a pile of boards on the back of the wagon. When he started up the little hill out of the lumber yard the wagon tilted backwards because the boards had been loaded too far to the rear. The front of the wagon lifted high in the air, jerking the horses off the ground. There they remained for an hour, suspended in the air by their harness while half the people in town gathered around to try to get them back down.

When he went to work in the bank, Percy came up with a shortage of $57,000. At the close of each day's work he just carried all the money into the safe and left it there. It never seems to have occurred to him to keep track of how much money he was putting in there. He just put it on a shelf and left it and the next morning he would start out fresh with an empty drawer. It took the bank examiners almost a month to straighten that out.

Even the simplest things caused trouble for Percy. In 1904 he bought a car, one of the earliest Ford roadsters, and my father gave him lessons in how to drive it. After the second lesson Percy decided he had the car well in hand and announced that he would drive the car home. He drove off up Main Street in a rather jerky fashion. When he came to his own driveway he made a wide turn and caught his sleeve in the gas lever, jerking it up. The car jumped ahead like a bucking bronco. Percy sat there in the driver's seat, pulling on the steering wheel with all his might, yelling, "Whoa! You son of a bitch! Whoa!" The car kept right on going, through Percy's barn, out the back wall, and down the riverbank, ending up in the water with a big splash. Percy never drove another car as long as he lived.

At the time Percy Benjamin went to work for the railroad, the depot was the most important building in the village. It most certainly was the most important station on the whole CS&M. It was the funnel through which the outside world poured into Flushing, not only because of the passengers who alighted from the trains there but because of the telegraph. In those days, before the widespread use of the telephone, the wires were the source of almost all the news. Over them came the first tidings of the San Francisco earthquake, the sinking of the *Titanic,* Willard's victory over Jack Johnson, and the daily baseball scores. In addition, the depot was the agency for both Western Union and Postal telegraph. As far as the railroad was concerned, Flushing was the only depot on the line outside of Saginaw that stayed open twenty-four hours a day. Trains rarely met in Flushing (no self-respecting engineer would be caught on a siding there because he might never get out again with those grades out of town), but it was a rare train that didn't get instructions there to meet another train at stations to the north or south. These instructions were all transmitted by the telegraph line.

The Flushing depot had a five-man staff, who took turns selling tickets, making out bills of lading, or loading baggage. If messages came in during the day, one or the other of them would sit down and take them. Year in and year out Percy Benjamin's primary concern was the telegraph. He came to work at nine o'clock in the evening, just after the northbound passenger train left town, and he had the place almost to himself until the next morning at six o'clock. From the time he came to work until the time he left, the line was alive with trains. With the disappearance of the passenger train, there were no trains working at the stations between Durand and Saginaw and the dispatcher released the flood of through freights and the orders for them kept Percy quite busy. Now and then Percy would work days and someone would replace him on the night trick, but this happened only at odd times and with no set pattern.

Although Percy worked nights, I saw a lot of him. On most mornings he would hang around the depot after work until the southbound passenger arrived. Quite often he would be around the depot in the afternoons. He took an interest in me. I suppose it was because I was what he had been as a boy. He patiently explained everything to me. He was the one who taught me to shinny up the wall under the ticket window and reach around through it to unlock the door so that I could get into the station agent's office. He took me out to the baggage room and showed me where all the train passage books were stored and often helped me to get one of the dusty old volumes down so that I could look through it and see what engines had gone through Flushing in the past. He tried to teach me the Morse Code, but I was still a little too young for that. About all I ever recognized were the various station calls. Percy got me my first ride in the cab of Burt Emans's engine and he saw to it that all the trainmen knew who I was. On those mornings when he had gone home before I got to the depot, he would always leave me a note.

"They had to use number 2292 on the southbound Flyer," a note would say. "Number 2245 has a bad air compressor." Or, "Extra South number 2263-2278 was a circus train."

My favorite spot in all the years I went to the depot was behind the telegrapher. I would drag a stool over and climb up on it and look over his shoulder. In Flushing the telegrapher sat at a low table in the front bay of the station agent's office. From his swivel chair he could look out a window and see the full sweep of the tracks as they curved into town from the north. By simply turning around he could also get an unobstructed view of the main line to the south. Above his head were two ropes that led up to the red semaphore arms atop the tower outside the windows. Without moving from his chair he could reach up and pull either of those arms out into the horizontal position. When either was straight out from the tower it meant that the telegrapher had orders for an approaching train. The clicking of the telegraph key never ceased and the telegrapher sat in his chair with the necessary materials spread out in front of him so that he could grab them when the Flushing call letters came over the wire. There were six basic things sitting on that desk at all times. There was a pad of Western Union telegraph blanks and a pad of Postal telegraph blanks. There was a big tablet marked "Grand Trunk Telegram." Messages that had to do with the railroad business such as Pullman reservations or lists of cars that would be dropped off by the local freight were copied on those blanks. There were also two pads of train order blanks, one of red tissue paper and one of green tissue paper. Last, to me, the most important item in the depot was that train passage book. The number of each engine and the exact time it arrived and left town were inscribed in it by the man on duty. I checked it several times a day.

The CS&M was a primitive railroad by present-day standards. It was a single-track line with no electric block system. Nor were there any other devices for automatic train control. The chief dispatcher in Durand knew where all the trains were and how they were made up. He controlled them through telegraphic orders that were transmitted to the various stations. At night, when all the other stations along the line were closed, these orders all came to Flushing. When the trains stopped to take water, the crews would walk back from the water tank and pick up the little slips of paper that told them what to expect along the line ahead of them. Once in a while a train would go through town without stopping. Light engines (engines that pulled no trains) or the two Flyers are examples. If the chief dispatcher sent orders to them, the telegrapher would write out the messages and attach them to big cane hoops, then go stand by the track. When the engines came into view the telegrapher would hold the hoops high over his head and the enginemen, warned by the red signal on the tower, would lean out of the cab and catch the hoops on their arms as the engines roared by. As soon as they got the hoop they would detach the message from it and throw the hoop back out the window and it would land beside the track a quarter mile or so up the right-of-way. (Percy Benjamin would always tell me in the morning if there was a hoop north or south of the depot and I would go and get it and bring it back.)

The CS&M operated without any wrecks for its whole existence in spite of its primitive methods. (The train wreck back of Henry Chatters's farm was not caused by the system of operation.) When Percy Benjamin came to work at the Flushing depot, however, things began to go wrong. Like the grades out of Flushing and the goat engines, Percy was just another added handicap. He hadn't been at work for more than a month before he broke both legs. Some friends came around to see him late one evening and brought him several bottles of beer. After the friends had gone he decided it would be nice if the beer was cold, so he walked across the tracks to a refrigerator car that was spotted on the main siding and crawled to the top of it. After some struggle he managed to get a fifty-pound cake of ice out of one of the reefers. In doing so he chipped off a piece and, as he turned to throw the ice down to the ground, he stepped on the chip. Percy and the ice and the tongs all fell to the ground together. Percy lay between the rails of the main line for half an hour, unable to move, and it was just by chance that the next train was from the north and stopped at the water tank or Percy would have been run over. (He learned something from this. After Flushing went dry and it became illegal to bring liquor into the county, Percy had a friend of his in Canada put a case of whiskey in a refrigerator reefer every now and then. The friend would wire the car number ahead and Percy would stop the freight and have the car set off the train for some reason or other. During the night he would climb up and retrieve his case of whiskey, then have the next train pick up the car.)

Not long after he got back to work after he broke his legs, Percy fouled up the whole Grand Trunk Railroad for a day. One evening he tried to move a boxcar with a pinch bar. The car got away and rolled down the siding past the depot, across Main Street, jumped the switch on the main line, and ran on out of town. It finally stopped about a quarter of a mile away and sat there in the dark. The southbound Flyer was due in twenty minutes and if it hit that boxcar there would be a fine wreck. Percy knew the Brent Creek operator had gone home for the night so he had the Flushing telephone operator get through to him at his house. The Brent Creek operator ran over to the depot and just did manage to flag the Flyer down. He held the train in Brent Creek for two hours while Percy put in a long-distance call to Saginaw and talked a friend of his there into sending a Saginaw yard engine all the way down to Flushing to push the boxcar on the siding. By the time the Flyer got through to Durand it was three hours late. Because it carried passengers and Pullmans that had to be hooked onto other trains, these other trains were all held at Durand. Percy was conducting all his business by long-distance telephone so that the chief dispatcher wouldn't overhear him on the telegraph. The chief dispatcher kept asking Percy where the Flyer was and Percy said he hadn't seen it. The longer the other trains were held in Durand the more trains were held up behind them. By the time the switch engine got that boxcar pushed back on the siding and the Flyer got to Durand, trains were backed up all the way to Montreal and Chicago. It was one of the worst messes the Grand Trunk ever had. A long time afterwards someone asked Percy why he hadn't let the engine of the Flyer push the boxcar onto the siding. He answered that he was afraid he would wake up all the passengers on the Pullman cars if the engine did any switching.

It was shortly after Percy came to work at the Flushing depot that the railroad was beset by one of the most baffling mysteries it ever faced. There were four switches on the main line through Flushing. Each one had a kerosene lantern on top of it. When the switch was open so that a train could take the siding, a red glass, lit by the lantern, showed up the track. When the switch was closed, a green light showed. About once a week a member of the depot crew would walk out along the track to the various switches and take down the lanterns and bring them into the baggage room and refill them with kerosene. After they had been filled they would sit on the baggage-room floor all day. Just before dark someone would come in and light them and carry them out and put them back on the switch stands. No one was ever specifically assigned to this duty. On the day the lanterns had to be refilled the station agent would just tell whoever didn't seem to be busy to go out and collect them, or do it himself. Toward evening he would pick out someone at random and tell him to take the lanterns back. One winter night in 1916 John Reardon came pounding down the track from Saginaw on the evening southbound passenger train and found a red light staring him in the face. He slammed on the emergency brakes and threw most of his passengers into the aisles. When Beans McAuslin, the fireman, climbed down from the engine cab and ran ahead to throw the switch he found that it was already closed. The lamp was sitting on the switch stand backwards. The same thing happened a month or two later, only on another switch. As the months passed it became a fairly regular occurrence. Every time it happened John Reardon would lose ten minutes.

Several times in the next five years the railroad sent detectives out to Flushing to find out who was tampering with the switch stands. One night a detective crouched behind the pickle warehouse for six hours watching the switch at the north end of the House track hoping to catch the culprit in the act. While he was watching it a train came to a grinding stop at the south end of the Team track a mile away, where the light was on backwards. Another time a detective came around to my house and questioned me about it. He seemed to think that some of the local boys were responsible. The mystery was never solved satisfactorily, but it was a cross that Percy Benjamin had to bear more than anyone else. It always seemed to happen on a day when he was working the early evening trick, and every time it happened John Reardon would come storming into the depot and pound his fists on Percy's desk and threaten mayhem. Every time he banged his fist everything jumped about a foot—the instruments, the pads of forms, and Percy himself.

Percy didn't get along with trainmen, generally. On an average night when he pulled the late trick he had to write between ten and fifteen train orders. The night northbound manifest might be ordered to meet the southbound Flyer in Montrose, two stations to the north, or an extra southbound freight might be ordered to meet a northbound extra at Lennon, the next town to the south. It was a busy railroad and on a single-track line like the CS&M, these meetings had to be carefully scheduled so that there would be a minimum of delay. Quite often a train that left Saginaw with orders to run straight through to Durand without meeting another train would be slightly delayed somewhere and when it got to Flushing it would get a change of orders ordering it to take the siding at Lennon to let another train pass. (When a train took a siding, according to railroad terminology, it went "in the hole.")

While most of the passing tracks along the CS&M could accommodate up to forty cars, it was the policy of the chief dispatcher to let the heavier freights have the right-of-way. The short trains, which could get under way easier after a stop, were usually ordered into the hole. By custom the chief dispatcher never spelled out elaborate instructions in his train orders. He simply prefaced each message with "red" or "green." When the telegraph key started clicking it would say, "Red for extra north number 2299-2262." Then it would go on to say, "Extra north number 2299-2262 meet Train number 96 south engine 2245 at Montrose." When that word "red" came over the telegraph key, the telegrapher at Flushing would grab the pad of pink tissue paper and write out the order on it. When the trainmen on extra north number 2299-2262 came over to the depot to pick up the order they knew that they would take the siding at Montrose. If the order was written on green paper, they knew that they would have the right-of-way and that the other train would take the siding.

From the time he went to work at the Flushing depot, Percy Benjamin seemed to be careless about which pad he grabbed. On some nights nothing would go wrong, but on other nights every train on the line would end up cowcatcher to cowcatcher while the crew argued about who belonged on the main line and who belonged on the siding. There was no real danger, of course, because trains always approached meets with some caution. If they saw a train coming at them with a headlight on they knew it was on the main line and they stopped or slowed to wait for the other train to clear. But a lot of time was lost. I could always tell when there had been a bad night on the railroad because some of the night freights were still coming through Flushing at noon. Fortunately for Percy, it took a long time to track this particular dereliction to its source and by the time he was found to be the culprit he was already gone.

Percy Benjamin was a convivial soul. While he wasn't a

drunkard by any means, he was famous in Flushing for liking a drink and was saddened by the decision of the village's voters to go dry. He spent a lot of time finding new sources of supply and he took some pride in being known as a man who could always provide a drink for his friends when they were in need of one. One of the most famous stories told about him had to do with a discovery he made one night while working at the depot.

The station agent was responsible for all the railroad employees who worked in Flushing and one of the most important CS&M installations was the water-pumping station. This station was tucked away down by the river on a shelf above the high-water mark. It was completely isolated from the rest of the village and very few of the townspeople had ever been there. It was housed in a corrugated iron shed and had a tall, thin smokestack sticking out of the top. About the only sign of life anyone ever saw around it was when the smoke came billowing out of the stack.

The pumping station was run by a man named Wes Bird. Wes was the nearest thing to a hermit that Flushing had. He had lived in the town all his life, but no one knew anything about him. My grandpa Perry once told me that Wes was the last person in Michigan who still hunted for his food. Whatever the case, I never saw Wes in his life when he was not carrying his shotgun under his arm and was not accompanied by his old hound dog. If he walked into a store in the business district, he carried the gun in with him and the dog tagged along at his heels. If he was seen on the street on a bright Easter Sunday morning he was carrying the gun and the dog tagged along at his heels. He never spoke to anyone and no one ever spoke to him. He couldn't read and he couldn't write. He never took a bath and he never changed his clothes. He must have shaved because he didn't have a beard, but he didn't shave often enough because his face was invariably covered with ragged bristles. He had a huge scraggly mustache and he always carried a huge chew of tobacco in his mouth and at odd moments would project a great stream of tobacco juice as he walked along.

The job at the water-pumping station was ideal for a man like Wes Bird. Every Saturday morning the local freight would spot a car of coal on the spur track that ran down into the village. Wes would go up and dump the hoppers and the coal would roll down the steep bank right up to the door of the shack that housed the pumping station. All he had to do was shovel it into the firebox under the boiler. When Wes first took the job he lived in a little wooden hut across the river from the pump house. Every morning he would row across to the pumps in a boat (in the winter he would walk across on the ice), tend his fires, and then go back home. While I was a small boy, however, the boat washed away in the flood one spring, so Wes simply dug himself a cave in the steep bank behind the pumping station, stretched a burlap curtain across the front of it, moved in a few old crates, and lived in it. In the wintertime, when it got bitterly cold, he would spread a few blankets out on the concrete floor of the boiler room and sleep there.

The pumps lifted the water from the river into a huge water tank that stood by the tracks. Wes Bird used to get up a head of steam every morning at daylight and pump the tank full of water. When it began to overflow he would bank his fires and shut off the pumps, pick up his shotgun, and wander down the riverbank for four or five miles looking for rabbits or squirrels or other small game. When he got enough for the day's food, he would come back to the pump station and start cooking. This was around one in the afternoon, as a rule, and at that time he would start the pumps going and fill the tank again. He would fill it for the last time after supper in the evening.

One night in the early fall a fireman from one of the night extras came walking over to the depot and told Percy Benjamin that the water tank was almost dry. Percy got a lantern and walked over the little-used path to the pumping station to see what was the matter. He found Wes asleep in the cave and roused him, then went down to the pump house to see if he could get the fires going. Percy had never been at the pumping station before and when he held up his lantern to look around, he could hardly believe his eyes. Wes Bird had turned the pumping station into a huge still. It pumped water, all right, but it made whiskey too.

Anyone else in Percy Benjamin's position would either have quietly told Wes to get rid of the still or reported its presence to Tom Bulger and let Tom take the responsibility for doing whatever had to be done. Percy's mind worked along different lines. *He* wasn't going to get rid of any still until he found out just how good Wes Bird's whiskey was. He told Wes that he wouldn't say anything about it if Wes would being him a jugful of the stuff the next time he made a batch.

Late one night, about three weeks later, just before Thanksgiving, Wes Bird came to the depot after everyone had gone home and shoved a jug of whiskey in through the ticket window. Percy thanked him for it and put it down under the counter. He was busy. There were several trains on the line and just before Tom Bulger had left that evening Mrs. Halliwell had called up. Her son was in the army and was stationed near Shreveport, Louisiana. Mrs. Halliwell had made up her mind, on the spur of the moment, to go down to Shreveport for Thanksgiving and she wanted to leave on the morning train. Tom had sent a telegram off to Chicago to get her a lower berth on the Illinois Central for the next night. He told Percy that when the reservation came in he was to make out the tickets so that they would be ready the next morning.

The reservation came in just after Wes Bird delivered the jug of whiskey and Percy went over and took down a long strip ticket. These tickets came in sections. Each section was separated from the next by a perforation. The more railroads a traveler rode on the more sections he needed. Sometimes these tickets would get to be five or six feet long. In Mrs. Halliwell's case, she needed only a relatively short one—six sections. The very bottom section would be taken up by the last Grand Trunk conductor before Chicago. The next to the bottom belonged to the Parmelee Transfer in Chicago. The third from the bottom belonged to the Illinois Central. The three remaining sections would be taken up in inverse order and would get Mrs. Halliwell back to Flushing. All these sections had to be filled out by hand, and before he got down the pen and the inkwell, Percy decided that while he was filling out the ticket it would be a good time to sample Wes Bird's whiskey. He poured a glassful and then sat down at the ticket agent's desk and went to work. He had got Mrs. Halliwell all the way to Shreveport and had started her back when a train order came over the telegraph for the southbound Flyer. Because that train didn't stop in Flushing, Percy had to get down the big hoops and go stand by the track. It was a cold night so he put on his overcoat, finished off the glass of whiskey, and went outdoors. By the time the Flyer had whizzed past and he had retrieved the hoops, he was thirsty again, so he poured himself another glass. Then he went back to work on Mrs. Halliwell's ticket. He got one more section of the ticket done when the telegraph key started clicking. When Percy scraped back the stool to go take the message he knocked over the whiskey glass and the liquid ran all over the ticket. When he came back to it he got down another strip of six sections and started all over again. He ruined the new ticket in about the third section when he inadvertently knocked over the inkwell. In one way or another he ruined three more tickets in the next hour. By that time he had finished off another glass of Wes Bird's whiskey. When he went to get still another six-section strip, he discovered there weren't any more. The next smallest one was an eight-section one. This worried him. He would have to use up those extra two sections somehow and the only way *that* could be done was by adding another railroad. He went to his telegraph key and sent off another telegram to Chicago. He canceled the Illinois Central reservation and asked for one on the Rock Island from Chicago to Kansas City and for a seat on the Kansas City Southern to Shreveport. He was pleased at this solution and poured himself another drink, then started the new ticket.

When Lloyd Way, the day trick telegrapher, came on duty at six o'clock the next morning, Percy Benjamin had gone home. He sometimes did this after the Lennon and Montrose operators came to work at 5:30 if the dispatcher gave him permission. He'd left a hastily scribbled note—at least Lloyd thought it was hastily scribbled because it was a little hard to read—saying that Mrs. Halliwell's tickets were in an envelope in the cash drawer. Lloyd was busy that morning and it did not occur to him to look in the envelope. When Mrs. Halliwell arrived, just before traintime, he looked at the amount written on the envelope and collected it from her. She put the tickets in her purse and got on the train. About an hour after she'd gone Tom Bulger found a big manila envelope under the counter. It was filled with about twenty void strip tickets, some of them six sections, some of them eight, ten, and twelve sections. Toward evening, while Tom was talking to Durand on the telegraph, the operator on the other end made some remark about people in Flushing not being able to make up their mind where they wanted to go, but the remark meant nothing to Tom and he let it pass. That night when Percy Benjamin came to work, he didn't mention Mrs. Halliwell at all, but he did take Tom off to one side and told him that he had just come up from the pumping station. Several weeks before, so he said, he'd discovered that Wes Bird had a still down there. After thinking about it for some time, he had sampled the whiskey, and it was terrible—real white mule. It wasn't safe to drink. Under the circumstances he had gone back down and told Wes to get rid of the still. He wondered if he had done the right thing. Tom Bulger thought about it for a while and then told Percy he guessed the whole business had been handled just about right. Nothing more would be said about it.

About two days after Thanksgiving someone in Flushing got a postcard from Mrs. Halliwell saying that she was enjoying her trip. It was postmarked from Denver, Colorado. The next day two other people got cards from El Paso and San Antonio. Quite a few heard from Mrs. Halliwell when she got to New Orleans. About a week before Christmas the neighbor who was looking after her fires got a check for another ton of coal. Mrs. Halliwell was starting for home, she said, but she would be a lot longer getting there than she had originally planned. She stopped over in Atlanta, Washington, New York, and Pittsburgh, and finally got home in the middle of January. She lectured about that trip to the women's clubs in Flushing for several years afterwards.

Percy Benjamin left Flushing unexpectedly in the spring of 1919. I suppose his leaving is one of the reasons why I always think of that period after the fire as being so dismal. In 1919 it was still the custom for railroad employees to be paid once a month by the paymaster. He would come along the line in an observation-type car pulled by an engine. When he came to a town like Flushing, all the depot employees, Wes Bird, and the section gang (track repairmen) would be assembled by the side of the track. They would file up the steps of the back platform, get their pay, and walk down the steps on the other side. It was a quick, efficiently handled business and the pay train never tarried very long in any one place. On that spring day in 1919, however, when the pay train came around the bend from Durand it had an extra car on it. Instead of taking their money and getting off the train, the employees were directed through the observation car to that extra car. There they found several doctors assembled and were all given physical examinations. When Percy Benjamin sat down in front of the eye charts he couldn't read some of them. He was color blind! The next day Percy was gone from the Flushing depot. There were no more lamps turned the wrong way on the switch stands and the trainmen always got the right colored orders.

Percy Benjamin's story *did* have a happy ending. He was transferred to the freight yards of the Grand Trunk at Lansing, where his telegraphy would be of some use and where his color blindness would not be a liability. Before he retired he rose to be freight agent in Lansing, a much better job than he ever could have got in Flushing.

CHAPTER TEN

DURING THE big fire at Hart's mill more than a thousand strangers came to town. They wandered up and down the streets in the dark and in many cases they entered homes to put out the small blazes. There was not one case of looting or petty thievery.

For most of its existence Flushing had very little police protection. As I remember it, no one in the village ever locked a door. All through my boyhood I wandered in and out of people's houses at will. Most of the time I didn't even knock. I just opened the door and shouted to see if anyone was home. I don't recall that I ever turned a knob and found a door locked whether anyone was at home or not. Our own house was never locked, day or night. Even when we went away in the summertime for a month anyone could have walked into our house and taken anything he wanted. Each summer, at the last moment, when we were all dressed and the car was packed, my mother would go to the front door and push the button that set the night lock. She was never sure when it was on and when it was off and would fuss over it for several minutes, opening the door and closing it from both the inside and the outside. After satisfying herself that the door was really locked, she would start looking for the key to the back door. She would range through the house, lifting up doilies, pulling out drawers, and opening cupboard doors. My father, meanwhile, would have got into the driver's seat and started blowing the horn. When this didn't get my mother to come, he would climb out and go in and join the search. Eventually my brothers and I would be helping, too. After about ten minutes my father would throw up his hands and say, "To hell with it." We would all troop down, get into the car, and go away, leaving the back door unlocked. We never did find the key to that back door and I doubt if there ever was one.

The village jail in Flushing had been built by my great-grandfather, Will Parmelee. Great-grandpa Parmelee was one of the village's authentic Civil War heroes. He had served in Phil Sheridan's cavalry and had lost a leg at the battle of Murphreesboro, Tennessee. He was picked up by Confederate soldiers after the battle and ended up in Andersonville Prison on a crutch made out of a hickory limb. He underwent two and a half years of starvation and pain and had the additional burden of seeing his own brother die in the prison. Will Parmelee had been a gay young man before he went off to the war and had married into the Niles family—the same family that Ira Sayre had married into. When he came back from his ordeal, he seemed determined to raise hell and that is just what he did for the next thirty years. From 1865 to 1894 he lived off the good will of his friends and the bounty of his wife's relatives. He worked one day in every seven and was drunk the other six days. Even when he was at his worst Will Parmelee was a greatly admired and a well-liked man. Although he wouldn't work for himself he would sober up and go to work in a friend's place if that friend became ill. He was always thinking up things to keep the villagers on edge. He once rode a log raft over the dam in the middle of the spring flood in order to win a dollar bet. Somehow, shortly after it was built, he managed to put a horse on top of Hart's mill. Although he had been dead for twenty years when I was a boy, a day rarely went by when I didn't hear some mention of him. On a ride through the countryside someone would point at a tree and say, "That is where Will Parmelee broke the record for tree climbing." On a walk through the village someone would point at a house and say, "Your grandfather Parmelee once put a skunk through the window of that place." On the day of Mrs. Halliwell's funeral everyone got to laughing about the time Great-grandpa Parmelee put a garter snake in her outhouse.

In 1876, through the good offices of his father-in-law, Will Parmelee was appointed village constable. He held that position until he died and the salary of $300 per year that he received for his services was the only money he ever earned. Shortly after he was appointed to the position he talked the village council into letting him build a jail, "in case a drunken Indian ever came to town." It was one of the most horrendous jails any town ever had. It was a wooden building with walls made of squared logs eighteen inches think (so tomahawks couldn't penetrate it, I presume). The four windows were small portholes so that no one could crawl through them, even if the bars were sawed off. It had only one room, eight feet wide and ten feet long. The ceiling was so low that an Indian couldn't even look dignified without bumping his head. There was a dirt floor and three wooden shelves on the wall in case anyone ever wanted to sleep. There was absolutely no room to move around. For eighteen years after the Flushing jail was built, Great-grandpa Parmelee was the only prisoner. Each Saturday night he would get rip-roaring drunk and be confined in his own jail. After his death no one occupied the jail again until the summer of 1919. Then for sixty days, while I was seven years old, I went down to the jail every afternoon and peeked timidly around the corner of the council chambers at the bearded faces of the men who were inside. Officially, the prisoners had been sentenced for disorderly conduct, but as far as I was concerned they were dangerous criminals.

I had heard rumors that the men in the Flushing jail were really there for kidnaping John Egan. John Egan himself claimed they had kidnaped him. The trouble with his story was that no one in Flushing thought he was worth kidnaping. The village had more than one famous drunkard—there were at least three of them in my boyhood—but John was a case apart. He worked in Frawley's poolroom as a counterman. When Frawley's poolroom had been Frawley's saloon, he had been a bartender. When Flushing and Genesee County went dry, Bill Frawley had the decency to change the *name* of his business, even if he didn't change the basic character of the place and John Egan changed the name of his occupation, even though he did the same old things.

Michigan had local option and Saginaw County, the next one to the north, remained wet. For the convenience of thirsty residents of Genesee County, a small disreputable collection of shacks had grown up on the Saginaw side of the county line near Chesaning, about fifteen miles north of Flushing. This notorious settlement was called Rattle Run and a steady stream of drunks staggered back from it to the neighboring villages. It is not particularly to Flushing's credit that very few of the residents visited this shanty town. They didn't have to, since anyone who wanted a drink could get one right in Frawley's poolroom. Frawley's didn't serve very good whiskey. It was known as white mule and I have always assumed that it was made right there in the basement.

The whole business was handled discreetly and no one ever mentioned it. My grandfather Love was the president of the village council and he played rummy in Frawley's every day. Frank Wilcox was the village constable and he occasionally ducked into the back room for a quick kick from the mule, as he quaintly put it.

John Egan's official duties under the dry regime included the frying of ham for fried ham sandwiches and the dispensing of soda pop, but I think his main job was tending the still. This involved a considerable amount of sampling. On almost any day of almost any week he would come out the front door of Frawley's and make his unsteady way across the bridge, turn into Emily Street, and climb the hill to his house up behind the West Side grain elevator. He never bothered to take off his white bartender's apron when he made this trip, and he always wore it when he came to work in the morning so that most Flushing people never recognized him without it. The only thing that ever varied in his public appearances was his degree of unsteadiness. This all depended on how busy Jimmy McNally was (Jimmy was the other bartender). If Jimmy got around to noticing that John was drunk by 12:15, John would walk home in a fairly straight line, holding himself under a tight rein, staring fixedly ahead. Under such conditions he would get up the hill without much trouble. However, if Jimmy didn't get around to looking at John until quarter of three in the afternoon, things were pretty hectic on the way home. John would stagger and reel from tree to tree. He would sing songs to the horses tied in front of the stores or make a speech to the flowers in Sarah Parmelee Perry Park. People used to refer to John as having a one-o'clock drunk or a two-o'clock drunk or a three-o'clock drunk.

On the whole the village of Flushing tolerated John Egan's weakness. His only trouble was talking. He never liked to drop a conversation once he had started it. He would follow a man right out of Frawley's, walk home with him, climb the steps of the front porch, and tag along right into the house. If the man sat down at the dinner table, John would sit down with him, grab a plate of food, and talk between bites. He actually did this once at Frank Niles's house, much to the horror of Frank's wife, who was the leader of the WCTU. (Frank Niles's wife always had trouble at mealtimes.) Under the circumstances most people in Flushing knew better than to engage John Egan in an argument. The traveling salesmen who visited Flushing didn't know about this tendency to talk and most of them got caught at one time or another. They would stop in at Frawley's for a quick drink on the way up to the depot in the morning and get to talking to John. He would follow them right out onto the street, across the bridge, up to the depot, and onto the train. About once a week Tom Bulger would get a telegram from the operator at Lennon or Montrose that John Egan was there and didn't seem to know where he was. Tom would tell the operator to put John on the next train for home. During all of my boyhood there was a glass bowl full of quarters in the cash drawer of the station agent's desk. Tom Bulger kept it there especially for John Egan. When the conductor helped John down out of the baggage car (he always came home in the baggage car), Tom would open the drawer and take money enough out of the bowl to give the conductor his fare.

In the summer of 1919 Saginaw County voted dry and Rattle Run was doomed. A great many people made pilgrimages there to pay their last respects. At some time during those hot summer days a group of Flint policemen decided to have an outing at Rattle Run. I've never been sure whether this was some kind of annual picnic or whether the policemen were absent without leave. The city of Flint was the only community in Genesee County with an organized, professional police force, and evidently the group that started for Rattle Run was the traffic squad, for they came roaring down East Main Street in a cloud of dust, mounted on motorcycles and riding in sidecars. There were ten of these vehicles and there was one policeman on each motorcycle and one in each sidecar. I was standing in front of the post office when they arrived and I watched them as they pulled in at the curb and dismounted. They all wore khaki-colored uniforms and brown leather puttees and long, brown, gauntleted gloves. They also had khaki, visored caps much like those worn by chauffeurs today.

The policemen were already in a holiday mood when they arrived in Flushing. They swaggered up and down the sidewalk with some braggadocio, helping themselves to apples or doughnuts in the stores as though they were at home in Flint. A few of them inevitably found their way into Frawley's poolroom where they tried to buy a drink to quench their thirst before continuing the hot, dusty ride to Rattle Run. John Egan knew better than to sell whiskey to a strange policeman and he told them, politely, that he had none. He was a wispy little man and nothing to be afraid of. One of the policemen boisterously jumped over the bar, elbowed him aside, and began looking under the counter for the jug of white mule. When this happened there was an ominous scraping of chairs at the rummy tables. Flushing had some rather noted ex-saloon brawlers like my grandfather Love and Sime Bresnahan and most of them could be found sitting around Frawley's in the morning. It had been a long time between fights for most of them and they were just the kind who would welcome a little boisterousness. Among those present was Frank Wilcox, the constable. He went over to the bar and showed his badge and suggested to the policemen that they leave quietly so that there would be no trouble. The man behind the bar laughed at Frank and went back to slamming cupboard doors. One of the other policemen grabbed Frank by the arm and roughly pushed him out of the way. That was enough for the rest of the regular crowd. They moved in determinedly, and before the policemen quite knew what had happened to them they were flying bodily through the air and landing on the sidewalk. When they got to their feet they were shoved along in front of a gathering crowd to their motorcycles. Frank Wilcox looked at his watch and told them they had just five minutes to get out of town. It was not until they sped off down Main Street to the iron bridge that someone discovered John Egan was riding in one of the sidecars. He was sitting on the lap of one of the policemen, his white apron blowing in the wind. Most of those who saw him at that moment seemed to think that he had simply gone along to continue his protestations that there was no whiskey in Frawley's poolroom.

It might be well to say a word about the two Wilcox brothers, Fred and Frank. They were the prosperous twin sons of old James Wilcox who owned orchards and berry farms all over the township. Both Wilcoxes were fond of politics and both served on the village council. Fred was a Republican and Frank was a Democrat. They used to sit across the council table from each other and whenever an issue divided the two sides they would almost come to blows. The rest of the time they acted as a team. They passed the office of village constable back and forth between them. Frequently no one knew from one day to the next who had the badge.

To most of the people in Flushing the Wilcoxes were objects of some affection and the common saying was that neither of them would hurt a fly. However, although they were approaching their middle fifties, both of them loved nothing better than a fight. Whenever trouble broke out in Flushing they seemed to smell it and would be there at once. Each of them had false teeth and upon arrival at the scene of a melee they would flip a coin to see who was going to join in. The loser would hold the other's teeth. If they could find some trustworthy third person to hold the teeth, *both* of them would get into the fight, but they were always careful of such a procedure. They gave their teeth to a third person once and then couldn't remember who it was. After eating soft food for several days and going so far as to order new teeth from Jerry Gibbons, the village dentist, they found the old ones. Mr. J. B. French, the village hardware dealer, had put them in the front show window of his store with a big sign over them announcing a sale of slightly used choppers.

On the day that John Egan was kidnaped Frank Wilcox was officially the constable and he took charge in the events that followed. The policemen reached Rattle Run without further incident and spent the afternoon and evening drinking. They started for home just as it got dark, guided by the flickering beams from the kerosene lamps that served them as headlights.

During their hours in Rattle Run their indignation against Flushing had been growing and they were ready to get even on the way back to Flint. Their trip was something of an epic. They were not seeing very clearly and they weaved in and out as they jockeyed for position in the semidarkness. The roads were narrow and dusty and the policemen ran in and out of the ditches and took off across the fields. They sang ribald songs at the tops of their voices as they moved drunkenly through the countryside. They stopped at a farmhouse or two and serenaded the farmers' daughters. They chased chickens around barnyards on their motorcycles. They let livestock loose from the barns. By the time they reached Montrose they were covered with dust from the road, mud from the ditches, and foam from the beer they had brought along from Rattle Run. Some of them were bruised from falling off the machines.

Montrose suffered mildly as this cavalcade passed through town. Some of the motorcycles were ridden up and down the board sidewalks. Two girls were chased off the street and up onto the front porch of a house. Obscene language was addressed to a few respectable citizens. As they turned the corner to ride toward Flushing, one policeman was heard to remark that Montrose hadn't seen anything to what Flushing was going to get.

Shortly after the drunken caravan roared out of Montrose, the telegrapher at the Montrose depot sent a warning to Bud Roof, the new station agent in Flushing. Bud promptly relayed it to my grandfather Love on the telephone. My grandfather Love got through to the State Constabulary in Flint and reported what he had heard. The officer in charge of the Flint barracks told my grandfather to do what he could until the troopers could saddle up and get to Flushing. In those days the troopers were mounted on fine horses and wore pith helmets. They had a reputation for excellence and were much admired throughout the state. They were a crack cavalry force and were the ultimate resort in times of violence. The Flint post of the Constabulary was located in the northwest part of the city at that time and was a good eight miles from Flushing. Although the troopers saddled up and galloped quickly, it would be a full hour before they could get to the village.

Frank Wilcox was quite put out with my grandfather when he found out that the Constabulary had been called in. He relished the thought of twenty drunken policemen trying to invade the village. It promised exactly the kind of free-for-all that he loved. As soon as he received the word he sent his brother Fred out to round up all the two-fisted men in town and while this was being done he began setting up a trap. There was no electricity, of course, and the village had no street lights of any kind. Flushing was dark and Frank Wilcox made it darker. One of the things I did that night was to run up and down Main Street and tell all the store owners to turn out their lamps. Some of my friends ran out along West Main Street and told all the people in the houses to turn out their lamps, too. It was a little like Lexington getting ready to welcome the Redcoats.

Frank Wilcox knew that the motorcycles would have to cross the old iron bridge and that their lamps wouldn't show very far ahead. He got a pile of railroad ties from the tracks that were then being torn up east of the railroad bridge and built a barricade across the end of the iron bridge nearest the business district. The ties were old and in the dark no one could see them from more than a few feet away. Frank wanted all the motorcycles to get right on the bridge before they stopped.

While the barricade was being built, Fred Wilcox got all the fishermen in town to bring out the big dip nets. These were stretched out on the roadway of the bridge to cover it completely and then wired securely together. Ropes were then tied to various parts of this big net and it was hoisted into the air so that it formed a canopy about fifteen feet above the roadway. Six of the men were stationed on top of the bridge with knives to cut the ropes that held up the canopy. The rest of Frank Wilcox's force hid behind the barricade, but other men were stationed along West Main Street at various places.

It took almost an hour to complete all these preparations. By the time they were done two forces were converging on Flushing. The State Constabulary were riding hard, about three miles away. The ten motorcycles were moving much slower, but they were nearer. They had arrived at Brent Creek, five miles away, and had left it. Brent Creek wasn't much of a town. It consisted of a railroad station, a general store, and six houses. It had footpaths instead of sidewalks. The policemen had ridden up to the front of the store, had broken the windows, had smashed the front door, then had entered and helped themselves to some food. One of the townspeople had made the mistake of trying to frighten them off by firing a twelve-gauge shotgun over their heads. This had reminded them that they were armed and most of them proceeded to pull out their revolvers and fire them into the air. One of the motorcyclists had ridden across a lawn and fired into the window of a house at a lamp. Almost every window in Brent Creek was broken and, to complete the reign of terror before he left town, one of the policemen had ridden his vehicle through the front door of the store, had turned it around inside, and had ridden out again. Nothing was left on the shelves and very little was left right side up. A full report came over the telegraph to Bud Roof as soon as the last motorcycle sputtered away toward Flushing.

The first flickering headlights appeared over Henry Chatters's crossing about twenty minutes later and came weaving down the Montrose Road toward Main Street. There wasn't a light showing in Flushing and the policemen must have noted this fact, for they stopped and held a council of war before making the turn into town and crossing the tracks. When they moved ahead they proceeded cautiously as though they were looking for trouble. When they started down the Main Street hill one motorcycle and sidecar branched off from the pack and rattled across the cinder-covered area between the depot and the railroad tracks, skidded around, and ran straight up to the door of the waiting room and banged up against it as though to ride right through it. As soon as the vehicle stopped, five Flushing men stepped out of the shadows with baseball bats upraised. There wasn't even a scuffle. The bats came down and the two policemen toppled over onto the cinders. Their hands were tied and someone brought a pail of water and threw it on them. When they came to they were yanked to their feet and marched down the hill.

Down at the bottom of the hill, where Main Street straightened out for the run to the bridge, another motorcycle branched off from the principal group and ducked down the little grade into the lumber yard. My grandfather Love, my father, and three of the yard men stood in the shadow of the sheds, each armed with an eight-foot two-by-four. When the motorcycle sputtered into the alleyway between sheds, the two-by-fours swung. The two policemen toppled over backwards and lay on the ground stunned. The motorcycle rolled on and turned over against a lumber pile. My grandfather and his helpers ran out, yanked the policemen to their feet, tied them up, and started for the bridge.

Things did not end quite so quickly or so easily in the center of town. The remaining motorcycles roared onto the bridge in a confused group and started across. When the flickering headlights of the first vehicle picked up the barricade the driver stood up in his saddle, jammed on his brakes, shouted, and tried to wheel around and go back. The motorcycles behind him either tried to steer around him and ran up against the bridge rail or else they ran into him. They ended up in a disorganized jumble, shouting at each other, and trying to get out of the tangle. In the midst of the tumult a whistle blew. From up above the net floated down over the motorcycle riders and a gang of men came whooping over the barricade like a tribe of Indians breaking out of ambush. Although the sixteen motorcycle riders were disorganized and taken completely by surprise they had no intention of giving up. While Frank Wilcox exhorted his posse to grab the edges of the net and pull it tight around the captives, two of the policemen struggled out from under it and one of them hit

Frank squarely on the jaw. The other began slugging it out with two of the net tenders. At that point the Flushing men forgot all about trying to pull the net. Some of them even lifted it up and crawled under it so as to get a clearer shot at their targets.

For ten minutes the free-for-all raged over the bridge, under the net and out from under it. It was so dark no one could really see what he was doing. One man recounted the next morning that he had been slugged behind the ear by Fred Wilcox who was just wading from one group of fighting figures to another swinging his fists in sheer exuberance. One Flushing man chased a policeman right up to the top of the bridge and down again and at least one man fell or was knocked from the bridge into the river which wasn't very deep at that time of year. Then, in the middle of the battle and the cries of the combatants, the State Constabulary came galloping down Main Street like the United States Cavalry, leaped from their horses, and ran into the midst of the fray swinging their riot clubs in all directions. One by one figures were dragged out of the pack and forced to stand along the barricade. Even Frank Wilcox, sporting two black eyes and a bloody nose, was lined up. It wasn't until my grandfather Love came walking up from the lumber yard that he was released. It was a good twenty minutes before the Flushing men were separated from the policemen.

The battle of the iron bridge was not quite over, however. An officer of the State Constabulary with a notebook started down the line of policemen to take their names and Frank Wilcox and his men began rolling up the net. When the officer reached the last three men in the line, they were ready for him. One of them came up with his fist and hit the trooper squarely in the stomach and another hit him beside the jaw. With that the three of them broke across the bridge. The movement took everyone by surprise and it was several seconds before anyone took up the chase. Even then the fugitives would probably have been caught if, at that precise moment, one of the motorcycles hadn't roared to life. It moved right through the midst of the pursuing troopers and they had to jump back out of the way. By the time the chase was resumed the escapees had disappeared.

The motorcycle was driven by none other than John Egan, a ghostly figure in a white bartender's apron. He turned left off the bridge and rattled up Emily Street. Instead of following Emily Street around the curve and up behind the West Side grain elevator to his house, however, John shot right up the steep hill that bordered the river. He soon disappeared from sight and sound at breakneck speed along the little country road that followed the high hills along the edge of the river valley to the east. Up until that moment, as far as anyone was ever able to determine, John Egan had never driven a motorcycle in his life. No one saw him again until late the next evening when a farmer on a wagon found him in a ditch beside the road, sleeping in the sidecar. He didn't seem to know where he was or how he had got there, but his memory returned as the days passed and he started to sample the white mule again. He claimed that he had not gone off with the policemen voluntarily. He had been kidnaped and had tried all day to get away. He had been asleep in the sidecar during the fight on the bridge and had awakened to find no one guarding him, so he jumped into the saddle and drove off.

The three escaping policemen weren't found immediately. They had jumped down to the riverbank at the west end of the bridge, had waded out to a small island in the middle of the stream, and had hidden in some bushes. After the excitement had died down and the villagers had gone home to bed, they waded the rest of the way across the river and hid in the village icehouse under a pile of sawdust. They remained there all the next day and night and on the second morning they came out, hungry and half frozen, and stumbled into the arms of Frank Wilcox. By that time there wasn't any fight left in them. They announced that they were ready to be taken to Flint to the county jail. They assumed, of course, that they would be tried in the county courts for what they had done in Brent Creek. Frank Wilcox thought that *someone* ought to be tried for blacking his eyes on the bridge. He went to my grandfather Love and recommended that his captives stand trial right there in Flushing and my grandfather agreed. The other seventeen, incidentally, had already been convicted and had been sentenced to sixty days in the county jail.

It wasn't easy to convict a man of anything in Flushing. To begin with, no one could remember who had been elected as justice of the peace. Frank Wilcox went up to the Flushing *Observer* and looked through the back files. He discovered there had been no election for justice of the peace for the past twelve years. Will Mutton had been elected to that office in 1888 and had been re-elected regularly without opposition through 1906. No one else seemed to want the job and no one ever came forward to run against Will, so after 1906 it was just left off the ballots. Frank Wilcox consulted with Ira Sayre and Ira was of the opinion that it was the intent of the people of Flushing that Will Mutton was *still* justice of the peace, so Frank Wilcox went out to Will's farm and brought him into the village council chambers to hold the trial. By 1919 Will Mutton was a small, stooped man of eighty-eight. He had, believe it or not, been engaged in the sheep-raising business all his life and, although he was still active in it, he was becoming absent-minded. He managed to fumble his way through his one and only case as justice of the peace, however, and he found the three policemen guilty of disorderly conduct. There was quite an argument at the end of the trial because when Will Mutton banged his gavel to announce his verdict, he said that he found the prisoners guilty of kidnaping.

"But you can't do that, Will," Frank Wilcox said. "They didn't kidnap anybody."

Will had visited Frawley's poolroom and he'd heard differently from John Egan. It took some argument before he banged the gavel again and announced that the verdict was guilty of disorderly conduct. He sentenced the prisoners to sixty days in the village jail. Under the conditions they had to put up with for the next two months, it might have been better if they *had* been convicted of kidnaping. At least they would have lived in the comparative luxury of state prison. There was one consistency in Flushing that should be remarked on, however. In its whole existence, the village jail was never occupied by anyone but policemen.

CHAPTER ELEVEN

At THE time the policemen invaded Flushing the village was in the midst of planning its single greatest celebration. For almost a year and a half everyone in town had been waiting for the day when the lights would come on again. Early in the summer the various organizations got together and agreed that something special should mark the moment when Bob Hart pulled the switch in his new concrete power plant.

After making certain that this event would take place in the early fall when the weather was still good, the Board of Commerce set aside an entire week for a street fair. The Order of the Eastern Star, the Odd Fellows, the Grange, the Ladies of the Maccabees, and the Knights of Columbus each scheduled a dance on successive nights. The Methodist church and the Baptist church announced that they would serve chicken dinners all week. The Chautauqua, which normally played Flushing in the summertime, arranged to come there for a special week. Ray Budd organized the best minstrel show yet. All the townspeople walked up and down through Stewart and Minard's furniture store buying new light fixtures. Along Main Street the old hitching rails came down and the new boulevard lights were installed. Strings of light bulbs were hung from one side of the street to the other and many of the householders near the center of town had gaily colored lights on their lawn. The empty lot where the old livery stable had been was literally flooded with candlepower. (The old hitching rails had been erected there, thus making it one of the first municipal parking lots, even if it was for horses.)

Aside from the actual ceremony of pulling the light switch, the villagers looked forward to two events with a great deal of anticipation. One was the big raffle which was to be held at the very end of the fair. The other was the opening of the New Ideal Theater. Of all the things that we had missed during those long months when the lights were out, the motion pictures topped the list.

The movies came to Flushing early. They were brought there by Mr. John Cuddeback, who opened the Ideal Theater on the ground floor of the Odd Fellows hall. He presented a midweek program on Wednesday and a weekend program on Saturdays and Sundays. All performances were evening ones. Because of those Wednesday evening performances, John Cuddeback was at war with half the parents in Flushing. It had nothing to do with the type of pictures he showed. Wednesday night was a school night and my parents, along with a lot of others, were against boys and girls going out and sitting up late when they had to go to school the next day. John Cuddeback wanted those dimes and deliberately presented pictures on Wednesday night which were calculated to draw boys and girls. Tom Mix and Hoot Gibson were Wednesday night men. So were Charlie Chaplin, Tarzan of the Apes, and Dustin Farnum. And when she finally came along, Clara Bow was a Wednesday night woman.

My father and mother were not taken in by this. John Cuddeback could have had all these stars in his theater in person and my brothers and I would not have been allowed to go to the Ideal Theater on Wednesday night. There was much grumbling in our house about the restriction and there was grumbling in the homes of other boys and girls who were similarly kept at home. This grumbling found an outlet in complaints to Mr.

Cuddeback, but he never changed his policy. Saturday night had its compensations, however. William S. Hart (we always pronounced it William Esshart) was a Saturday night man, as were Douglas Fairbanks and Fatty Arbuckle. There were honest arguments between the Wednesday night theatergoers and the Saturday night ones over which stars were the best. Because I always had to defend Hart against Mix and Arbuckle against Chaplin, I eventually got to dislike both Mix and Chaplin. I have never thought Chaplin was as funny as a lot of other people say he was.

Aside from acquiring those rather irrational prejudices and the necessity of sitting through a lot of mushy pictures with dopey women like Elsie Ferguson, Colleen Moore, and Lillian Gish, we didn't really suffer from going to the movies only on Saturday night. We got *all* the epics. We could always tell when a picture was going to be an epic because on such occasions Mrs. Cuddeback brought her violin and played along with Mrs. Banning at the piano. Mrs. Cuddeback was very good on "Hearts and Flowers." I think her repertoire was quite limited, but she could handle that one piece as well as anyone I ever heard.

Shortly after the fire John Cuddeback decided to take advantage of his long, forced vacation to build a new theater. He bought a store building in the middle of the business block and tore it down. He advertised that the New Ideal Theater would be the finest theater in the state and the villagers believed it. It had two projectors. In the old Ideal Theater a person would just start to get interested in a film when a sign would come on the screen that said, "End of Reel One. Reel Two will follow immediately." Then the lights would go on and people would run up and down the aisles or twist in their seats and talk until John Cuddeback got the reels changed. There would be no more of that. The picture would continue from beginning to end without interruption. Other innovations in the New Ideal Theater included slanting aisles, seats that turned up, and electric fans along the wall. A popcorn machine, run by young Delford Cuddeback, was placed in the lobby. (I had good reason to remember both the fans and the popcorn machine. The next summer after the New Ideal Theater opened one of the fans came off the wall in the middle of Fatty Arbuckle's comedy and fell on my head, knocking me unconscious. I was eating a big bag of popcorn at the time this happened and for some unaccountable reason I never cared for popcorn again. I never liked Delford Cuddeback, either.)

The big attraction at the New Ideal Theater was the Mighty Wurlitzer Orchestra. It was installed a few days before the theater opened and the whole celebration of Flushing's festival of light might be said to have begun on the day that John Cuddeback invited the townspeople to attend a concert that was to be given by the representative of the Wurlitzer Company. People flocked into the theater in their best clothes one afternoon and sat primly in the lighted auditorium while a man came out and bowed and sat down at the keyboard. My father took me to hear this performance and I sat in the front row where I could see everything that went on. I have never heard anything quite like the Wurlitzer Orchestra in the whole forty-six years since that afternoon. I have certainly never seen anything that resembled it once it got going. The Mighty Orchestra came in a huge, square case with windows on three sides so that people could see what was going on inside. There were two violins that were actually bowed, two cornets whose keys went up and down, a xylophone, a saxophone, a bass drum, a snare drum, a pair of cymbals, a banjo, and several other instruments that were buried down in the bottom of the case. When all these instruments started playing at once, I couldn't take my eyes off them. No matter how many times I saw it, there was so much to watch that it was always as good the second time through as the first.

The box was connected to a piano-like instrument that sat in the pit. Theoretically, the piano was played like any piano and the sounds of a piano came out. If the pianist wanted a violin accompaniment, he just pulled a knob above the keyboard marked "violins" and kept right on playing. The violins would join in. Any other instrument could be brought in the same way. The only time I ever heard the full orchestra was on that afternoon when the Wurlitzer representative played for us. It sounded quite good then. It may have been the first full orchestra I ever heard, but I don't think so. We must have had one on the Victrola. The next day, when the New Ideal Theater opened officially, Mrs. Banning, the regular pianist, took over. I am convinced that the whole contraption baffled her. She would play along, as she always had done, keeping one eye on the screen. When she began to get excited she would reach for a knob. She invariably pulled the wrong one. William Esshart would be chasing Indians and a violin would start playing. Norma Talmadge would be dying to the rat-a-tat-tat of a snare drum. Strongheart (there was a dog for you) would be barking like a xylophone. It got so bad, finally, that John Cuddeback told Mrs. Banning to leave the knobs alone. He even brought back Mrs. Cuddeback with her violin.

To celebrate the opening of the New Ideal Theater and inaugurate the festival, John Cuddeback had arranged for an epic. He advertised that the first picture would be one in which the village could take pride. Flushing would be the first town in the state to see it. About a month before opening day, however, John Cuddeback had to change his plans.

On that Monday afternoon when Hart's Mill burned, a big sign had just been put up over the front of the Ideal Theater advertising the coming Wednesday night's picture. It was wartime, then, and the huge colored lithograph showed the *Lusitania* sinking by the bow. The four orange and black smokestacks belched smoke and flame and the water around the ship was filled with swimming people and floating wreckage. After the fire that poster hung up on the billboard for eighteen months. The sign blistered and strips began to peel off it. The colors faded and the images became blurred. Every day for eighteen months I stopped and looked up at that picture. I counted the lifeboats. I counted the people swimming in the water. I memorized every detail of the *Lusitania.* I wasn't the only one. All the people in Flushing took to gazing wistfully up at that billboard.

After John Cuddeback announced he was going to open the New Ideal Theater with an epic, a delegation of businessmen called upon him. They said that they had been watching the *Lusitania* sink for eighteen months and thought that Mr. Cuddeback should show the picture he had been advertising all that time. He had to send all the way to Hollywood to find a print of the old film, but he managed it. When the New Ideal Theater opened its doors, people fought to get in. He had to run the picture four times that first night and seven times the next day—the first matinees Flushing ever had—and finally every night for a week. It did a bigger business than any other film ever shown in the village. It wasn't a very good picture, but everyone liked it and almost everyone started hating the Germans all over again, even though the war had been over for almost a year.

The raffle that took place on the last night of the celebration was one of the most memorable events in my life. Raffles had a peculiar place in the regard of the people of Flushing and it all had to do with Dummy Garner. Flushing didn't have very many problems. There was no village idiot, as I recall, and there were no crazy people, or anything like that. There was only Dummy Garner. In his own way Dummy represented a tragedy and in his own way he was a problem. He was already an old man when I was a little boy and he had lived in or near Flushing all his life. He was a short, squat, sturdy man with a bald head and a huge white mustache. He was born deaf and dumb and in his whole life he had never heard a sound nor had he uttered one. His family had been well-to-do farmers who owned a place about four miles east of town and a house at the end of Elm Street to which they retired each winter. Dummy had been sent away to the Michigan Institute for the Deaf and Dumb when he was a very small boy and had acquired a fairly respectable education for a person of his time. He was equipped to cope with life, but the people of Flushing were not equipped to cope with Dummy. Most of his early life was spent in frustration and isolation.

Dummy Garner inherited his family's land and was never in want. He married a girl who was afflicted as he was. He tried to work his farm, but I think he was defeated by the animals, especially the horses. He was not able to control them. He had several bad accidents. Once his team ran away on Main Street and almost wrecked the business district. In about 1890 Dummy sold his farm and moved into the house on Elm Street for good. I believe he thought he could find a way of life in town, but it took him twenty years to adjust. He could not communicate with people and they could not communicate with him. In all the various things he tried to do, from clerking in stores to manual labor, communication was important and most people simply did not have the patience to spend the extra few minutes required to write their needs and desires on the pad that Dummy always carried with him and Dummy did not know how to teach them the quicker, simpler methods available to him. He was affable and well-liked, but when people found themselves in a position where they might have to deal with him they went somewhere else to save time and trouble.

I don't think the people of Flushing realized that they were being cruel or selfish or thoughtless. Dummy Garner knew what was happening and he saw himself being shoved farther and farther out of the main current of life in the village. He could have retired to his front porch and lived out his life in comfort, but he didn't want to do that. He wanted to be part of the town and he worked at it. As one thing after another failed, he decided that he'd have to find some kind of occupation in which he could do something that people wanted done and yet which would not bring him up against the habit of evasion practiced by most people. For centuries the refuge of the handicapped has been in the handicrafts and to some extent this was the direction in which Dummy Garner started. He had been forced to develop his powers of observation to a remarkable extent—and his memory, as well—and he began watching everyone closely to see how things were done. He soon began some cabinetmaking and when people saw how good his work was they asked him to do more. If someone wanted a cupboard put over the kitchen sink, they would send for Dummy. The cupboard making led to remodeling work of other kinds. By the time he was sixty-five, when I was a boy, he was building houses. Every morning I would see him hurrying along the street, his big toolbox in his hand. There was a jauntiness about him that seemed to impart itself to everyone he met for, by that time, nobody avoided him any more. He had become a part of the community and was leading a useful life.

There was another side of Dummy Garner. He was one of the greatest unconscious comedians I have ever seen; unconscious, because I don't think he ever tried to be funny. Indeed, he probably did not realize he was being funny. His comedy grew out of the powers of observation he had developed so assiduously, and out of his memory. He became a first-class mimic. He could imitate the walk of everyone in town. He could blink his eyes like everyone, he could wave his arms like them, move his head as they did when they talked, make up faces like they did when they said certain words, and, wonder of wonders, he could even dance like them. The dancing was the thing that tickled the fancy of Flushing residents more than anything else. Dummy belonged to all the lodges—the Masons, the Odd Fellows, and the Grange. For many years he attended all the meetings, including the social ones. When he started dancing at some of them, people could not believe their eyes. It took everyone a long while to realize that he *still* couldn't hear the music. He was just doing exactly what he saw everyone else doing. When someone jiggled up and down he jiggled up and down. When someone kicked a foot, he kicked a foot. He got a great deal of enjoyment out of dancing and continued to dance until he was eighty years old. Whenever people got to talking about dances and Dummy Garner they would start giggling. At parties they imitated Dummy imitating themselves.

There was one thing about Dummy Garner that baffled the people of Flushing. It started way back in 1890 when he first moved to town. He was the luckiest man who ever trod the village streets. Legend held it that he had won every raffle ever held in Flushing. While this may have been an exaggeration, it was close enough to the truth so that people discussed it in wonder. The members of the Baptist church seemed to think that his luck was some kind of a boon granted to him by God to compensate for his affliction. Nonchurchgoers, like my grandfather Love, were a little less charitable. They thought he had some kind of system. It became a way of life in Flushing to keep Dummy Garner from buying tickets in raffles. It was generally felt that once he got even one lone little chance the raffle was already over.

All kinds of things were tried. In the beginning prizes were bought that could be of no earthly use to Dummy. He was a naturally thrifty man and it was reasoned that he wouldn't waste his money by buying a chance on something that he couldn't use. This approach never worked. Dummy bought the tickets anyway and when he won he insisted on keeping the prize no matter how incongruous it was. The most famous prize he ever won was given away in about 1900, when telephones were a new thing in Flushing. The raffle committee at the Masonic Lodge thought up the idea of giving away a wall telephone, along with a one year's subscription for service. When Dummy won it he insisted that it be installed in his house. Mr. French, as the village hardware dealer, had charge of installing telephones at that time and he sent off to Chicago for the biggest gong he could find and put it in Dummy's living room. Every time that telephone rang it could be heard three blocks away. Everyone on Elm Street except Dummy knew when he had a telephone call. He would sit on his front porch in his rocking chair, completely oblivious to the fact that his phone was ringing. His neighbors would sometimes come running out of their houses, up the front steps of his house, and go into the living room and lift up the receiver. For many years it was one of the big jokes in Flushing to give strangers Dummy's telephone number. Addie Badger, who approached her job conscientiously, always rang it. Sometimes, if she was grouchy, she would keep ringing it for half an hour or more. Of course, most people in town thought the whole thing would end at the close of the year's free subscription, but it didn't because Dummy kept right on paying the bills until the day he died. Of course when people really wanted to get hold of him they always sent a note up to his house.

Later, at another raffle, the first prize was a new Victrola and Dummy won that, too, along with ten records. He played these records over and over again until his neighbors almost went out of their minds. When one of them complained about it, the complaint got back to Mr. French. He suggested to various people that it might be a good joke if everyone gave Dummy a new record for Christmas that year. Almost fifty families did that very thing and, because Mr. French was also the dealer in phonograph records, they bought them all from him. He sold them all the same record, "Cohen at the Telephone." At almost any time of the day or night for the next few years, people who walked past Dummy Garner's house could hear Cohen talking on the telephone. Dummy never knew it because Mr. French had carefully changed all the labels.

When it came time for the big raffle in 1919, Dummy Garner was naturally the subject of much discussion. My father was the chairman of the raffle committee and he had chosen a Ford touring car for the prize. When the time came to announce the raffle and sell the tickets for it, all the ticket sellers were called into conference. They agreed to keep the whole business a secret as long as they could. It wasn't very hard to keep a secret from Dummy because, before a person revealed it, he had to go to the trouble of getting pencil and paper and writing it down. This removed the element of impulse which accounts for most secrets being leaked. Of course, my father expected that Dummy would find out about the raffle eventually, but he fervently hoped that all the tickets would be sold before that happened. It worked out much as my father hoped it would. By the time Dummy learned that anything was afoot, most of the salesmen had exhausted their books and had turned in their stubs and their money. For a week before the drawing, poor Dummy ran around the town waving dollar bills in front of people's faces, trying to get some chances on the Ford, but up until the morning of the day on which the tickets were drawn, he hadn't been able to purchase a single ticket.

It was Mr. J. B. French, of course, who ruined this conspiracy. He had purchased a few extra raffle tickets quite early in the sales campaign and on the morning of the drawing, as I was on my way through his store to the depot, he called me into his office. He said that he understood I delivered special delivery letters for the post office and he wanted to know how much I got for it. I told him that I received eight cents. He shook his head sadly and said that it was too much for him to pay. *He* had a special delivery letter to go out and he couldn't afford that much. He would give me a nickel. I knew Mr. French well enough by that time to make him bargain with me so I said my rock bottom price was seven cents. He thought about this for quite a while and offered me six cents. Then he shook his finger at me. He had an idea. His letter was going to Dummy Garner. He would stick a note in it recommending that Dummy give me a little something extra. Maybe I would get *more* than seven cents. I agreed. He scribbled out a note on a piece of paper and stuck it in the envelope.

"Now you be sure and tell me if Dummy doesn't give you any more," he said.

I ran up Elm Street as fast as I could go and found Dummy sitting on his front porch. I handed him the envelope and waited for him to tear it open. He started to grin when he saw what was inside and he bowed and nodded at me, then took out the raffle tickets, counted them, and handed me one. Then he showed me the note Mr. French had written. It said that if he wanted the tickets, it would be a good idea to give the boy who delivered them the extra one enclosed. Mr. French knew that I wouldn't waste any time telling people that I had got a raffle ticket for delivering an envelope to Dummy Garner. He knew, also, that I would spread the word around that Dummy had some tickets. I did just that. It didn't take the word long to get around Flushing. My father even came home in the middle of the afternoon to question me about it.

There was a good deal of consternation about those raffle tickets. Just before supper that evening my father headed a committee that went up to Dummy's house and tried to buy them back. He wouldn't sell them. That night, right after supper, someone walked into Mr. French's store and punched him in the nose for sending them. I don't think Mr. French quite expected that. It was probably the first time one of his little jokes backfired.

The drawing for the Ford was the last event of that gala week. Early in the evening a big barrel with all the stubs in it was placed on the bandstand. Frank Fuller and his Flushing Cornet Band played a concert and a big crowd gathered around, but most of them paid little attention to the music. They just watched the barrel. Every once in a while, between numbers of the concert, someone would get up and give the barrel a spin. Once three men climbed up and lifted the barrel out of its cradle and shook it up and down. At about eleven o'clock most of the booths and the exhibits closed and the rest of the people in Flushing gathered at the stand. My brother John, then only three years old, was to draw three numbers out of the barrel and the last one would be the winner. By the time my father lifted him up and turned him upside down so that he could reach down inside for the third number, there wasn't a sound on Main Street. My father read the numbers off slowly and everyone looked down at their tickets and then, when they realized that they didn't have the winning number and the silence still continued, everyone turned to look at Dummy Garner who was standing near the back of the crowd. It suddenly began to dawn on people that he couldn't hear the numbers. Someone finally got up courage enough to go over and look at his tickets. When the man finally looked up and shook his head, the whole crowd sighed; then, as one man, everyone looked down at his own tickets again. Someone shouted to my father to read the number again and he read from the stub. No one said a word. As my father waited to hear a shout and none came, he looked puzzled. Then, all of a sudden, he grinned. He reached in his own pocket and pulled out some tickets, looked at them carefully, and then triumphantly held one up in the air.

At first there were a few shouts, and then one or two boos, and finally a deep buzz. My mother was standing down near the edge of the platform and she held up her finger to my father and beckoned to him. He raised his arm to the crowd to be patient a moment and then went over to bend down and talk to my mother. She pointed out to him that he had organized the raffle and that his son had pulled the winning ticket out of the barrel. I could see that my father was very disappointed, but he did what he had to do. He held up both hands for silence and explained that he already owned a Studebaker so he wouldn't need the Ford. (There was a certain amount of irony in this announcement because the very next night my father and mother drove over to Flint to see a motion picture and the Studebaker was stolen. It was never found.)

Before my brother John drew the second set of three stubs out of the barrel, I happened to look more closely at my own ticket and right then and there I knew who was going to win the Ford. My number was 2315, the number on Burt Emans's engine. I grasped the ticket firmly in my hand and waited.

"Number two-three-one-five," my father called out.

I let out a yell and began dancing around and around the stage. My father just stood there and scratched his head. My mother started chasing me and on about the third time around the stand she finally caught me. The next fifteen minutes were pretty hard on me. I can't remember all the arguments that were used on me, but I wasn't having any of them. I didn't care if my own brother *did* pull the number out of the barrel and I didn't care if I was too young to drive, that Ford was my car and I was going to keep it. I lost out in the end, though. My father finally said he would *buy* me a Ford touring car when I was old enough to drive, but that I couldn't have *this* one. I knew when I was beaten and finally said all right, but that my father wasn't to forget his promise. My father straightened up from the edge of the platform with a strained look on his face and held up his hands. He announced that three more numbers would be drawn, but he was damned if anyone in *his* family was going to draw them.

The next master of ceremonies was Jerry Gibbons, the dentist. His son Denis, who was two, was still awake, so Denis took over the drawing. He promptly reached into the barrel and pulled out three numbers, holding the last one high over his head. As the numbers were read off, Jerry Gibbons's face began to turn red. Without saying a word, he picked Denis up and jumped off the platform. Everyone in the crowd was in hysterics by that time and some of them called out that Jerry should keep the Ford, but he just shook his head and wouldn't say a word.

Joe Gage was president of the Board of Commerce that year and he crawled up on the stage and stood there smiling, waiting for the crowd to quiet down. When he held up his hands and spoke, he announced that the next set of three numbers would be drawn by Dummy Garner. When the crowd heard this, the people started to yell and shout. They got the idea right away. If Dummy drew his own number, he'd *have* to give up the car the same way as my father and Jerry Gibbons had done. Dummy was boosted up to the platform and bowed all around at the crowd to much applause, then walked over to the barrel. He reached in and quickly pulled out a ticket, looked at it, and handed it to Joe Gage. He did the same thing with the second number. When he pulled out the third number, he looked at it and beamed. If anyone thought Dummy Garner was going to give up that car he was sadly mistaken. Other people could do what they pleased, but he had the car and he intended to keep it.

There were a lot of people against Dummy's having that Ford simply on the grounds that he had won another raffle. There were some who thought he would be a genuine menace in an automobile. In spite of the fact that he had just turned the car down, my father offered to buy it from Dummy on the spot. So did Jerry Gibbons and Joe Gage. Dummy just shook his head stubbornly and wrote out a note to Bill Frawley, the Ford dealer, instructing him to deliver the car on Monday morning.

As long as the good weather lasted that fall, the Ford was enshrined on Dummy Garner's front lawn. Every morning Dummy came down off the front porch and polished it from end to end. Often, in the pleasant fall evenings, instead of sitting in his rocking chair, he would open the back door of the car and climb in. There he would sit, smoking a big black cigar, reading the evening paper.

Quite a few people in Flushing felt sorry for Dummy Garner. Among them was Mrs. Harvey Dunn, our next-door neighbor, a gentle, hard-working farm woman who had been brought up as a

Quaker, and who firmly believed that every person had his rights. Toward the end of October, when the Dunn family moved into town for the winter, Mrs. Dunn quietly ordered her son Sidney, who was then fifteen and had just got his driver's license, to stop by Dummy Garner's every afternoon on his way home from school and offer to take Dummy for a ride. Sidney would crank up the Ford and Dummy would come down out of the house, climb into the car, light up his cigar, and away they would go. Sometimes Dummy would sit in the front seat and sometimes he would sit in the back. No matter where he sat, his ride through the village resembled a progress. No one acted more lordly than he did when he rode in that car. He would bow and tip his hat to all the people he passed, and grin in triumph.

Dummy Garner may have been a dummy, but he was no fool. While he was riding around in that car and bowing and beaming at the people, he was keeping a close eye on everything Sidney Dunn did to make the car go. In November, after a month of observation, he decided he could drive a car himself. One morning, just as it was getting daylight, he came down the front steps of his house, cranked up the Ford, climbed into the driver's seat, and drove off down Elm Street. He had no trouble at all. He turned left on Maple Street for a block, got to Main Street, and headed west across the bridge. He was all the way up the West Main Street hill before anything went wrong. The car began to sputter and spit and buck and finally slowed down. Dummy hadn't understood quite *everything* about his Ford. He was out of gasoline at this particular moment and had no way of guessing what the trouble was. The car jumped ahead a few more feet and came to a stop exactly in the middle of the railroad crossing. At that precise moment the engines from the northbound manifest were bearing down on the crossing. It is true that they were coming in to take water and were not moving very fast, but the lead engine was already blowing its whistle and Dummy couldn't hear it. He sat there in the front seat pulling levers and pushing pedals, trying to understand what he had done wrong. He never once looked up. The engineer on the leading engine had seen the car drive on the tracks and stop. He grabbed his whistle cord and held it down, then let it go and applied full brakes. Lloyd Way, the morning telegraph operator, had seen the whole thing. He threw up the window by his telegraph key and shouted, then saw who was in the car, and dove right out onto the cinders and started running. He arrived at the car just as the engine did. He reached out and shook Dummy by the shoulder and pointed up. Dummy turned his head and there was the cowcatcher and boiler of number 2296 not two feet away. Dummy's jaw dropped and he fainted.

Dummy Garner sold his Ford that same afternoon. It was the first time in anyone's memory that he had ever given up anything he had won. Of course, he made a deal that was characteristic of him. He sold the car to George Packard, the township supervisor of roads, for about half what it was worth, but he made a stipulation that George would have to come over to his house once a week and take him for a ride. As long as Dummy lived he never missed that outing and George was never allowed to trade the Ford in. Both Dummy and George lasted well into the 1930's and that old 1919 Model T did, too.

My father never did buy me a Model T touring car, by the way. I just forgot to ask for it.

CHAPTER TWELVE

After Flushing celebrated the return of electric lights, the people of the village entered into a dizzy social whirl that lasted well into the next summer. If a social whirl gets dizzy enough it can get people into trouble, and both my grandpa Perry and I had our difficulties. Grandpa's embroilment was pretty serious. Mine only seemed serious, but it gave me some pretty bad moments.

At the time I was born, Flushing had two churches, a Baptist church and a Methodist one. There was a Presbyterian church *building,* but no practicing Presbyterians. There were practicing Roman Catholics, but no Catholic church building. My family had no pronounced views on religion. My grandmother Love was a Christian Scientist and spent an hour each morning with her Bible and Mary Baker Eddy, but she never mentioned it outside her own house. She certainly did not try to impose her views on the rest of us. My grandfather Love had a *negative* view. He hated Methodists. I never heard him refer to just a plain Methodist. He always called them "God-damned Methodists." I suspect it had something to do with Prohibition. Like Oren Hart, he associated the Methodist church with the WCTU, which he always called "The Hens of Hell." It should be added, in justice to my grandfather, that, although he seemed to be a blasphemous man, he was the exemplification of rockbound honesty and moral principles. He lived a godly and an upright life in almost every respect. God just didn't have anything to do with it.

As in most families, whatever religious observance there was in our house was supervised by my mother. She had attended college in her youth and had been exposed to the Episcopal Church. All that pomp and ceremony fitted in exactly with her natural leanings. For the rest of her life she considered herself an Episcopalian. What is more, she considered her sons to be Episcopalians, too. The absence of an Episcopal church in Flushing did not deter her. In her own mind she didn't have to go to church to be a staunch Episcopalian. Having declared her preference, she was prepared to wait until an Episcopal church opened in the village, or until she moved someplace where there was an Episcopal church. In the meantime, after my youngest brother was born, she took all of us over to Flint and had us baptized at St. Paul's Church.

Of course, my mother had no intention of letting any of us grow up to be heathens. We were farmed out to the Baptist church in Flushing at an early age to learn what we could. Unfortunately, Flushing had more than its share of bad luck with Baptist ministers. Throughout my boyhood there was a whole succession of them who went wrong. One turned out to be a drunkard. One turned out to be a crook who sold stock in a perpetual-motion machine. Another ran off with the wife of a member of the congregation. I was never apprised of the exact details of these various errors, but it seemed to me that the only class of people about whom my mother and father consistently conversed in whispers were Baptist ministers.

Because of the transient qualities of Baptist ministers the church was left in the hands of Art Freeman for long periods of time. Art Freeman was an elder of the church, a short roly-poly farmer with pink cheeks who was ideally suited for the role of Santa Claus, which he played every Christmas. He bounced around the village, giving off sparks of energy, first organizing things and then running them. There was nothing sanctimonious about Art Freeman. If anything, he was a little short on theological information. This did not bother him, nor did it bother the Baptists. Everyone was so busy that no one had time to think about what was going to happen to him in the hereafter. Weekly chicken dinners, Boy Scout meetings, wiener roasts, camping trips, dances, fairs, and paintup-cleanup campaigns followed each other day after day. The Baptist church sponsored anything that looked as though it might be worthwhile, from the annual Chautauqua to the Board of Commerce. Art himself ran the dinners, washed the dishes, stoked the furnace, rang the bell, helped dig Baptist graves, acted as Scoutmaster, and sold pies at the bazaars. In the church he was officially the superintendent of the Sunday school and lay reader. He preached the sermons during the long periods when no minister was in residence. He led the hymns at all times. He played the organ for weddings. As far as he was concerned, the Baptist church should be a place where people wanted to come, and he kept it that way. Under his direction the attitude of the Baptists could best be summed up in the hymn he led every Sunday, "Brighten the Corner Where You Are."

I loved Art Freeman for a lot of things, but I loved him the most for his annual parties at his sugarbush. His farm, about four miles west of town, had the biggest stand of maple trees in the county and Art was one of the most successful producers of maple syrup in our part of the state. He had constructed a sizable plant for boiling the sap. This sugarbush was located deep in the woods behind his farmhouse. From the time the sap first began to run in the winter, it was the custom for each Sunday-school class, in turn, to have a sugaring party at Freeman's farm. (No Methodist Sunday-school class had anything like it, a fact which gave the Baptists a chance to lord it over them to some extent.)

The festivities of that winter after the lights came on again began with a trip out to Art Freeman's farm. Art announced that a new minister had been appointed to run the church and that the whole Sunday school would get an extra turn that winter to celebrate the appointment. On a Friday night I walked up to the Baptist church just as it got dark and found a big, flat-racked sleigh waiting for us. I climbed aboard and nestled in the hay and we soon started out to the sound of sleigh bells. As we glided through town Art Freeman, who was driving the team, burst into a hymn and all of us joined in. One song followed another as we rode the four miles out into the country. When we got to Art Freeman's farmhouse, we tramped a mile through the snow to the shack in the woods. There were two rooms, one with a big fireplace and tables scattered around in front of it. The other was a bare room with a vat full of boiling sap in the middle of it. Benches ran around the wall and most of us went straight to them and marked out a place for ourselves. As soon as I got my coat off I ran and got a bowl and spoon from the shelf and went to the vat and dipped out a big cup of the hot sap, then went to sit on the bench and stir it. After considerable stirring a bowl of sap would become maple sugar. I finished my second bowl and had two nice big lumps of maple sugar tucked away in a bag in my coat pocket before I got tired of stirring. I went into the big room and sat at a table and played dominos for a while, then stirred another bowl of sap. (There was never any limit to how much we could take.) After that I went outdoors and played pom-pom-pullaway in the deep snow. I was back inside and just finishing my fourth bowl of maple sugar when Art Freeman came in and held up his hands to tell us to clear the tables. Then he and the teachers from the Sunday school came in carrying huge stacks of pancakes and platters of sausages. I used one cake of my maple sugar to spread on the pancakes and poured hot syrup on my second and third batches. When the meal was done and the pancakes were just about to come out of my ears, Art Freeman led us in a little prayer and we all tramped back through the snow and climbed aboard the sleigh. I was asleep long before we got to the church and someone shook me awake. I walked sleepily down Elm Street trailing hay after me and clutching my three remaining cakes of maple sugar. My mother was waiting up for me and told me that it was after midnight. It was the first time in my life that I had ever sat up that late. I went to bed thanking my lucky stars that I was a Baptist.

The big trouble with the Baptist church, the way Art Freeman ran it, was that it was long on activity and a little short on God. I went there for eight years and can't remember hearing anything about God at all. In the earlier grades we colored pictures of angels and in the later grades there was some talk of Jesus. I heard all the usual stories about the Babe in the manger and the three wise men. I knew that Jesus could heal the sick, and I was quite impressed to learn that He could walk on water, but the *principles* of religion were scattered very thinly about the basement of the Baptist church. I carried away the idea that if I was good I would go to heaven. If I was bad I would go to hell, a vague sort of nether region in the bowels of the earth noted chiefly for its heat. The very fact that I *still* cannot remember the exact wording and order of the Ten Commandments gives a pretty good idea of the ineffectiveness of that early religious training. I don't know what happened upstairs in the church after the collection was taken and we marched down to the basement for Sunday school, but I always had the feeling that most Flushing Baptists had the same vague ideas that I had. Now and then one of the itinerant ministers would view this scene with horror and shake everyone up with a little fire and brimstone. That is exactly what happened in that spring after the lights came on again. The new minister took one look at us and decreed that there would be a revival meeting. He sent off and requested the services of a traveling revivalist.

I'm not sure, now, how I happened to get involved in that

revival meeting. The True Blue class, of which I was a member, may have been invited or I may have attended the first meeting thinking it was something like the Epworth League. It always irked me a little that the Baptists never had anything like *that.* Whatever the case, once I had attended a revival meeting I was fascinated. The revivalist, a complete stranger to everyone in Flushing, roared and pleaded and tore his hair. He stomped around the front of the church and pointed his finger at people. He would stop in the middle of his roarings and sing gentle songs or drop down on his knees in the aisle and pray beside some guilty-looking person's pew. The whole performance was completely different from the "Brighten the Corner" business that I was used to. By the end of the very first hour of the very first meeting, the whole congregation began to act as if it was hypnotized. Everyone got down on his knees and rocked back and forth and sang and shouted right along with the revivalist. Then, just when it seemed that everyone was going to fall over in a trance, the minister said, in a hoarse voice, that the meeting was adjourned. Everyone was to come back the next evening and bring his friends and neighbors.

Up until the time of the revival I'd never gone to the Baptist church on a week night (except to eat a chicken supper). After that opening I wasn't going to miss it if I could help it. Evening after evening the singing and the shouting continued and more and more people kept coming. Even Indian Joe Walker showed up. Indian Joe hadn't been sober a day in his adult life until he had almost burned himself up in a fire at Christmastime, and I think it is significant that right after the revival he started getting drunk all over again. Along toward the end of the first week the revivalist began exhorting people to renounce their sins and give themselves to God. At first only a member here and there rose haltingly and stumbled forward to kneel before the minister. The newly saved cried in open grief and the people who still remained in their seats held their heads in their hands, swaying, and whimpering a little. Once the stream started forward it grew in size. On the second Sunday evening there was almost a mad rush to get down in front when the revivalist beckoned. Although I must have been completely innocent of any evil thoughts or actions at that stage of my life, I was quite moved by all this and marched down the aisle to renounce whatever sin I had. The minister patted me tenderly on the head and I began weeping along with everyone else.

I took this action without consulting my parents. They had not gone to the revival meeting, and were probably not even aware that a revival meeting was in progress. My mother knew that I was going up to the church every evening and she thought it was nice that I did so, but I suspect she thought I was attending some kind of initiation for new members of the True Blue class.

On the Sunday evening I gave myself to God I walked in the front door of our house, my eyes wide with wonderment. I went to stand in front of the card table where my mother and father were playing their usual Sunday evening game of bridge with Doc Davis and his wife. All of them put down their cards and politely listened to the announcement I made. My mother smiled in a good-natured way and patted me on the head. My father said he guessed it wouldn't hurt me any. When I tried to explain that this had been quite a significant move on my part, my mother shushed me up and shooed me off to bed. It would have been better for everyone concerned if they had paid a little closer attention to what I had to say. As it happened, in the hurly-burly of my ordinary activities during the next week, I forgot to mention the subject again.

On the third Sunday evening, as the revival ended, I presented myself at the rostrum in the front of the church along with all the others who had gone down the aisle to give themselves to God—a sizable number by this time. Back of the Bible stand, where the three red velvet thrones usually stood, things had been cleared away to reveal a rather large bathtub. It was filled with water and Art Freeman and the revivalist stood in it up to their hips. As his name was called, each convert walked gingerly down a set of steps into this bathtub, clothes and all, and was seized on either side and dunked beneath the surface of the water. When my name was called—just ahead of Indian Joe Walker's—I did as the rest had done and was properly immersed. I walked home in my drenched clothes, singing, "Brighten the Corner Where You Are," dripping water all the way. I opened the door and went to stand in front of the card table. *That* was the only time I ever broke up the Sunday evening bridge game. Whatever hell there was still left in Flushing after the revival was concentrated right there in our living room for the next hour. My father raved and threatened because the Baptists had ruined my best Sunday suit. My mother was mad because I had walked all the way home on a chilly March evening in clothes that were soaking wet. There was much scurrying around, in which Doc Davis took charge. Although he was only the village horse doctor, he seemed to know exactly what to do. I was hurried out of my clothes and into a hot bath, then put to bed, still blithely reaching around between my shoulder blades to see if my wings had started to sprout. I'm sure that if the Baptist church had owned a telephone that night the elders would have heard some hell-fire and damnation from a couple of experts.

When I awoke the next morning without a cold, some of the elements of crisis disappeared, but it was a good two weeks before I was allowed to go back to the Baptist Sunday school. I was placed in the strange position of having to argue for this privilege. Religious devotion had nothing to do with it. I simply did not intend to lose my rights to attend those sugaring parties, nor did I want to forgo the annual summer camping trip of the True Blue class.

My baptism made something of a hero out of me at school. I received about the same amount of attention as a boy with a newly broken arm. I was the only boy in my grade, and for two or three grades above me, who had gone through the ceremony, and I was the center of a heated theological discussion. It was about whether the sprinkling of water on one's head was enough or whether true baptism required complete immersion. I was in an enviable position because I had *both.* I spoke with the authority of a boy who is completely safe and my views impressed many of my friends. The next year, when another revival was announced, two Methodists, one Roman Catholic, and Art Ailing, who was a heathen, attended and let themselves be dipped in the Baptist tank.

My mother's gnawing doubts about the advisability of my returning to the Baptist Sunday school *did* have some religious basis. She remembered that I had already been baptized in the Episcopal church and she wondered whether the Baptist ceremony wiped out the earlier one. She might have done something about it if a new crisis had not arisen in our family at this precise moment to take her mind away from my problem. As it was, I was never rebaptized as an Episcopalian. For all I know, when the time came, the Episcopalians may have confirmed a Baptist.

The new crisis was brought on by my grandpa Perry. As far as I am concerned, Grandpa was two different men. He could have been the kindly, understanding, somewhat lonely man that I remember or he could have been the stiff, somewhat pompous old man who was given to puttering around at inconsequential tasks that many people thought him to be. He was sixty-five years old when he came to live in our house after Sarah Parmelee Perry's death and it was not expected that he had many years left. As it turned out, Grandpa's declining years were years in which he refused to decline.

Edmund Perry was born in 1851. He was the great-great-grandson of Commodore Oliver Hazard Perry. He came to Flushing in 1881 to trade with the Chippewa Indians at their annual encampment. He met Sarah Parmelee and married her, bought out a store in the village, and ran it for twenty-seven years. It was the most prosperous business in western Genesee County and Grandpa became a moderately wealthy man. He had served as president of the village council for twenty years before his retirement in 1908. He had built up the reputation of being a rather colorless, proper small-town businessman who lived in the shadow of a forceful, personable woman. He was respected, but not greatly loved. It is amazing how little the people of Flushing knew about him after seeing him and doing business with him nearly every day for thirty-five years. Even my mother underestimated him.

Grandpa Perry's outstanding trait was amiability. He took the attitude that he might just as well do what other people wanted him to. He enjoyed life as it came to him and took pleasure in almost everything, and if it made others happy when he let them have their way it made him happy, too. I think he had loved Sate Parmelee. If his assumption of the role of a community leader made her happy, that was good enough for him. As long as she lived he went along with her desires, letting her play the tune and dancing with right good will. After her death he was thrust into a new role. His daughter and his grandchildren were the only people that mattered to him and he moved into our house to be near all of us. He had been retired for eight years at that time. He was expected to be docile and give obeisance to his betters—anyone who was younger than he was, and carrying the load of the world on his shoulders. When Grandpa moved into our house, my parents seem to have assumed that he needed care, like one of their children. And they somehow expected that he would obey orders, also like one of their children. There were signs that Grandpa still considered himself a grown man from the time he came back to live with us, but everyone ignored them.

One night a few months after Sate Parmelee Perry's funeral he walked into Darby's poolroom and sat down on a chair to watch the pool players. Up until that moment he had never entered a poolroom in Flushing because it was unthinkable to do so under his wife's code of conduct. He watched several games from his chair, then approached the table and observed that it looked like an easy game and that he was surprised that grown men would waste so much time at it. Having made his opening gambit, he allowed himself to be talked into several games of rotation pool at a penny a point. He didn't get a ball, but he was still of the opinion that the game was easy. In the next three weeks he allowed every pool player in town to trounce him badly, first at a penny, then at a nickel a point, but he managed to improve a little, as the series ended—enough to make him bolder. He was willing to raise the stakes. The pool players rushed to get some of Grandpa's money. Having set the whole village up in this fashion, he proceeded to clean everyone out at a dollar a point. It took a long time for people to realize that they had been taken in by a bona fide pool shark. It eventually came out that Grandpa had played pool and billiards for money in every town in the West long before he ever came to Flushing and that he had been considered by many as a champion. Ten years later he was to play a series of exhibition matches with Willie Hoppe in Detroit and very nearly beat him.

Grandpa was a handsome man. Although his hair was thinning and was gray around the edges, he carried himself like a man many years younger. He stood ramrod straight and moved briskly. He was in excellent health. Indeed, during the fair that celebrated the return of electricity he entered a foot race that was advertised as being for middle-aged men. He was sixty-nine at the time, but he still thought of himself as middle-aged. He won the race even though most of his competitors were thirty years younger than he. He was always a great walker. He clipped off five or ten miles a day in hot weather and cold weather, wet weather and dry weather, until four months before his death on his ninety-first birthday.

Grandpa had no secret for longevity. Many people thought he stayed brisk and healthy because he was an abstemious man. Nothing was further from the truth. He liked a good cigar and he smoked several of them a day. He also liked a drink and had one each morning as long as he lived. It was a fact not generally known. My mother didn't know it, but *I* knew it when I was still a small boy.

It was Grandpa's custom to put me to bed each night. My mother would undress me and put me in my pajamas in front of the fireplace in the living room. Then Grandpa would take me by the hand and lead me up the stairs to the bedroom, tuck me in, and lie down beside me. He would sing me a song, or tell me a story, or read to me from a book until I dropped off. He was a wonderful storyteller and his songs were usually sad ballads about soldiers who rode up hills and never came down again—all of them Civil War songs. I loved bedtime for the stories and songs, but I loved it for another reason. Grandpa smelled nice. I've never known a man since who smelled so good.

That smell was always there. As I grew older and the bedtime sessions ceased, it never changed. Grandpa always had an assortment of goodies hidden in his bureau and one day when I was snooping around to take inventory of his stock I found a dish with a half dozen eggs tucked away in the shirt drawer, next to the bay rum bottle. I was certainly curious about those eggs, but I didn't dare admit to Grandpa that I had been snooping in his dresser, so I couldn't ask him about them. All I could do was keep a close watch and see what he did with them. I soon discovered that it was even more mysterious than I thought. Grandpa would take one of the eggs and the bottle of bay rum and his shaving mug and go down the back stairs to the bathroom each morning. This was peculiar because I knew that Grandpa got a shave at Joe Gage's barbershop each day at eleven o'clock. Finally, I made believe I was building a castle on the back porch. I put two or three washtubs and a bench on top of one another and climbed on them so I could see through the little bathroom window. What I saw was interesting. Grandpa started out by breaking the raw egg into his shaving mug. He sloshed it around a minute, then poured some bay rum into it. Then, all of a sudden, he gulped the whole thing down, poured a little more bay rum into the mug, and swallowed that. After having completed this part of the ceremony, he took several Sen-Sen tablets from an envelope and put them in his mouth. Then he bathed his face in cologne water. It was no wonder he smelled so good. I couldn't discuss any of this with my family. If I had, my father would have given me a whipping for peeking in the bathroom window. I *did* find out, later, that the bay rum bottle did not contain bay rum—it contained straight bourbon whiskey.

For almost two years after Sate Parmelee Perry's death, Grandpa fell into the role that was expected of him in our household. He worked around the house and rarely went into the outside world. Then, in the winter of 1918, he was selected on the panel of jurors for the February term of circuit court in Flint. Because of the severity of the weather that winter he elected to take a small apartment near the courthouse and was there through both of Flushing's major disasters. He came home in the spring looking more chipper than I had ever seen him. In the next several months he took part in many affairs that concerned the village and in the fall elections he ran for village councilman. His service on the council caused a minor disruption in our family because he ran on the Republican ticket and immediately became a thorn in the side of my grandfather Love, who had been running things without much opposition for several years.

The major explosion in our house didn't come until that winter after the lights came on again. Grandpa had made no secret of the fact that he enjoyed jury duty. It was permissible in Michigan for citizens to volunteer for this duty and Grandpa had left his name with the county clerk when he left Flint at the end of his service. His second call came in January, 1920, and he left to take up his residence in Flint at about the same time I went on the sugaring party at Art Freeman's farm. We didn't hear very much from Grandpa the rest of the winter. There was a good reason. The jury panel on which he served was one of the first in the history of Genesee County to contain women and on that panel was a young woman from the village of Montrose by the name of Ardele Streator.

Ardie Streator was an extremely attractive person of about thirty. She ran an insurance and real estate agency in her village and considered herself a successful businesswoman. Because Flushing was near to Montrose she was known to a good many Flushing people. Unfortunately, Ardie had a bad reputation. The big black mark against her was a divorce. It is hard for a person of this day and age to visualize the position of a divorced woman in a small midwestern village of that era. No matter what the grounds for divorce had been, a divorcee was only one shade less scarlet than Hester Prynne. One can get some idea of how bad Ardie's reputation was by the very fact that I became conscious of it, and about all I ever heard was a stray word, here and there, in conversations that were always conducted in whispers. In justice to Ardie, I never did see anything wrong with her. I liked her. She had a way with small boys and was good to me in many ways. Of course, in addition to her reputation, whatever it was, Ardie was six years younger than my mother and forty years younger than Grandpa. That was some kind of scandal in itself.

Grandpa married Ardie Streator before the jury term was over and before anyone ever knew or suspected what was going on. He came walking into the house alone one evening after supper and announced what he had done. His announcement created the greatest storm our house had ever seen. My mother wept and said, "Papa, how could you?" My father raged through the house, saying, "There's no fool like an old fool." Poor Grandpa just stood in the middle of the floor looking downcast. My mother continued to weep for two days and was on the verge of tears for a week after that. My father didn't go through a door for a month without slamming it. Grandpa just kept quiet and finally disappeared for a few days. I suppose he went on a honeymoon. At the end of it he just came into the house and moved back into his room and resumed his usual ways.

I don't think Grandpa ever intended to bring Ardie to our house to live. As it turned out, he never *did* live with her. But he didn't give up, either. He just set his chin and weathered the storm that raged around him. He handled the whole affair in his own patient way. He bought a Model T Ford roadster and learned to drive it. Once or twice a week he drove over to Montrose and spent a day or night at Ardie's house. Occasionally, if my mother and father went away for a day, Ardie would drive over from Montrose and spend a day at our house. More than once I came bustling into the living room to find Ardie sitting on Grandpa's lap.

Grandpa Perry's marriage to Ardie Streator changed many things in my life. It even had a part in changing the village of Flushing. To begin with, the relationship between Grandpa and my parents was never quite the same. My mother still loved her father and was kind to him, but she seems to have seen him as an adult for the first time in her whole life and she became increasingly cautious about trying to influence his life. My father was more overtly hostile. His criticism of Grandpa was a shade more caustic and there was never any doubt that he thought Grandpa was in his dotage. I loved Grandpa. I thought he was the kindest, gentlest man I knew and for the rest of my boyhood I became increasingly close to him. He sensed this and appreciated it. Whenever he had some special treat in the way of a trip or an adventure he always sought me out.

As far as the village of Flushing was concerned, Grandpa knew he was in some disfavor, especially with all the people who knew and remembered Sate Parmelee Perry. On the other hand, he got support from an unlikely quarter. All the pool players and not a few of the older males in the village took his part. He was reelected to the village council in 1920 and again in 1922. The amiable man that he had always been was still there, but he proved that he was no rubber stamp, and he stood up to my grandfather Love.

Grandpa Perry's relationship with Ardie Streator continued for almost four years. He waited for several months until the excitement died down and then he and Ardie were divorced just as quietly as they had been married. The divorce, when it was announced, created almost as much of a storm as the marriage, primarily because Grandpa gave Ardie three of his houses and a considerable amount of cash. The peculiar thing about the divorce was that it did not change things between Grandpa and Ardie at all. He still went over to Montrose to see her every week and she came over to our house when the coast was clear. A year after the divorce Ardie took the cash Grandpa had given her and moved to Detroit, where she opened a candy store. After she'd gone, Grandpa went over to Montrose every week and collected her insurance premiums and looked after her rental properties. He did other business for her, too. Although the three houses were now in her name, Grandpa kept right on repairing them, painting them, and collecting the rents for her. Every month he would take the interurban from Flint down to Detroit and deliver the money to her and help her with her books. I often went with him, and those were the greatest trips of my boyhood. I loved interurbans next best to trains and used to ride out on the back platform all the way to Detroit. After we got there, Ardie and Grandpa and I would go to see the Detroit Tigers, to the movies, and eat in Chinese restaurants. The best thing of all was that I was left to wait on the customers in the candy store and could eat as much candy as I wanted to whenever Grandpa and Ardie retired to the back room—and in all delicacy, they spent a lot of time in that back room. I couldn't help but like Ardie.

Ardie died suddenly just before we moved away from Flushing. She gave Grandpa back all his houses in her will, along with two that he hadn't owned before. I don't recall that Grandpa threw that "old fool" business back at my father, although he might well have done so. He just wasn't the kind of person ever to hold a grudge.

CHAPTER THIRTEEN

ONE SUMMER day in 1920 I had been at the depot riding around in the cab of number 2315. Burt Emans had finished taking water and had chugged out of town to the north and I was standing by the water spout watching the caboose disappear across Henry Chatters's crossing. Grandpa Perry came rattling up the Main Street hill in his Model T and beckoned to me. He told me he was going over to Montrose to see Ardie Streator (none of us ever called her Ardie Perry) and wondered if I would like to ride along with him. I climbed in and we clattered along the road out of town. We sped along at a reasonable twenty-five miles an hour and reached Brent Creek where I saw Burt Emans switching, but he didn't see me. When we got to Montrose, I jumped out of the car and ran for the depot and arrived there just as Burt Emans pulled in. He looked down at me in some surprise.

"What are you doing *here*, George?" he asked me.

I think Burt Emans thought I had stowed away on the cow-catcher or in the caboose or something. When I told him that I had ridden over to Montrose in a car with my grandpa, he shook his head as though he didn't believe it. Twice, while I was riding in the cab as we switched around Montrose, he asked me how fast my grandpa had been driving.

I often think of that trip as a landmark. I not only got to ride on the engine twice in one day, but for the first time that I knew of an automobile had actually got somewhere faster than a train. I didn't realize it at the time, but it was the beginning of a new era. Just two years before that no one would have thought of driving a car to Montrose, especially my grandpa. He would have taken the train. In that two years cars had improved just enough so that a man could get into one in Flushing and reasonably expect to get all the way to Montrose without having to stop and change a tire, put some water in the radiator, or repair something. The secret of our prompt arrival at Ardie Streator's house was not speed, but steady driving.

Most historians seem to think that America's entry into the automobile age progressed as the cars improved technologically. I think the roads had more to do with it. When my father bought his first Ford roadster in 1904 he tried to drive it to Port Huron. In one ten-mile stretch between Lapeer and Imlay City he got stuck in the middle of the road eight times and each time he had to be hauled out by a farmer with a team of horses. When he got to Imlay City he had the Ford put on a railroad flatcar and sent it back home. It was seven more years before roads improved enough so that he dared try it again.

Not only were the roads bad, they were unmarked. There was no such thing as a road map. The farther we got from home the more my mother and father would argue about road directions. My mother would insist that we had turned at a certain corner the last time we came that way and my father would insist that she was thinking of another corner. One night there was a detour on the road to Owosso, which was only twenty miles away, and my father and mother got completely lost. It seems incredible that anyone could get lost only twenty miles from home, but everyone did.

During most of my boyhood Flushing was a village of dirt streets. There were no pavements, of course, and the only graveled street was Main Street, east of the river. Each day, in dry weather, Grandpa Perry would get out the garden hose and water down the street in front of our house to keep the dust down, but at no time before the war did the traffic get heavy enough so that it was a major problem.

The big change in the village came mainly through the efforts of George Packard. It seems fitting that another branch of his family gave its name to the Packard Motor Car and the Packard Electric Company, which later contributed so many of the inventions that made the automobile what it is today. But George himself was an unsuccessful farmer and several years before I was born he began driving a team of horses for my grandfather Love at the lumber yard. He still worked there when my father took over the yard. When my father bought his first truck, George learned to drive it and hauled most of the lumber for the Flint business that my father built up. For quite a few years George was the only driver in Flushing who had a chauffeur's license. He used to wear the little metal badge proudly, in the center of his cap, like a policeman's badge.

The first truck my father bought was a Republic with a chain drive and hard rubber tires. It served well enough on the haul to Flint, but every time George Packard had to haul a load of lumber to a farm on one of the country roads he got stuck. At the close of the war, on George's advice, my father bought a Duplex. It was one of the first four-wheel-drive trucks manufactured for commercial use. It could go anywhere. The front wheels were directly under the cab and the steering wheel stuck straight up out of the floor. George would sit there with his arms wrapped around the big wheel in a bear hug as the Duplex lumbered along the road. When he turned a corner he would tug and pull to get the front wheels turned and then tug and pull the other way to get them straightened out again. I rode around with George quite a lot on that old truck. When we were on a country road and came to a gooey rutted stretch George would stop the truck, pull out a plug of tobacco, take a big chew, spit on his hands, rub them together, shove the gears into four-wheel-drive, and go to work. I would sit there beside him and hang onto the side of the cab as he fought the wheel. As we wallowed into the mud, the front wheels below me would spin and slither and drip mud and water as they pulled the load through the ruts and holes. It seemed that nothing could ever stop that old Duplex, and George used to talk to it and coax it along through the worst going. When we came to dry land again he would stop, spit out a big gob of tobacco juice, reach over and pat me on the knee, and chuckle in triumph.

A lot of George Packard's life had to do with mud, even before my father got the Duplex. The lumber yard was at the bottom of the hill on West Main Street. The road leveled out there and ran for a block across the river flats to the bridge. This short stretch ran along a causeway that had been built to keep it from washing out in each spring flood. It had never been graveled. It served well enough before the automobiles came, but after cars started using it there was a problem. In any rainy spell it became a morass of sticky mud. The first car to venture through it would leave deep tracks. The second car would make the tracks deeper. Eventually the tracks would be hub-deep and cars would start getting stuck in the middle of Main Street. Because he worked in the lumber yard and had a team of horses handy, George would always haul the cars out of the mud. On some days he would rescue ten of them. As time passed, he tried to alleviate his work by bringing plows, disk harrows, stone floats, and rollers in from his farm. With these he would turn the dirt over, manicure it, scrape it, and pack it down. The ruts would disappear and in dry weather the street would be fairly smooth, but the next time it rained the ruts would be deeper than ever.

In the summer of 1919 George Packard suffered his greatest defeat. The Duplex got stuck in the middle of this stretch of Main Street. George stormed into the village council meeting that night and informed the members that he was damned if he was going to pull another car out of the mud or do any more work on the street. My grandfather Love tried to pacify him and the council finally agreed to pay him to gravel the stretch and get it into good condition. He set to work on it at once, taking two weeks off from the lumber yard to do it. He had a box wagon which he used to haul gravel from the pit east of town. As usual, I was there. He had a big spring seat up on the front of the wagon and I used to sit up there beside him and hold the reins. Sometimes I actually drove the horses. The floor of the wagon was made up of closely fitted two-by-fours. In order to dump the load all one had to do was turn these two-by-fours on their sides and the gravel would trickle to the ground. I wasn't strong enough to turn them, but I was strong enough to put them back in place while George was spreading the gravel around with his shovel. On the way back to the gravel pit I would sit on the end of the long tongue that stuck out behind the wagon. This was my favorite place to ride because it jiggled up and down.

George did such a good job on West Main Street that the township supervisors agreed to pay him money to gravel some of the main county roads when he suggested it the next spring. He bought the old Republic truck from my father, took off the lumber rack, and built a dump box. For the next two years he graveled all the township roads. In the summer I spent a lot of my time riding around with him on that dump truck. When I revisited Flushing more than forty years later I found all the roads paved, but there wasn't a single one of them that I hadn't seen the gravel put on. The memory of riding along on that old truck and coming to the stretch where we had last dumped a load of gravel and making the first tracks through it is still fresh. The things I recall best were the little marks George would make on the top of the truck cab when he dumped a load. It was the first time I had ever seen the 𝍸 𝍸 method of keeping tally. I was quite impressed by it.

As the road in front of each farmer's house was graveled, a

little of the old life disappeared. The farmers soon discovered that they wouldn't get stuck in the mud and began buying automobiles to take them into town and back. One by one the horse-drawn vehicles disappeared. Soon there weren't any horses at all. I can't remember, today, just how long it took to gravel all those roads, but I know it began that summer when George Packard graveled West Main Street and I know that the ride I took over to Montrose was one of the first by-products of it. The only other time, before that, that I had been to Montrose in a car, my father slid off the road into a ditch when he tried to turn the corner north of Brent Creek.

George Packard went on to become the supervisor of roads in Flushing Township. He got a tractor with a big scraper blade on it and wherever you were around Flushing, there he was with his tractor, scraping the gravel he had put down. It was many years before he got a snowplow, though. All the time we lived in Flushing, some roads were still impassable in the wintertime. But still, I have often thought that George Packard did more for the automobile industry than any of the more famous members of his family.

The increase in the number of automobiles that came to Flushing in the first three years after the war created a new problem—dust. In the summertime things began to get pretty bad. For two years the village council did a lot of arguing about it. One summer a big wagon with a tank on it was bought from the city of Flint and it ran up and down the streets spurting streams of black oil onto the gravel and dirt. The oil kept the dust down, all right, but it was worse than the dust. There was a big puddle of it in the street in front of our house and one day a car ran through it and spattered oil all over my mother's dress as she was working on her flower beds. My youngest brother, John, fell in another of these puddles over on Cherry Street and tracked oil all through the house. The experiment wasn't tried a second year. The next summer the village council bought a carload of a chemically treated salt. It worked fine, but before long my father began to notice holes appearing in the fenders of his car. The chemicals ruined half the fenders in town.

All through these years the village council discussed the ultimate solution: the paving of Main Street. From the time Bob Hart gave the boulevard lights to the town the paving had been in everyone's mind, but my grandfather Love didn't want to spend the money for two reasons. One was that there still weren't enough cars in Flushing to warrant it. The other was that he suspected Ira Sayre was going to get his finger in the pie somehow. By the summer of 1920, however, the situation had changed so radically that even Grandfather had to start thinking about doing something. On the ballot that fall the proposition was put to the voters and they approved it.

Before the paving could begin the old iron bridge on Main Street had to be replaced and the decisions surrounding this brought on another crisis in village affairs. My grandfather Love had run the village for ten years at the time the bridge question came up, but in the 1920 elections the Republicans had almost taken control of things away from him. His majority was reduced to 6-5 on the council and the leader of the opposition was Grandpa Perry. My two grandfathers had never been very cordial to each other. Grandfather Love was still of the opinion that Grandpa Perry was something of a fussbudget and he strongly suspected that Grandpa was a tool of Ira Sayre. It was true that Grandpa had always been friendly with Ira Sayre. Sate Parmelee and Julia Sayre were cousins and had grown up together, but I doubt that Grandpa ever took any orders from Ira. In the winter when the question of the bridge came up, Grandpa was still in the midst of the disrepute that his marriage to Ardie Streator had brought on and he was being stubborn about a lot of things. Grandfather Love would have had trouble with him even if there had been no Ira Sayre.

The decision to replace the old iron bridge had been made.

The plans for the new bridge had been accepted. Bids had been submitted by several companies and an agreement had been made to let the contract. George Packard was called in and told to build a temporary bridge that would cross the river down by the lumber yard. This temporary bridge was a long wooden span that rested on wooden piles that had been driven into the stream. It was flimsy at best and could not possibly survive the spring floods, but everyone thought that by the time the high water came the new Main Street bridge would be completed and in use. As soon as George Packard and his crew finished the temporary, a wrecking company came in and began tearing down the old iron bridge. It was at that moment that the trouble came. Henry Chatters died of a stroke. Henry Chatters was my grandfather Love's right-hand man on the village council and his death left the council deadlocked at five to five. Unfortunately, one formality connected with the new bridge had not yet been completed. Although the firm had been selected to build it, the actual contracts had not been signed. A Flint law firm had been retained to look into the fine print and had only just forwarded the contracts to Flushing for signature when Henry Chatters died. When it came time for Grandfather Love to get the approval of the council for his signature, he had lost his majority and the newly deadlocked council wouldn't give it to him.

A considerable howl went up from my grandfather Love. He accused Grandpa Perry of all kinds of things, not the least of which was being crooked. He claimed that Ira Sayre wanted to substitute another firm to build the bridge because he would get a cut out of it and that Grandpa Perry would get paid off, too. I've never been sure whether or not Ira Sayre had anything to do with the fight that ensued, but I suspect he did. However, I do not think he had any corrupt motives. I think that he saw a chance to get even with my grandfather for all the indignities that had been heaped upon him over the years and that he decided to take it. He advised Grandpa Perry in the matter and somehow or other he convinced Grandpa that a firm other than the one selected should build the bridge.

Week after week went by and at the meetings of the council two rows of men sat grimly across the table from each other and glared. The iron bridge was gone and the temporary was in use. It was obvious that no one was going to get across the river when the flood came the next spring if the new bridge wasn't started soon. The temporary was sure to wash out and the nearest bridges were ten miles away. Tempers in Flushing became pretty heated and people began calling the councilmen harsh names. My mother and father heard most of these names and became the focal point of a lot of the indignation because both of their fathers were on the council and leading the opposite sides.

My mother knew she would have to do something, but she had a problem. In all the years of her marriage to my father she had only been able to get Grandfather Love to come to our house once or twice for formal occasions. Although Grandfather was fond of my mother and welcomed her to *his* house warmly, and although he sometimes stopped in for a cup of coffee in the kitchen in the mornings, he simply did not like to run the chance of meeting Grandpa Perry. This attitude was the result of Grandpa Perry's long and rather warm friendship with Ira Sayre. Ira Sayre was Grandfather Love's horned enemy, and under his code any friend of Ira's was also an enemy.

My mother did some conniving. She searched through her memory until she found an occasion for a party that Grandfather Love couldn't possibly refuse. She picked on his fortieth wedding anniversary. She didn't invite *him.* She invited my grandmother and got an acceptance. There wasn't much Grandfather could do. My mother put a big meal on the table and made a festive occasion out of it, but she meant business. When the dinner was over, she took Grandfather Love by one arm and Grandpa Perry by the other and led them to the parlor, sat them down in chairs facing each other and then went out, closing the sliding doors after her. She told them that they weren't going to be let out of that room until the bridge question was settled.

My two grandfathers sat in the parlor for an hour without speaking. Grandpa Perry finally asked Grandfather Love if some neutral party couldn't make the decision as to who was going to build the bridge. Grandfather Love said he guessed that some neutral party could, but that he'd have to be absolutely impartial, absolutely honest, and absolutely smart. At that point they started naming names. Grandpa Perry would mention a name and Grandfather Love would shake his head. Grandfather Love would mention a name and Grandpa Perry would shake *his* head. They could not agree on any of the more prominent men of the village, so they put on their hats and walked down to the council chambers where the voter registration books were kept. Each one opened a book and read names from it aloud. As each name was read, one or the other would shake his head. When Grandpa Perry said, "Joe Gage," Grandfather Love closed his book with a bang. They got up, shook hands, lit each other a cigar, and walked up to Joe Gage's house together. That was how Joe Gage became president of the village council, the highest office Flushing had to offer. He held the office until the next election and then declined to run again. He accepted it only on the condition that he would be allowed a free hand, and he was given it. He solved the bridge problem by awarding the contract to an entirely new firm. The bridge was finished and in use before the floods could wash away the temporary one next spring. It still stands and I think it will stand for a good many years.

In telling me about this incident a long time afterwards, Grandpa Perry said that on the way up to Joe Gage's house that evening, Grandfather Love had made the statement that Joe was the *only* man in town with the wisdom to handle *any* job in the village and that he was probably the fairest man that had ever lived there. Joe Gage served two other interim terms on the council in later years, but that was after my family had moved away from Flushing. Each time he served it was because some knotty problem had to be solved. At the time of Joe's death, when he was a very old man, someone suggested they ought to erect a monument to him. The matter was lost, but my father used to think they already had one. Every time we drove across that bridge, he always said, "Well, here we go across Joe Gage's bridge."

CHAPTER FOURTEEN

When my father died in 1962, he left me a drawerful of odds and ends. When I went through them I found a picture I had drawn in 1921, when I was nine years old. In its own way that picture told the story of the most exciting day in the history of Flushing. At least I thought it was the most exciting day, at the time, though I don't suppose very many adults would have thought so. If they did, they wouldn't have the same reasons for doing so. My grandpa Perry always referred to it as the day all the Knights Templar came to Flushing. I always referred to it as the day all the engines came there.

One of the institutions of small-town America was the Sunday baseball game. Every town had a semiprofessional team made up of local heroes and one or two imported lights. Charlie Gehringer, KiKi Cuyler, Joe Kuhel, and several other major league stars of twenty or more years ago all got their starts on these village teams. The three ballplayers I have named all came to Flushing on one or another of those summer Sunday afternoons and played in the ball field that the Wilcox twins had constructed out behind one of their berry patches. Year in and year out, Flushing always had a good team. Our biggest rival was Durand with whom a home-and-home series was played each summer. Durand always had a big advantage over most of the towns because it could send fairly large crowds wherever its team played. The railroad simply hitched an engine to several day coaches and ran a special train out to the scene of the game. At the game played in Flushing in 1921, more than two hundred people came over to watch it.

There were certain simple rules governing a game between towns like Durand and Flushing. Each town furnished one umpire, for instance. During the first inning the Durand umpire would call balls and strikes and the Flushing umpire would handle the bases. In the second inning they would change places, moving back and forth in each succeeding inning. For Flushing Frank Haskell, the village paint and wallpaper dealer, had handled the umpiring duties for years. The regular umpire for the Durand team was a man called Freckles Deal. Freckles was a brakeman on the Grand Trunk Railroad and in 1921 was senior enough to stand at the head of the extra list. This meant that he got first call as a brakeman on any nonscheduled train out of Durand, or he was the first called to replace any brakeman on a regular run who was incapacitated for any reason. Freckles was a well-known figure all over Michigan because he got to most communities. Although he was a sober, competent brakeman on weekdays, he wasn't very well liked. He had red hair and a nasty temper. When he got to drinking, as he often did on a Sunday, he was a mean customer.

On the afternoon when Durand came to play Flushing in 1921, Freckles Deal had imbibed too much whiskey before he arrived at the ball park. He couldn't have told a strike from a captive balloon. The Durand manager took one look at him and dismissed him for the day, then asked Jerry Gibbons if Flushing could furnish the second umpire to take Freckles Deal's place. Jerry Gibbons suggested my father and the offer was accepted at once.

My father had a rather unique place in the sporting life of our part of Michigan. Stature might be a good word for it. In his early days he had been a familiar player and the fact that he had gone on to play professional ball and to reach the big leagues gave him considerable prestige. When the Durand manager found out that my father was available to umpire the game, he raised no questions.

The invitation to umpire the game that Sunday came at one of those rare moments in my father's life. My mother had got him out of bed at an early hour. One of her nieces was being baptized in the Episcopal Church in Flint and she and my father had been asked to be godparents. They had driven over to St. Paul's Church and had eaten breakfast after the ceremony. They had arrived back in Flushing just in time to come out to the ball park. My father still had on his best gray suit and still wore his fancy black and white sport shoes. He was really dressed up, but there was more to it than that. He was bemused. His infrequent visits to church did something to him. It may have been the hymns or it may have been my mother's complete rapture (it certainly wasn't the sermons), but whatever it was, he came out a changed man. Sometimes he stayed a changed man for several days. Under the circumstances, he was in no mood to umpire a baseball game that afternoon and it took a considerable amount of coaxing to get him to take on the job.

The ball and strike umpires did not stand behind the catcher in those days. They stood out on the pitcher's mound directly behind the pitcher. My father went to stand in the middle of the diamond at the start of the game and Frank Haskell went over to hover around first base. There was trouble on the very first play. The Durand fans had taken up a position along the first base line where the Durand bench was. The Flushing fans were along the third base line. The real crux of the trouble was Freckles Deal, who had refused to accept the verdict that he was unfit to umpire. He took the attitude that his dismissal was part of a conspiracy to keep Durand from winning the game. Along with three of his friends he had taken a place near the first base bag and proceeded at once to make himself obnoxious. On every play he issued a long series of catcalls which he directed at the umpires. At first he directed his insults at Frank Haskell, who was frail-looking and sixty-five, but in the third inning, when his language became abusive, my father stopped the game momentarily, walked over to him, and told him to quit picking on an old man. Thereafter, with his attention focused on my father, Freckles Deal turned the air blue. Because my father was up on that lofty cloud on which he had floated out of the church, he simply ignored the whole thing and concentrated on umpiring the game.

Things worked up to a crisis. The Durand fans kept shoving closer to the first base line and gradually took up the chorus. The Flushing fans, who ordinarily watched the game from their cars parked behind the fence along third base, were aware of what was happening. One by one they got out of the cars and crowded the base line, heckling the Durand fans and players. In the fifth inning the tenor changed. The Flushing fans began to concentrate on my father. They encouraged him to go over and beat the daylights out of Freckles Deal. No one in the park understood that my father had been taking his churchgoing to heart and that he was turning the other cheek. He remained calm and in the end this began to irk the Flushing fans as much as it irked the Durand fans. They began to ride him. My grandfather Love was worse than anyone else. *He* was all for a fight *any* time and he invaded the Durand side of the diamond waving a ten-dollar bill. He was willing to bet that the umpire could whip any three of the Durand rooters. When the sixth inning passed and my father still showed no inclination to join in a fight, my grandfather changed his offer. He was willing to bet ten dollars that *he* could whip any three Durand rooters.

At the beginning of the eighth inning my father moved over to the first base line to take up his duties as base umpire. By that time the fans had moved so far forward that they were standing right on the base lines. On the first play a Durand batter hit a ball to the shortstop and on the throw the Flushing first baseman had to fight the crowd for possession of the ball. Things had gone as far as they could go. My father stepped over to first base and held up his hands. He announced that the game would not go on until the crowd moved back several yards from the base lines. There was a moment of impasse and then the people began to back up—all except one of them. That one was Freckles Deal. In a spirit of reckless defiance he took a step forward, placed his feet on the first base bag, and folded his arms.

"If you want me to move back, you yellow bastard," he told my father, "you move me."

My father didn't have much choice. He could pick Freckles Deal up and carry him back or he could push him back. He chose the latter. He doubled up his fist and swung and hit Freckles Deal on the chin. Freckles did a backward somersault and ended up the required distance away. He lay there, stretched out on the ground, as his fellow townsmen gathered around him.

My father had had enough. In his exalted frame of mind, with hymns still flitting through his head, he felt he had disgraced himself. Without even looking back he walked down to home plate and resigned as umpire. Then he walked to his car, got in, and started for home. By the time someone threw a pail of water on Freckles Deal to revive him, my father was all the way through Wilcox's berry patch. When Freckles came to, he scrambled to his feet, doubled up his fists, and rushed out onto the diamond like a tormented bull, only to find that his assailant had escaped him. He stood there for several minutes before he was led away by friends, vowing to come back and get even. It didn't help matters any that Flushing won the game.

Freckles Deal returned to Flushing much sooner than he had thought he would. During that Sunday night Mac Durfee, the regular brakeman on the local freight, came down with the grippe. Freckles Deal, number one man on the extra list, got the call. When number 2315 came rolling up to the depot the next morning, Freckles was sitting on the cowcatcher. I was at the depot as usual and I soon discovered that the local freight had brought a carload of two-by-fours for my father's lumber yard. Ordinarily I would have crawled up in the cab of the engine while it was at the depot, but that car of two-by-fours changed things. I always asked my father for the privilege of telling the brakemen where a car should be spotted on his siding at a moment like this. I told Burt Emans that I would catch him later and copied down the number of the boxcar on a piece of paper and ran down the Main Street hill as fast as I could go. I burst into my father's office to tell him the news and he went to his old filing cabinet to dig out the invoice and see what was in the car. Then he led the way down the track to the two-by-four piles and put a stick in the ground to show me exactly where the car should go. After that he went back to his office and I went to stand next to the Main Street crossing to wait for the train.

It should be explained that the spur track that ran down into the village from the main line was still in use even though the railroad bridge had been blocked off three years before. There were still several business establishments on the *west* side of the river that got carload freight, among them the grain elevator, an oil-distributing company, a coal yard, a brick yard, and my father's lumber yard. The railroad men had never liked the spur track because of the grade. The hills on the main line were bad enough, but the one on that spur line coming out of the river valley was almost impossible. It was at least a six percent grade, perhaps steeper. The rails and ties were flimsy and an engineer had to keep his driving wheels from spinning. If they spun, the rails might spread and let the engine drop on the ground. Every locomotive had sand spouts that ran down from a dome atop the boiler and when an engineer started up the hill out of the river bottom he would turn on the sand and leave it on all the way up the grade. On the goats the sand spouts poured the sand out on the rails just ahead of the front driving wheels. It didn't do any good at all if the engine was backing up. For that reason no southbound trains ever did any switching on the spur. If they ever got in there with the front of the engine headed downhill they might not get out again. Furthermore, the trainmen never tried to climb out of the spur with more than three cars. On busy mornings they often made two or three trips down the hill to bring out all the cars. Over the years every freight crew had trouble on that spur. Engines or cars were always running off the track. All over the Grand Trunk Railroad, the Flushing spur was known as The Hole and the trainmen uttered the phrase as though it was the Black Hole of Calcutta.

The worst part of The Hole was the side track that ran into my father's lumber yard. It was a switchback that branched off the main spur right at the Emily Street crossing. It curved sharply to the north and crossed Main Street at the very bottom of the hill that came down from the depot. The minute it got across Main Street it straightened out and ran steeply downhill to the river. Any car of lumber that was to be delivered to the lumber yard had to be hooked on the front end of the engine and pushed around that curve, across Main Street, and down the hill to where it belonged. Trainmen tried to keep the engine from going down the hill. They would put two empty freight cars between the engine and the car to be delivered so that number 2315 didn't have to go too far down the grade. They would have put more empties than that ahead of the engine, but since the railroad bridge had been blocked off there wasn't room enough between the switch and the big mound of dirt at the end of the span. As it was, Burt Emans had to back right up against the block in order to clear the switch when he had three cars ahead of him.

On the morning that the car of two-by-fours came for my father, number 2315 came backing down into The Hole with three cars behind it and three cars in front of it (two of them empty). I watched it cross Main Street on the hill above me and waited at the corner of the office. For several minutes it switched around over by the grain elevator. Then the engine, with the three cars on the head end, came squealing around the curve. Freckles Deal was hanging from the ladder of the first car. As it rumbled across Main Street, he held out one arm in the stop signal and dropped to the ground. He turned and saw me standing beside the track.

"George," he said to me, "run in and find out where they want this car spotted."

"I know where they want it spotted," I said, and led the way down the track to where the stick was stuck in the ground.

Freckles Deal looked around for an adult, then shrugged and turned back to the engine. He grabbed up the stick to use as a wheel chock and raised his right hand and wiggled it in the air as the signal for Burt Emans to advance cautiously. Burt released the brakes in the engine cab and the cars rolled slowly forward. When the car of lumber reached the marked spot, Freckles Deal lowered his arms abruptly and Burt applied the brakes. By that time the engine had moved across Main Street and had nosed into the steep grade that ran down to the river. The back of its tender was flush with the edge of the street. Freckles Deal bent over and shoved the chock under the wheels, then straightened up and walked back up the track to grab the uncoupling bar between the lumber car and the empty next to it.

It was at this precise moment that my father walked out of his office. He had his bankbook in his hand and was on his way to town. He looked down the track to see if the car was spotted in the right place and waved his hand when he saw that it had been, then turned and walked around the corner of the office to his car. I don't think he gave Freckles Deal a thought. He didn't even recognize him. Freckles Deal recognized my father all right. He stood there for a moment, his mouth open in surprise, then doubled up his fists and started up the track. The trouble was that Freckles had already whirled his arm in the back-up signal to Burt Emans as he reached for the coupling drawbar, but he hadn't actually pulled the bar to uncouple the loaded lumber car. Number 2315 could have yanked two empty cars out of that grade with no trouble, but pulling two empties and a loaded car was something else. The engine backed slowly for a foot or two, taking up the slack between cars, gave its first chug, and then the wheels began to spin on the rails. There was a series of sharp staccato chugs before Burt Emans could shove the throttle closed. In that short instant the damage was done. The rails spread and number 2315's driving wheels dropped to the ground.

Everyone knew at once what had happened. Freckles Deal had got to the door of the office, opposite the engine, and was within five feet of the wheels when they dropped. He stopped and gaped at the big drivers. Burt Emans leaned far out of the cab, looked down, and swore. He climbed down from the cab and stood wiping his face with his bandanna handkerchief while he studied the situation. About the only person who didn't seem to realize that the engine had run off the track was my father. He had got into his car and as Burt Emans climbed down from the cab, he backed out and sped away. As it turned out, he never came back to his office that day at all.

Burt Emans and Freckles Deal and the fireman got down on their hands and knees and crawled around under the engine for several minutes. Then Burt climbed back up in the cab and blew several short blasts on his whistle, a signal that meant trouble. Pete Ronald came over from the grain elevator switch where he had been waiting and John Strauble, the conductor, came hurrying down from the depot where he had been unloading less-than-carload freight. Pete and John crawled around under the engine in their turn. When they had finished their survey, John Strauble instructed the brakemen to unhitch the engine from the three boxcars and get it back on the track. He was going out south of town, where the rest of the train had been left standing on the main line, to protect it with a red flag.

The four trainmen now went to work on the engine. They took the two big cast-iron "frogs" from the hooks on the tender and placed them carefully behind the driving wheels. The drivers would climb up on them and then slip back onto the rails. When the frogs had been carefully adjusted so that the flanges on the wheels were up against the indentations, Burt Emans pulled himself back up into the cab and took his place at the throttle. Pete Ronald moved down to the cowcatcher and took a firm grip on the coupling drawbar, ready to pull it and release the boxcars. Freckles Deal crawled on top of the nearest empty boxcar and stationed himself at the hand-brake wheel. The maneuver that was about to take place was a relatively simple one. When the engine ran off the track, the boxcars were still coupled to it. It would have been next to impossible for the engine to pull itself up onto the frogs and at the same time pull the boxcars along with it. Therefore, the cars had to be uncoupled and, if possible, pushed a few feet out of the way. All that was needed, on a steep grade like that, was a little nudge to get them rolling. When everyone was in place, Pete Ronald raised his hand cautiously and wiggled it at Burt Emans. Burt had already shoved the big direction lever in the cab to the forward position and he now gave a quick yank on the throttle, then shoved it shut again. The effect of this quick pull was to produce one violent chug. The engine lifted itself up for a moment, shuddered, and subsided. This nudged the three boxcars, and they began to inch forward down the grade. Pete Ronald yanked the drawbar, then moved around beside the cars and replaced the stick of wood that had served as a wheel chock. Up on top of the car Freckles Deal gave a quick twist of the hand-brake wheel. It spun free; it wasn't connected to anything! There was a crunch and the wheels of the car rolled right over the wheel chock. Freckles Deal shouted something down to Pete and ran along the top of the car to the hand-brake wheel on the second car. Pete looked around quickly for another wheel chock and grabbed up a piece of a thick, round cedar post. By this time the cars were moving down the grade at the rate of speed a man could walk. On top of the second car, Freckles Deal began tugging frantically at the hand-brake wheel. It wouldn't turn at all. Pete Ronald threw this piece of cedar post under the wheels, but it was round and the wheels just nudged it aside. Freckles Deal straightened up from his struggle with the hand-brake wheel, looked around for a moment, then skipped along the runway on top of the car to the brake wheel on the third car. Pete Ronald ran a few steps, hurriedly grabbed a two-by-six off a lumber pile, and sprinted after the cars. By this time the cars were moving about as fast as a man could trot and Pete had a hard time catching them. He threw the two-by-six but it slithered across the track and the wheels missed it completely. Freckles Deal was turning the third hand-brake wheel and the clank of the brake shoes could be heard as they began to take hold. It was too late. Pete Ronald shouted something from below and Freckles Deal straightened, looked around, and dove for the ladder on the side of the car. He came down it like a cat and jumped to the ground. A moment later the three cars ran off the end of the track and plowed into the river with a magnificent splash.

Pete Ronald and Freckles Deal stood there on the track with their hands on their hips arguing with each other for several minutes. They might have come to blows if Bud Roof hadn't come running down from the depot with a piece of paper in his hand. John Strauble had sent out a telegram to stations north and south warning them that the local freight was blocking the main line just out of Flushing. The chief dispatcher had monitored this message and was now wiring back to inform the crew of the local that two special trains of Knights Templar would be leaving Saginaw within the hour. The crew of the freight was to get that engine back on the track in a hurry and pull the train onto a siding until after the specials passed.

The frogs had already been put in place, so the crew went

right to work. Burt Emans pulled the big direction lever in the cab into reverse and leaned out the window to look down. I knew what was coming next and I scurried over to the cement shed and peeked back around the corner to watch. When Burt Emans was sure everything was ready, he opened two steam pet-cocks on the cylinders over the pilot wheels. Jets of steam shot out horizontally with a deafening roar. I had seen this before, but I never could get used to it. It always seemed to me that the engine was going to blow up. Like some prehistoric dragon spitting streams of fire, number 2315 began waddling backwards over the ties. It raised itself up onto the frogs and there was a triumphant shout from Pete Ronald. Number 2315 was back on the track again! Burt Emans shoved in the throttle and shut off the steam jets, then left the cab and began to climb down to the ground. Just as he did so, a terrible thing happened. With a rasping sound the whole engine tilted forward. The pilot wheels had reached the point where the rails were spread of course, and they now slipped to the ground. The four trainmen all stood beside the engine angrily shaking their heads and muttering. They got back down on their hands and knees and adjusted the frogs behind the pilot wheels. When all was in readiness, Burt got into the cab again and I retired behind the cement shed once more. The steam jets began to roar and Burt pulled the throttle. This time number 2315 did not waddle backwards. It just stood where it was and the driving wheels spun. There was another jar and the whole engine dropped to the ground. All of number 2315 was off the track! Burt Emans stood beside it and shook his head. He told Pete Ronald that the only way they'd get number 2315 back on the track now was to get another engine and pull it on.

Burt Emans and his fireman stayed with number 2315, but the two brakemen trudged up to the depot and I plodded along beside them. When they got to the top of the hill they separated. Freckles Deal went into the baggage room and got the big red flag and some torpedoes. He then sauntered out along the track north of town to intercept the two specials. Pete Ronald went to send off the bad news to the chief dispatcher in Durand. An answer to his telegram was not long in coming. Extra freight, northbound, number 2265, was already made up and waiting to follow the northbound noon passenger train. The original plans had called for this freight to meet the two specials in Lennon. (The passenger train was supposed to meet them in Brent Creek.) Now number 2265 would come on into Flushing and wait there for the specials. After they had gone by, number 2265 would go down into The Hole and pull number 2315 back on the track. Only a few minutes after this message came in it was amended. The passenger train would wait for the two specials in Flushing. John Reardon's engine, number 2248, would push the cars of the local freight onto the siding to get them out of the way.

Pete Ronald had always been my favorite railroad man outside of Burt Emans, so I tagged along with him after the messages came in from Durand. We walked out to the southern limits of town where two switches led off the main line. One of these two switches led into a long side track that paralleled the main line all the way through the village. It had been built originally as a passing track, but when the decision was made not to have trains meet in Flushing, except in emergencies, the siding was converted to other uses. Several businesses were located along it and freight cars were parked there for loading and unloading. It was called the House track. The other switch was only a few feet away from the south House track switch. It led into a siding that branched off on the other—east—side of the main line. It followed the main line tracks right down to the depot, where it ended abruptly about thirty yards short of the baggage room. It had been built thirty years before to serve two canneries that were then in existence, but the two canneries had long since gone bankrupt. In all the years that I had lived in Flushing this track was rarely used. Once in a while in the sugar beet season some gondola cars would be parked on it and farmers would drive alongside them and fork sugar beets into them—it was called the Team track for this reason—and quite often the local freight would set out a car at the upper end of it so that it could be picked up easily by one of the fast freights. Most of the Team track was covered by heavy weeds and unless one knew it was there he was unaware of its existence. A single wooden tie was wired across this dead-end track as a sort of block to keep runaway boxcars from crashing into the depot, but even that was covered by thick grass.

When Pete Ronald and I reached the switches at the south end of town that summer day, he went over to the House track switch and unlocked the padlock and turned the switch so that the cars of the local freight that were still standing on the main line could be pushed into the siding when John Reardon would finally come along. Then we went back and sat down on the bank of the cut, almost behind the West Side school, and he told me all kinds of things about the railroad. We had been sitting on the grass for about three quarters of an hour when we heard John Reardon's engine whistle, far off to the south. Pete Ronald got up slowly, brushed himself off, and walked over to the track. Soon afterwards a boxcar came gliding silently down the track toward us. It was the head end of the local freight that was being pushed into the siding by the passenger train. I could barely hear number 2248 chugging far back at the end of it. John Strauble was standing on top of one of the cars to relay hand signals to the engine, and as the first car went by Pete Ronald swung onto the hand ladder. There were several freight cars standing along the House track that day and as the train came up to each one of them it had to slow down before bumping it and pushing it on along the siding. Pete Ronald, riding the head car, had to run ahead each time and open the couplers before the cars bumped. After each coupling, he would raise his arm in the go-ahead signal and John Strauble would relay it back to the engine. As the cars rolled on down the siding and more of them were added to the train, it became harder and harder for John Reardon to pick up speed again. I stood beside the switch where Pete Ronald had left me and within a few minutes number 2248 came into view, chugging hard.

There were fourteen cars on the local freight that day, counting the caboose. There were six cars parked along the House track. The passenger train had three cars. Number 2248 was pushing or pulling twenty-three cars by the time it reached the switch and began to nose into the siding. This was a bigger load than a goat was meant to handle and it was barely moving. Just as it came opposite me it slowed to pick up the last car and, when John Reardon pulled his throttle to move on ahead again number 2248 couldn't move at all. It just stood where it was and spun its wheels. John Strauble climbed down from his boxcar and walked back along the track to find out what was the matter. He and John Reardon and the passenger conductor talked things over and finally decided that they would have to unhitch the passenger cars, thus lightening the load enough to enable number 2248 to push the freight the rest of the way onto the siding. John Reardon became very angry during this discussion because John Strauble made some disparaging remarks about his engine. Tempers weren't improved any in the next few minutes. Unhitching a passenger train from an engine is not a simple matter. Two or three hoses and a cable had to be detached and Beans McAuslin, John Reardon's fireman, had to get down between the tender and the mail car with a wrench and undo them. In the process he broke his goggles.

While the passenger train was being unhitched, the first of the two specials whistled, far to the north. I decided I had better go down and watch the specials, so I left before John Reardon finished pushing the freight onto the siding and went back to get his own cars. The first of the two trains full of Knights Templar roared across Henry Chatters's crossing just as I reached the depot. As they turned for Flushing the engines ran over and exploded the torpedoes that Freckles Deal had put out and blew two short blasts to acknowledge the red flag. They slowed down immediately and by the time they reached the water tank they were barely crawling. The engine numbers of the doubleheader that pulled the eight coaches of the special were 2243 and 2294. I hadn't seen either of these engines at that time, so I went over and talked to the engineers while they walked around the engines and poked away with their oil cans. I didn't learn very much except that number 2243 usually pulled a regular passenger train on a railroad that was called the Turkey Trail.

After taking water for several minutes, the two engines pulled their train slowly up the track to the south and stopped near the Team track switch to wait for the northbound extra freight. At just about the time the last coach glided past the depot, the second special whistled to the north. It exploded two more torpedoes as it passed Henry Chatters's crossing and acknowledged Freckles Deal's flag. When it got to the water tank I was pleased to discover that it was pulled by number 2245 and number 2299. Number 2245 came to Flushing quite often and number 2299 usually pulled one of the fast manifests during the night.

While the second special was taking water, northbound extra number 2265, which was to pull number 2315 on the track, whistled for the crossing south of town. I went over to stand in front of the depot where I could see it better. It came slowly around the bend and drifted almost to a stop as it approached the Team track switch, its white flags blowing in the breeze. The head-end brakeman was hanging from the cab ladder and he dropped to the ground and ran ahead of the engine to throw the switch. When he raised his hand in signal there was a belch of smoke from the stack and the engine nosed slowly into the siding. Number 2265 felt its way through the weeds of the unused track, chugging leisurely downgrade, the fireman leaning far out his window and peering backwards to catch the signal of the brakeman when the caboose cleared the switch. The engineer had one hand on the throttle and one hand on the brake and his eyes were glued on the fireman, waiting for the relay of the signal. Number 2265 chugged across Emily Street and down the track toward the depot. It was not until the engine was thirty yards from the end of the track that anyone realized that the caboose was not yet in sight. Something made the engineer look around and he saw the depot looming up before him. He had run out of track. He jammed in his throttle and applied full brakes. Under any kind of ordinary conditions the train would have stopped before it was too late. It certainly was not moving very fast and the engineer had acted hastily, but competently.

Unfortunately, there were weeds on that track and the weeds were slippery. When the brakes were applied, the wheels locked and slid along. There didn't seem to be any change of speed at all. The cowcatcher scooped up the tie from the end of the track and the engine and tender slid right out into the roadway that ran around the depot. It came to halt in a cloud of dust with the front coupler wedged squarely up against the wooden walk of the baggage room. Number 2265 was *really* off the track and as it rested there on the ground its wheels slowly sank into the clay and cinders. There was more to the predicament of number 2265 than that, however. The caboose and four cars still stuck out on the main line to the south. One car stood at an angle to the main line on the Team track switch itself and the caboose effectively blocked the exit from the House track. There were now five trains and seven engines in Flushing and not one of them could move. Thirty-one trainmen manned those five trains and not one of them knew what to do. All thirty-one stood out at the south end of town and argued for twenty minutes and then came trouping down to the depot to send a telegram to the chief dispatcher, telling him that they needed another engine. After the telegram was composed, no one could agree on who was to sign it and Bud Roof just sent it off without any signature at all. After a long time an answer came back from Durand. An extra engine would be sent out but it would take at least an hour and a half to assemble a crew, fire it up, and get it under way. The rescue train could not be expected in Flushing for at least two hours. The chief dispatcher was pretty unhappy.

It was now nearly one o'clock in the afternoon. It would be nearly three o'clock before help arrived. This brought up a new problem. Neither of the two specials had a dining car, nor did the regular passenger train. On board the two specials were about 1,800 hungry Knights Templar and on board the passenger train were another 200 hungry passengers. Most of these people had been leaning out the open windows of their cars, watching the drama unfold, and it didn't take them long to learn that it might be several hours before they arrived at a place where they could get something to eat. They began leaving the trains in small groups at first and then they moved in a body. They streamed down the Main Street hill toward the business district to look for food.

The two thousand strangers who now invaded the village equaled about double the population. The town was poorly equipped to feed such a horde. Mrs. Gage could squeeze thirty people into her hotel dining room and the two poolrooms could serve about ten people every half hour. Consequently, the visitors had to make shift. They invaded the grocery stores, the bakery, the candy store, and the meat markets. Frankfurters, which came in big bunches like bananas, were carried down to the corner at Fred Graves's barbershop. A huge bonfire was built there and crowds of white-plumed men milled around it, trying to roast hot dogs, marshmallows, and steaks on the ends of long swords.

There were other complications in Flushing that afternoon. Not the least of these was the traffic situation. Only two streets led into the village from the farming community west of the river. One of these was Main Street, but Main Street was now blocked. In the morning, when number 2315 had been struggling to get on the track, it had backed up, and in backing it had ended up with its coal car squarely across Main Street so that vehicular traffic could not move in either direction. The only other street that could be used was Emily Street which branched off at the end of the bridge and ran up around the grain elevator and came out west of town near Frawley's coal yard. When number 2265 ran off the track, it pulled its train of cars across the Emily Street crossing so that it effectively blocked *that* means of ingress and egress. No one could get into town or out of town on the west.

The people of Flushing and the stranded travelers may have been having a hectic time, but I was having a picnic. I solved my own eating problem by getting some bread and jelly at my grandmother's house and then went back up to the railroad and started climbing in and out of engine cabs, cabooses, passenger cars, and even Mr. O'Brien's mail car on the passenger train. I talked with engineers and firemen, brakemen and conductors. I even helped John Reardon polish the bell on number 2248.

The rescue train arrived in Flushing at a little after three o'clock. It was pulled by number 2277 and the dispatcher, evidently alarmed by what was happening to all his trains, had sent along a wrecking crane and a full crew. It ran up behind the caboose of the northbound extra and hitched on, then slowly pulled all of number 2265's train back out of the Team track onto the main line. At that point everyone had to stop and scratch his head again. There was nothing to do with this train because all the sidings were full. The only place to put it was down in The Hole. If number 2277 ever backed down into *that* track with all those cars and then tried to push them out later, it might never get out. The only other alternative was for number 2277 to back up all the way to Lennon and pull the train into a siding there. That was too far away and, because number 2277 would be pulling *two* trains up a long grade it might never get there. The trainmen—there were thirty-six of them now—all stood around and argued again. Number 2277 finally pushed number 2265's train back onto the Team track. The caboose and the last four cars were then unhitched and number 2277 pulled them back out onto the main line. It had been decided that number 2277 could probably push *that* many cars up out of The Hole, but it meant that the two special trains would have to back a mile or two out of town so that the switch down into The Hole would be uncovered.

In straightening out this situation, the trainmen on the two specials gave some consideration to the Knights Templar who were now wandering all over Flushing looking for food. The conductors wanted all these people back on the trains as soon as possible so that they could leave town when the track was clear. In order to save time, it was decided that the engines on both specials would give warning by blowing their whistles and ringing their bells while they were backing out of number 2277's way. By the time they came back into the depot all the Knights Templar would be assembled there, ready to get aboard. With four engines blowing whistles and ringing bells there was quite a din, and it was added to when John Reardon decided to use the same method to call in the passengers of *his* train. After the specials backed off and number 2277 started to move through town and out to the switch that led down to The Hole, it had to pass through the depot area where milling crowds had started to gather, so it blew its whistle and rang its bell, too. That made *six* engines in Flushing, all blowing whistles and ringing bells at once.

The only silent engines in town were number 2315 and number 2265. All through the late forenoon and early afternoon, number 2315 had been sitting patiently in the lumber yard waiting to be rescued. Burt Emans and his fireman had whiled away the time by reading the newspapers or magazines. Every once in a while the fireman got up and threw a few shovels of coal on the fire. At about three o'clock, after one of these stokings, he looked at the water-level gauge on the boiler and told Burt Emans that they'd better do something about getting a little more water. Burt folded his newspaper and crawled down out of the cab to trudge up the hill to the depot. He arrived there at the moment when the two specials were backing out of town. Two or three hundred people were milling around inside and outside the waiting rooms and most of them were badgering Bud Roof with questions about when the trains were going to leave or where they could get something to eat. Bud was a little harassed.

Burt Emans had no particular sense of urgency when he elbowed his way through the crowd into the waiting room. He simply wanted to borrow a fire hose from the fire department, attach it to the nearest hydrant, and fill his tender with water. He started out by asking Bud to call someone in the village who could lend him the fire hose, but his request was lost in the din of jabbering people, blowing whistles, and ringing bells. Bud Roof didn't hear it, so Burt tried again. He repeated his request in a little louder voice and it was still ignored. The third time he thundered. Bud looked up at him in annoyance and asked him if he *had* to have the hose right then. Burt was a little annoyed himself by then and he said that Bud had damned well better get the hose or be responsible for number 2315 blowing up. Somehow it got through to Bud that number 2315 was about to blow up. As the enormity of the catastrophe dawned on him, he grabbed the telephone and told Addie Badger that he needed the fire department and he needed it quick. Addie knew one way to get the fire department and that was to pull the switch on the fire whistle. (It had been moved to her office after the fire.) The trains were still whistling and ringing their bells and now the fire whistle started blowing.

Flushing had its new Reo fire truck in 1921. Fred Graves still had the job of getting to the firehouse and opening the doors. The driver of the truck was supposed to be Pick Parsell, one of the village butchers, but if Pick happened to be in the icebox of his shop he couldn't hear the fire whistle and he was sometimes a little tardy in running down the alley to the firehouse. Fred Graves had had a secret desire to drive that truck from the time it was bought and he learned how to drive just so he could realize his ambition. He was a terrible driver, but he didn't let that bother him. He would run over to the firehouse, open the doors, and count a quick ten. If Pick Parsell wasn't in sight by the time he finished, Fred would jump in the driver's seat, start the motor, and run the truck out of the firehouse. Usually, before he got to the corner of Main Street, Pick would come running down the alley and shove him out of the seat and take over, but on the day Burt Emans wanted the fire hose, Pick was besieged in his shop by all those Knights Templar and he didn't get out on time. Fred Graves called Addie Badger and she told him the fire was up at the depot. (Bud Roof hadn't said so, but she assumed it was because *he* had called.) Fred did his fast count, jumped in the driver's seat, started the siren going, and wheeled the truck out of the firehouse. He made it to Main Street, turned the corner, ducked down over the bridge, and headed west. The Reo had an exhaust whistle in addition to a siren, and with all these going, it added immeasurably to the general din.

By the time the fire whistle started blowing, most of the Knights Templar had heard the train whistles and most of them had started for the depot. There were mobs of white-plumed Knights moving west, all jabbering. Many of them were rattling swords. When the people of Flushing heard the train whistles, followed a few minutes later by the fire whistle, and finally by the siren and exhaust whistle on the fire truck, and when they saw the mobs of people moving west across the bridge, they naturally assumed there was some kind of disaster up at the depot. Almost everyone dropped what he was doing and headed west, too. Within ten minutes nearly three thousand people were moving on Main Street, talking excitedly, and raising a thick cloud of dust as they tramped along the road.

Fred Graves moved the fire truck slowly west through the

crowd until he came to the lumber yard at the foot of the hill. There he found his way blocked by number 2315, so he had to turn around laboriously and fight his way against the stream of people back to the bridge and then turn up Emily Street. He sped around the turn past the grain elevator and up the hill. It wasn't until he reached the top of the hill that he saw his way blocked by the cars of number 2265's train. He drove up as close to them as he could to try and see what was on fire at the depot. By leaning down he could see through the trees and what he saw wasn't encouraging. Number 2265 was leaning up against the walk that ran around the baggage room. Fred is reported to have told somebody who came running by at that moment that a train had run right through the God-damned depot.

Fred backed the Reo up and turned into the driveway of the old cannery and whizzed around the end of the building, then tried to cut across Charlie Cotcher's vegetable garden. The ground was soft and he got no farther than the radish patch before he bogged down. He jumped down and ran around to the back and started to drag the hose off the truck. By this time hundreds of people were climbing the hill toward the depot and Fred shouted for some of them to help. Several of the Knights Templar swarmed over to the truck and helped Fred carry the hose toward the depot. Fred had the nozzle and he lugged it around Henry Stout's house and through a fence and into the back door of the waiting room. He pointed it straight at Bud Roof.

"Where's the fire?" he yelled.

"Not here!" Bud yelled. "Down at the lumber yard."

Fred and his Knights Templar pulled the hose back out of the depot and started down the hill. While they'd been up at the depot, some of the other members of the fire department had caught up with the Reo and had grabbed the other end of the hose and carried it to a fire hydrant. Now as Fred and his helpers struggled down the hill, someone turned the hydrant on. The hose began squirming and before the men carrying it got control of it, they had wet down a good hundred people who were coming up Main Street. Some of the other firemen came rushing up and got the nozzle pointed away from the street and helped pull it down toward the lumber yard. While all this had been happening, the rescue train, number 2277, had chugged north of town and was now backing down into The Hole. Its caboose reached Main Street at just about the time the firemen had finished dragging the hose down to the lumber yard and the wheels ran over the hose and cut it. That left the loose end flopping around like a snake and a lot more people got wet.

Although the fire department was having a hard time, the railroad was finally clear. When number 2277 got into The Hole, the main line was open for the first time in four hours. The first of the two specials now moved back into town and the engines stopped at the water tank again. The whistles were still blowing and the bells were still ringing. Off in the distance the fire whistle was still screeching, and on the side of the Main Street hill wet and bedraggled Knights Templar were trying to find a way to get past the wildly flopping fire hose.

When the first special finished taking water it moved across Main Street to the depot and people began climbing aboard. With all the noise and milling crowds and excitment, I don't think anyone knew which train was which. A lot of people got on the wrong train. Some of those who boarded the first special were passengers who had debarked from the regular northbound passenger. As soon as all the seats were filled, the conductor gave the signal and the train pulled out of town. Some of the people on that special found themselves back in Durand, which they had left at eleven o'clock that morning.

The second special followed the first one by twenty minutes and at least one Flushing resident managed to get on this one. He was John Egan, who had followed some drinking Knights out of the poolroom to continue whatever discussion was under way.

John didn't get back to Flushing for three days and when he *did* get back he had a plumed hat and a sword to go with his bartender's apron.

After the second special had left, John Reardon backed the passenger train out of the siding and came down to the depot, loaded up, took water, and headed for Saginaw. A lot of Knights Templar got on the passenger train, by mistake, and ended up in the wrong city. My father always said, afterwards, that there were Knights Templar wandering up and down our railroad for a week, looking for their convention.

There were still a lot of problems to be solved after the passenger train left Flushing. Number 2315 still had to be put back on the track. Burt Emans had finally convinced the fire department that there wasn't any fire and they brought a new hose and filled his tender. While this was going on, the crew from the wrecking train had gone down to the lumber yard and placed frogs and jacks under the engine. They were expert at taking care of *little* wrecks and they knew just what to do. Number 2277 put the wrecking train on the grain elevator siding and then ran around the curve and hitched onto number 2315. It took just one good yank and there was number 2315 back on the track and ready to go. Both engines now went up to the depot and the wrecking crew started to work on number 2265.

There was still a lot of confusion at the depot. Although all the out-of-towners were gone, most of the Flushing residents who had gone up to see the disaster were still there. They had discovered number 2265 and hung around to watch the wrecking crew get it back on the track. A legend had already grown up about number 2265, even before the wrecking crew went to work. The way people were describing it, number 2265 was right *in* the baggage room and in later years people always described that day as "the day the engine ran into the baggage room." It would be hard to convince anyone in Flushing today that the cowcatcher was only touching the walk that ran *around* the baggage room.

The rescue of number 2265 did not take long. It was about five o'clock when number 2315 and number 2265, now coupled as a doubleheader, pulled out of town. Number 2277 went back to Durand at about the same time. The three boxcars were still in the river, of course. A day or two after the excitment subsided, the section crew went down to the lumber yard and repaired the track. Shortly afterwards, number 2277 came out from Durand with the wrecker and went into the siding. The big hook fished the cars out of the water and put them back on the track. By that time my father's two-by-fours were soaked. When he unloaded them and put them on his piles, the sun came out and warped them all into corkscrews. The whole carload was ruined.

My father wasn't any angrier about his two-by-fours than Freckles Deal was about the punch he had received on the jaw at the ball game. On the day the engine ran into the baggage room, Freckles had gone down to the lumber yard after he intercepted the two specials. He crawled up in the cab of number 2315 and sat with his feet on the window sill, waiting for my father to come back to his office. My father had gone over to Flint on business, however, so Freckles waited in vain. He *did* carefully take down my father's name from the sign over the office and three weeks later he sued my father for hitting him. He claimed his eyes were injured, somehow. I had drawn a picture of all the engines that came to Flushing that day and had shown it to my mother, explaining just how it had all happened. She made my father listen to my explanation and the minute he heard the part about Freckles not pulling the coupling drawbar, he sued the railroad for ruining his two-by-fours. Nothing ever came of either suit, but my father must have put the picture away in case he ever went to court. He forgot about it and it was still there, forty-one years later, to remind me of the biggest day in my young life.

CHAPTER FIFTEEN

THERE WERE two other boys in Flushing who spent a lot of time around the depot. Paul Cotcher, who lived next door to it, and Ed McKenzie, the blacksmith's son, rode on the engines and knew all the trainmen. Occasionally they went into the station agent's office and sat on the stool to watch the telegraphers. They were both in my grade and we were good friends. We exchanged a lot of information and ran sort of a little club. In the summer of 1922 another boy began to hang around the depot. His name was Nick Sponto and he was two grades behind us.

The Sponto family lived at the west end of the Main Street bridge. They were foreigners of some kind. I think they were Romanian, but it didn't make any difference. We called the Spontos hunkies. At one time all foreigners in Flushing were called hunkies, but after Steve Polovich beat a few of us up, and after we got to know the rest of them better, we dropped the name. Only the Spontos kept the opprobrious label.

All the Spontos were cordially disliked in Flushing. They seemed to go out of their way to make people angry. Nick Sponto habitually dressed like a gypsy. He wore a red bandanna handkerchief around his head and he had a small gold earring. He was mean and he was tough. He once got into a fight with a boy at school and pulled a knife. He swore and he smoked and he chewed tobacco. His sisters—he had five of them—were just as nasty and vicious as he was. Stella Sponto was in my grade and after some other girl had spelled her down one day, Stella clawed and scratched her until she bled. One or the other of the Sponto children was always stealing tablets or books or pencils from children in the lower grades.

Tony Sponto, who had fathered all these monsters, was something of a monster himself. He established a reputation for drunkenness and untrustworthiness shortly after he arrived in the village. When he was drunk, he was mean and quite often his children would come to school with black eyes or bloody bruises. In 1912 Tony bought five acres of land along the riverbank and tried to run a vegetable garden there. The soil was good, but the river flooded it each spring and it was under water just long enough so that the growing season was precariously short. In three of the first five years Tony Sponto's garden was a complete failure. In 1917, when the war broke out, Tony went into the junk business. All the rest of the time we lived in Flushing, he kept acquiring more and more scrap metal. Huge piles of rusting iron and tin grew higher and higher. Pigs, chickens, goats, geese, dogs, cats, and rats wandered among the piles and wallowed in the mud. Tony Sponto's place was an eyesore and it smelled bad. The people of Flushing cordially detested Tony Sponto and I think he hated the people of Flushing.

Most of the foreigners who came to Flushing in the first fourteen years of the twentieth century were hard workers. They had been poor peasants and wanted land of their own, and they would put in long hard hours to earn a few dollars to put toward the purchase of that land. The Nagys and the Poloviches and the Supaks never played baseball or football or watched trains with the rest of us because as soon as school was out they were out working. Tony Sponto sent his family out to work, too, but he used the money they brought in to buy whiskey. Soon after

World War I, Tony bought an old Model T truck with a wide, flat rack. It had no cab and no driver's seat. A cushion was stretched out over the gasoline tank, but Tony never sat on it. He drove the truck standing up. This was in the day when the speed of a vehicle was still regulated by means of a gas lever on the steering wheel so that the feat wasn't quite as difficult as it seems. Whenever Tony wanted to put on the brake, he simply stepped forward and onto the brake pedal. The rest of the Sponto family, all women, stood in the middle of the flat rack, all huddled together and hanging onto each other. Nick, the only boy, would squat beside his father on the gasoline tank. Wherever they went, whether it was out to a farm to work in the fields or to collect junk, they always rode this way. It was quite a sight to see them arrive at some house at the request of a family to clean up the junk. The minute the truck rolled to a stop, the Spontos would explode out of their huddle and run off in different directions. Within a few minutes they would pick a yard or a barnyard clean. They would come back to the truck carrying old pieces of wire, pump handles, sheets of tin from water troughs, or lengths of pipe. Of course, they never confined themselves to junk. Unless they were watched they would grab anything they came to, including chickens, sleds, working machinery, or furniture. It was impossible to watch all of them so that they got away with considerable thievery over the years.

With this background, it was understandable that we were a little surprised when Nick Sponto began showing up at the depot every day. He got there before I did in the morning and he stayed there until after the evening passenger train went north. He was sneaky about it, too. He hid behind the baggage room or lay in the weeds over by the water tank. He had a little tablet and was forever writing things down in it. He left that tablet lying on the baggage wagon one morning and I looked in it. He had all the trains listed, and the engine numbers and the arrival and departure times. He had how many cars each train had on it and he even had the number of times a train whistled for the Main Street crossing. Before I had a chance to see what else he had written down, he caught me looking through the pages and grabbed the tablet, kicked me in the shins, and ran. I didn't bother to chase him. I just made up my mind *he'd* never ride on Burt Emans's engine.

Paul Cotcher and Ed McKenzie and I might have discussed the unusual behavior of Nick Sponto a little more that summer if we hadn't had other major preoccupations. A new bridge was being built across the river and we had to watch it. As if that wasn't enough, Ira Sayre bought a radio in August. It was the first radio in Flushing and it created a sensation among boys my age. None of us knew quite what a radio was, or what it could do, and we used to sit on Mrs. Niles's hitching block in the evening and watch the long aerial that Ira's hired man had strung up from a high pole in his yard. I don't know whether we expected to see the sound come and light on that wire or not.

One night after we had finished playing run sheep run, Ed McKenzie dared me to go over and look in Ira Sayre's window. He thought we might actually get a look at what the radio was like. Ed McKenzie had heard that it was kept in the library which was on the first floor. We sneaked across the street from Mrs. Niles's hitching block and up Ira Sayre's driveway to the big bay window of the library. By standing on tiptoe we were able to see over the sill. The room was dimly lit and Ira Sayre was sitting in his big armchair, his eyes closed, his hands folded across his enormous stomach. On his head was something that looked like a pair of earmuffs. They were connected by a long wire to a little black box from which three orange glowing light bulbs protruded. We had just taken all this in when two arms reached down from above and grabbed us by the back of our shirts. The arms belonged to Ira Sayre's hired man. He dragged us around to the back of the house and in through the kitchen door, then stood us on our feet in front of the big armchair. Ira opened his eyes and squinted at us, then leaned forward to get a better look.

"It's against the law to peep in windows," he said, then looked at me and scowled. "Aren't you George Love's grandson?"

I knew I was in trouble then. If he'd asked me if I was Ed Perry's grandson, I would have been all right. He turned to the hired man and told him to bring the razor strop. When it was brought into the room, Ira Sayre heaved himself to his feet with great difficulty and motioned for me to bend over the arm of the chair. Ira could make that strop sting, even if he was in poor health. He gave me four good lashes with it and then it was Ed McKenzie's turn. When the whipping was done, Ira Sayre gave the strop back to the hired man and motioned me toward the chair.

"Sit down!" he rumbled at me.

I sat down and Ira picked up the earmuffs and carefully adjusted them to my head. I heard someone singing. Then I heard the music stop and a voice uttered words that I will never forget as long as I live. "This is radio station WCX, Detroit, Michigan. Please stand by for two minutes for ship signals." There followed a long period of crackling and crashing that hurt my ears. It was static, but I thought the static was as wonderful as either the music or the voice. In the middle of the static Ira Sayre reached over, yanked the head set off, and motioned for me to make room for Ed McKenzie. It has always interested me that I was present at Ed McKenzie's introduction to radio, for he was to become Detroit's most famous disk jockey twenty years later. We became pretty famous in our age group *then* because we were the only ones in Flushing who had heard a radio. No other boy or girl got into Ira Sayre's library although some of them got all dressed up and knocked on the door and asked.

On the Saturday afternoon before Labor Day I had a dull time. The workers on the bridge had taken the afternoon off and there weren't many trains. Number 2315 came down from Saginaw quite early. I climbed into the cab and we moved from the water tank up to the south end of town. Burt Emans backed into the House track to pick up a car that had been set out there and then told me I'd better climb down because that was all he had to do that day. Even the local freight was a fizzle.

I walked along the railroad track and finally wandered out the Montrose road to Sleepy Murray's house. It was about two blocks north of the depot and was the last one in town. Sleepy was always building things or smoking woodchucks out of holes. He was on the bank of Cold Creek fishing when I found him and he said he was glad to see me. He was thinking of building a dam and he needed help. We carried rocks for a while and then Sleepy got his beebee gun and we went hunting squirrels. At about quarter of six, his mother stuck her head out of the back door and called him in to supper. I started back down the Montrose road to the depot.

The railroad crosses the Montrose road at Henry Chatters's farm and then runs along beside it all the way into the depot, a distance of a mile. At no point in that whole stretch is the track obscured from the road except at the very point where the Montrose road turns east and enters Main Street. There, in the angle where the two roads join, stood a one-story shed that served as a pickle warehouse. It was built on stilts and a person could get down on his hands and knees and look under it to the other side. For one brief moment a driver in a vehicle coming south along the Montrose road had his vision of the tracks obstructed. Main Street formed the stem of a Y. The Montrose road was one arm of the Y and the Seymour road was the other arm. A driver on the Seymour road could also see a train coming from the north until he made the turn and the pickle warehouse got in his way. His view was obstructed for only an instant, however.

There was no watchman at the crossing, nor were there any gates or signal lights. Although automobile traffic had been increasing steadily for several years, it was still not very heavy. Such traffic as there was consisted almost entirely of local vehicles. Outsiders rarely entered Flushing from the west. The local people were well aware of the crossing and its dangers and approached cautiously. Most of them came to a full stop before venturing out onto the tracks. The trainmen on the line also were cognizant of the danger. Most trains approached the crossing with whistles held down. There had never been an accident on that Main Street crossing.

On the afternoon after Sleepy Murray's mother called him to an early supper, I shuffled along the road toward the depot. There were no sidewalks in that part of town and I walked down the middle of the gravel road, kicking a tin can ahead of me. I stopped occasionally to throw a rock at a telephone pole. When I reached the pickle warehouse I perked up. Tony Sponto's old Model T truck was parked behind it in the little driveway where the farmers ordinarily unloaded their cucumbers. There were no Spontos in sight. I assumed they were all over on the other side of the tracks working in Bill Kaiser's bean field. As long as they couldn't see me, I looked upon this happenstance as a real opportunity. I had watched Tony driving around town while standing up and it seemed to me that this method might solve some of my driving problems. (My father would not give me driving lessons because I couldn't see over the cowl of his car.) I looked around carefully to make sure that I hadn't missed any Spontos and then clambered onto the truck to try the standing method. I planted my feet firmly on the gasoline tank, grasped the steering wheel in both hands, and made a sound like a motor running. I was just turning the wheel in a long imaginary curve when I heard Tony Sponto's voice. It sounded mean.

"Get offa that truck, keed, or I keel you."

I didn't even look around to see where the voice was coming from. I ran back across the flat rack as fast as I could go, jumped to the ground, and kept right on running. When I finally reached the middle of the Montrose road, I stopped and looked back over my shoulder. Tony was crouched under the pickle warehouse shaking his fist at me. I knew better than to get mixed up with Tony Sponto. I didn't even dignify things by thumbing my nose at him. I just walked along the far side of the road, giving the pickle warehouse a wide berth, and crossed the railroad tracks to the depot.

It was now almost time for the southbound passenger train. On this hot summer Saturday afternoon there was hardly anyone at the depot. No passengers were going anywhere, but Mr. Sutton had driven up to meet Mrs. Sutton, who was due home from Saginaw where she had been shopping. Mr. Sutton had parked his car near the waiting room and was sitting in the front seat reading a magazine. Bud Roof had carried two cans of motion-picture film out and put them on the cinders where the baggage car usually stopped and Charlie Thompson had put the one small bag of outgoing mail a little farther up the tracks so that he could throw it in the door of the mail car. When I came across the tracks that day, Charlie was leaning through the open front windows of the depot showing Bud Roof the new forty-five revolver that the government had just given him. I asked Charlie to let me see it and he held it up for me to look at before he put it in the holster that hung from his hip. I then climbed a few steps up the ladder of the semaphore pole and looked down on the scene. I was still hanging up there by one arm when the passenger train whistled far off in the distance. The minute I heard that whistle I knew my long, dull Saturday was over. That whistle did not belong to John Reardon's number 2248. It belonged to either number 2243 or number 2246. I knew that John Reardon had gone north with number 2248 on the noon passenger train that day and it did not seem possible that he would come back with anything else. Something unusual *must* have happened. I climbed farther up the ladder and turned so that I could see the train when it came across Henry Chatters's crossing. John Reardon blew the long station whistle and the engine rumbled across the Montrose road and turned for the south. The minute it came out into the open I knew that it was number 2243 because it had a shorter smokestack than number 2246. It came roaring down the grade into town and John Reardon blew his customary warning for the Main Street crossing—two longs, two shorts, and one long.

It was just at the moment that he blew his whistle that I caught a movement out of the corner of my eye. Tony Sponto's truck had emerged from behind the pickle warehouse and was heading for the crossing. All the Sponto women were standing in the middle of the flat rack in a huddle as they always did, hanging onto each other for support. Tony was standing up and driving, and young Nick was squatting beside him on the gas tank. From the minute I saw the truck I knew that it was going to drive onto the track in front of the train. I don't know how I knew it, but I suppose it was the determination with which it moved. Charlie Thompson sensed it, too. He had been leaning with his back to the depot, his elbows resting on the window sill, when he saw the truck, only a moment after I did. He straightened up and yelled and took an involuntary step toward the crossing. Mr. Sutton had put away his magazine and was backing out of his car when he heard Charlie yell. He turned and looked and he yelled, too.

The truck kept on coming. The train, although it was actually coasting into the station, seemed to be rushing at a headlong speed. The two met in the middle of the crossing. The engine hit the truck broadside, squarely in the middle. The truck tilted on its side and was dragged up the track, plowing up the cinders in front of it. The Sponto women were dumped off in all directions at the moment of impact. Some of them fell to the ground on one side of the train and some of them fell to the other side. Tony Sponto hung onto the steering wheel and seemed to ride along, pushed up against the front of the boiler. When John Reardon brought the train to a stop, Tony was still standing there with the steering wheel firmly gripped in his hands although it was no longer connected to anything. The only unlucky Sponto was Nick. He was trapped in the wreckage, pinned between the twisted truck and the cowcatcher. When people tried to remove him it was discovered that he was caught. John Reardon climbed up into his cab and backed away carefully, almost an inch at a time. When Nick was freed he was unconscious and covered with blood. It was the first time in my life that I had ever seen a mangled human body.

Everyone acted promptly and efficiently. The train's crew and passengers came pouring down out of the cars. Bud Roof rushed into the depot and called Doc Logan. Doc came speeding up Main Street in his car, his horn blowing, and arrived just in time to tend to Nick after he had been pulled out of the wreckage. Most of the passengers tried to help the Sponto women. They had been skinned up and their dresses were torn and there were some bruises, but Doc Logan looked them over and said that none of them were hurt seriously. Tony Sponto was found to have a broken arm and several broken ribs. He also had a deep gash on his head that required stitches. Nick was the most seriously hurt. One leg was broken and the other was badly torn. Both arms were broken. He had suffered a heavy blow on the head and Doc Logan was afraid that he had a fractured skull.

The baggageman on the train pushed a stretcher out the door of his car and Nick was placed on it and carefully lifted back into the train to be taken to the hospital in Durand. Tony was also helped onto the train, but when Doc Logan and the trainmen tried to get Mrs. Sponto to accompany them she stood back and called them vile names. Without even waiting for the doctor to fix up her bruises, she turned and shooed her daughters down the hill. About every fifth step she turned around and shook her fist at the crowd and shouted something nasty—most of it in a foreign language. By that time quite a crowd had gathered and the men all gave a hand and pulled the wrecked truck off the track. John Reardon blew his whistle and number 2243 chugged up the hill to the south and Durand.

I rode home with Charlie Thompson that evening. I was late for my Saturday night bath and I held up supper, but my family forgave me under the circumstances. My whole family listened to my description of what had happened. Among those who heard me was Grandpa Perry. For some reason, however, as the days and weeks passed, everyone forgot that I had been there. I more or less forgot it myself, so I guess I shouldn't think it was strange.

Nick Sponto came home from the hospital in December. He was in a wheelchair for several months and when he did get out of it he was never able to walk normally again. Shortly after Christmas my father came to supper one night with the announcement that the Spontos were suing the Grand Trunk Railroad for $150,000 and that they would surely get it because the crossing was unguarded and dangerous.

The railroad made no settlement in the case. Ira Sayre was asked to defend it. He had been drawing a big retainer for more than forty years and this was the first case that had ever been given him. I think Ira could have begged off if he had wanted to. He was dying that winter. He had gone downhill badly since the summer. He still made the trip to his office every few days, but it was agony for him. He shuffled along the sidewalk, barely able to put one foot in front of the other. Before the case actually came to trial he had a light stroke and took to a wheelchair. He was never to get out of it. For some reason Ira was insistent that he be allowed to try that one last case. I suppose he felt that it would be some kind of proof to the world that he actually was a lawyer and that he hadn't taken all that money for nothing. He gathered what strength he had left and subpoenaed all the witnesses he could find and prepared the case for trial in February. I was not called because no one remembered that I had seen the accident. I doubt that Ira Sayre would have called me even if he had known.

As usual in Michigan, the month of February was a nasty one in 1923. The blizzards blew in from the north and the snow piled up and the temperature kept going down. Grandpa Perry had volunteered for jury duty as he always did in those days and had been instructed to report to Flint for the February term of court. The weather was so bad that he took a small hotel room in Flint and prepared to stay there until the end of the term of court.

I cannot remember the national events of that winter, but I think there had been a long coal strike. It had caused a crisis in Flushing because the village coal supplies were dangerously low. In an effort to conserve what there was left for home consumption, the township school board decided to close down the schools for two weeks. This was the first time in my memory that we had ever had a vacation in the middle of winter. I was ready for a vacation at any time, but my father didn't welcome this one with any enthusiasm. My mother had been in increasingly poor health that winter and had spent several weeks in bed. In an effort to lighten the load on her shoulders, my father suggested that I might like to go over to Flint and stay with Grandpa. I liked the idea immensely. Flint had streetcars and cafeterias, two of my favorite things.

The first night I was in Flint my grandpa took me for a streetcar ride *before* supper, to a cafeteria *for* supper, and to a Tom Mix movie *after* supper. This was my idea of the best possible vacation. The next morning we got up and went to *another* cafeteria for breakfast and then took a streetcar up to the courthouse. Grandpa had to check into the big jury room every morning until he was excused for the day. We sat around with a lot of other people and finally someone called out Grandpa's name. He took me by the hand and turned me over to a court bailiff and gave me explicit instructions to sit quietly in the courtroom while he was examined to sit on a case. By a remarkable coincidence, the case turned out to be the Sponto case and my grandfather was one of the first chosen for that jury. I have often thought, since, that he could have disqualified himself or that he could have been challenged on the basis of past association with Ira Sayre, but the thought never seems to have occurred to him, and the Spontos' lawyer could not have guessed about his long friendship with Ira. From all I know about Grandpa, I am sure he thought of himself as able to render a perfectly impartial verdict.

I did not pay any attention to the early legal moves in that trial. I was eleven years old and this was the first time I had ever been in a courtroom. I scarcely understood what was going on. There was an even better reason for my indifference, however. Once the bailiff led me into the court I found it to be full of all my good friends. John Reardon was there. Charlie Thompson was there. Bud Roof, Doc Logan, Mr. Sutton, Mr. O'Brien, the railway mail clerk, and even Beans McAuslin, John Reardon's fireman, were all there. I went and sat in a seat next to John Reardon and he whispered to me about number 2248. I was well entertained.

The actual trial did not begin until after the noon recess. The first witness was Tony Sponto. Under questioning by his lawyer, he said that he and his family had spent the day working out on Harlan Bruner's farm. They had finished about six o'clock and had all got on the truck to drive home. They had driven along the Seymour road from the south. They couldn't see the tracks because of the trees and the buildings. There was no warning device of any kind on the crossing and no train whistle had been blown. Tony had turned into Main Street and had looked along the tracks, but couldn't see anything because the pickle warehouse was in the way. There was no way he could possibly know that a train was coming. Tony's lawyer had a big map that showed where all the buildings were and everyone watched while Tony pointed things out. By the time he had finished Tony had proved pretty well that the crossing was dangerous. Ira Sayre sat in his wheelchair and asked Tony some pretty sharp questions when it came his turn. He asked how long the Spontos had lived in Flushing and how many times they had driven over that crossing. He asked whether Tony didn't know that a train was due at that time of day. Tony said that he was a poor ignorant foreigner and that he didn't understand American ways. He had no idea when trains were due and he couldn't even tell time very well.

After Tony got off the stand, all the other Spontos got up and said almost exactly the same things. Then the lawyer began calling other people. He called a doctor to tell how badly Nick Sponto was injured and the doctor said that Nick might not be able to walk again and that he certainly would never be able to earn a living. Just as the afternoon ended, Harlan Bruner testified that the Spontos had worked at his farm all day. Ira Sayre asked Mr. Bruner what time they had left the farm, but Mr. Bruner didn't seem to know. He was under the impression that it was sometime between five and six o'clock, but that he hadn't checked the time. He had paid the Spontos off and told them they could go home as soon as certain things were done. He'd been in the barn when they left. He didn't seem to think they were far off as to the time they said they left, but he couldn't be too sure.

When the judge banged his gavel and got up and left for the day, all the jurors got up and came out into the courtroom. Grandpa reclaimed me from the company of John Reardon and talked for a few minutes with Harlan Bruner about something to do with the weather. When we got out of the courthouse, it was early for supper so we got on a streetcar and rode all the way out to the end of the line and back. We got off in downtown Flint and went to a cafeteria for supper. Then we went to see a Hoot Gibson movie. In all that evening Grandpa never said one word to me about the Spontos or the accident or the trial. After we got in bed that night he told me one of his stories about when he was buying and selling furs in the West. He turned out the light about 9:30 and rolled over on his side to go to sleep.

Grandpa's room was on the top floor of the hotel and there was a skylight right over the bed. I wasn't sleepy at all and I lay awake looking up at the glass for quite a long time and as I lay there I thought about everything I had heard during the day. About half an hour after he had turned out the light, Grandpa lit a match to see what time it was by his watch. I was glad that he was awake.

"Grandpa," I asked him, "what happens to people who tell lies in courts?"

"They go to jail," he said. "Now you go to sleep."

I thought about that for a few minutes.

"Good," I said.

"Good, what?"

"All the Spontos are going to have to go to jail."

I have often wondered, in all the years since, just what effect this pronouncement had on Grandpa at the moment I made it. The light was out and I couldn't see him. Whatever else he was, Grandpa was a conscientious man. He took literally the judge's admonition not to discuss the case he was hearing. He had not said a word about it to anyone and here he was trapped in a hotel room with a grandson and the grandson had made a statement he couldn't possibly ignore. He must have remembered by that time that I had seen the accident and had come home and discussed it at the supper table. He put his hands under his head and lay there in the dark for a long time, looking up at the ceiling. He must have been fighting the temptation to ask me what I had meant, but he couldn't win. He reached over and turned on the light, got up from the bed, and lit himself a cigar. Then he paced the floor in his nightgown (over his long underwear, as usual) and turned to look at me.

"Maybe you'd better tell me about it," he said.

I told him that Tony Sponto hadn't been out at Bruner's farm before the accident. He'd been hiding under the pickle warehouse. I told him about Nick Sponto's notebook and all the material that was written in it. When I went to sleep Grandpa was still pacing the floor, puffing on his cigar. I don't think that Grandpa went to sleep at all that night. He woke me up quite early and helped me to dress, then rushed me down the stairs and out onto the street. He was in such a hurry and was so preoccupied that he didn't even take me to a cafeteria for breakfast. Instead of taking a streetcar ride up to the courthouse, we walked there. Grandpa walked. I had to run most of the way to keep up with him.

When we got to the courthouse we went down a long hall and knocked at a door with glass in it. The door was opened by a man in shirtsleeves and suspenders. It was the judge I had seen the previous day. Grandpa introduced himself and he and the judge argued for several minutes. The judge didn't want to talk to Grandpa and he didn't want to let Grandpa in until Grandpa said that he wanted to disqualify himself from the case. After we got inside the judge was pretty mad with Grandpa. He wanted to know why Grandpa hadn't disqualified himself before the trial began. Grandpa pointed at me and told the judge that I was his grandson and that I had spent the night with him. I had given him some information and he felt that it would prejudice his verdict. He couldn't help listening to it and now that he had heard it, he wanted to disqualify himself. The judge looked at me and asked me what I had said, so I told him the whole story. When I finished the judge looked at me thoughtfully.

"Is this boy a truthful boy?" he asked Grandpa.

Grandpa nodded. The judge paced up and down the floor of his office for several minutes. He finally thanked Grandpa for coming and said that, under the circumstances, he would disqualify him. That meant that he would have to declare a mistrial. (There were no alternate jurors in those days.) Before he did so he wanted to investigate the truthfulness of what I had said. He felt that perjury was involved. If it was, he would have to take certain steps. He asked Grandpa to stay in a separate room when court convened and not to see or speak to the other jurors. After saying this, he called a bailiff into his office and instructed him that the jury was not to be brought into the courtroom.

When the judge walked into the courtroom that morning he led me by the hand and told me to sit down on the witness stand. After he got up on his own chair, he put on his glasses and looked around the court. He beckoned to the Spontos' lawyer and to Ira Sayre and they came over to the bench. He spoke quietly to them and said that something had come up that involved testimony given in the court. He wanted to assure himself of certain things before he proceeded and he asked the two lawyers for their indulgence. He said that he would see them in his chambers at the close of the session. I could see Ira Sayre looking at me. He was scowling. The other lawyer seemed puzzled. They both went back to their tables. (Ira was still in his wheelchair.) The judge rapped for order and asked for all the witnesses to the accident to stand up. When they were on their feet, he pointed at Charlie Thompson and asked him to look at me closely. Had Charlie seen me at the scene of the accident?

"He's *always* at the depot," Charlie said, "but I can't honestly remember whether he was there that day or not. He could have been."

The judge looked at me and scratched his head. I raised my hand like I did in school and he nodded at me. I told the judge that Charlie had his new revolver that day and that he showed it to me. The judge looked at Charlie. Charlie grinned.

"He's right," Charlie said. "He was there."

The judge pointed at John Reardon. John said he knew me and that I was probably there, but that he had been so busy he couldn't remember me. I raised my hand again and told John that he had been driving number 2243 that day. John said I was right. The judge seemed a little put out about that. He asked John Reardon how *he* knew he had been driving number 2243.

John said it was the only time he had ever had that engine. Number 2248 had developed a leak in an air line that afternoon and he had to change engines.

The judge looked at me for quite a long time after that, then banged his gavel and said that court would stand recessed until after noon.

After we got back to the judge's office, Ira Sayre and the other lawyer came in and the judge told them that he was going to disqualify a juror and that he would have to declare a mistrial. He then looked at Tony Sponto's lawyer in a very stern manner. He said that he had reason to believe that certain witnesses had given perjured testimony. He then turned to me and told me to tell both lawyers exactly what I had told him. I told about Tony's truck behind the pickle warehouse and about Nick's tablet. Tony Sponto's lawyer started to ask me questions. He was pretty mad. The judge stopped him. He told the lawyer that he would have a chance to cross-examine me on the stand because he wanted Mr. Sayre to call me as a witness. He said they would proceed to the selection of a new jury at once. He recommended that the lawyer re-examine his own witnesses and remind them of the penalties for perjury because if perjury had been committed, he intended to turn the matter over to the prosecuting attorney.

Ira Sayre stayed in the judge's office after the other lawyer left that morning. He looked at me for quite a long time.

"Aren't you Ed Perry's grandson?" he asked me.

There wasn't any second trial. Tony Sponto and all his family ran away and the lawyer dropped the case. The Spontos were found in Detroit about a week after that morning in the judge's office. Tony beat up his wife and some of the girls to keep them from talking, but the story came out. Tony had rigged up the accident so that they would all be rich. Nothing ever happened to them for lying on the witness stand and even though all the

Sponto girls and Tony's wife had been badly abused, they were loyal to him. They came back to Flushing and took up right where they had left off. About a year after that day in court, Tony was arrested for bootlegging and spent some time in jail. While he was in jail one of his daughters, or it may have been his wife, became involved with the man who ran the flour mill on the riverbank. Tony found out about it and one dark night he and Nick went over to the flour mill and stabbed the miller to death. I've never been sure of the details of that case, because we had moved away from Flushing by the time it happened. Nick was acquitted of the murder, but Tony was sentenced to life in prison and died there in 1955. His crime was the first capital crime committed in Flushing since the murder of Thomas Brent in 1839.

One thing happened to me as a result of that case. About a month after it ended a man came to our house one day and asked for me. He had a big box and in it was a radio. It was just like the one that Ira Sayre owned. I became the second person in Flushing to own a radio set.

I never saw Ira Sayre to thank him for his present. He died that spring.

CHAPTER SIXTEEN

ONE MARCH day in 1923, less than a month after the conclusion of Tony Sponto's lawsuit, I came out of the West Side school one afternoon just in time to hear a train whistle in the distance. I was electrified by the sound of that whistle because no engine whistle like that had ever sounded on the CS&M before. There was a driving snowstorm that afternoon and I plunged into it and ran for the railroad tracks. I had almost reached the depot when a snowplow pushed its way around the bend at the south end of town. It came slowly down the grade to stop at the water tank and I stood there and looked up at the engine in some awe. It was numbered 1452.

The arrival of number 1452 marked the end of an era in Flushing. I think it marked the end of my boyhood. Number 1452 was no goat. It was a jack engine. It had its headlight in the center of the boiler. It had three driving wheels on each side. It had only one pilot truck. It was a modern engine in every respect and it was powerful. It could pull fifty freight cars at one time and the grades out of town were no real obstacle to it.

I didn't know it but the goats had been wearing out for several years. In my little book many of the numbers I had written down so carefully were just memories—engines never to be seen again. Out of the original eighty goats, only thirty were left that spring of 1923 and twenty of those last survivors were marked for scrap before the end of the summer. Number 2315 disappeared before the end of April. It was succeeded briefly by number 2277 and then that wore out. The last goat driven by Burt Emans was number 2288. John Reardon's old number 2248 had less than six months to live. One fall day it was hauled down from Saginaw at the end of the southbound local freight. One of its boiler tubes had burst. I was never to see it again, nor did I ever see John Reardon again.

In the spring of 1923 a work train came through Flushing putting down heavier rail. For a month a pile driver worked on the bridges across Cold Creek north and south of town, strengthening them. The local section crew put new ties and rails on the sidings and in The Hole. One morning in June Burt Emans came into town with a jack engine on the local freight. And, just to make the change complete, the Grand Trunk began repainting and renumbering all the engines. I was soon completely lost. The first jack engine on the local freight was number 705 (it had once been number 1449). Burt Emans soon replaced it with 700, then 699, and then settled down permanently with 678. I rode in the cab of number 678 for more than a year. I liked number 678, but I didn't have the affection for it that I had felt for the old goats.

The appearance of the jack engines on the CS&M had a profound effect on the railroad. A doubleheader of jacks could pull a hundred cars up to Saginaw. That equaled three of the old trains. There was no longer any need for all those extra freights. As time passed, the afternoon manifests disappeared also. The work trains that had formerly taken care of the sugar beets and the livestock and the sand and gravel were no longer necessary. All that traffic could be handled by the jack engines on the local freight. Very soon, by the winter of 1923-24, the number of freight trains on the CS&M had narrowed down to two each way. Just two short years earlier there had been as many as fifteen.

Other influences were operating to reduce the CS&M from a bustling, busy railroad to a lonely stretch of track. After 1920 the population of Michigan rapidly changed to automobile transportation. The two night flyers were taken off in 1922. In the fall of 1923, all but two of the other passengers ceased operating. The force at the depot was reduced from five men to three and Bud Roof closed it and locked the doors every night at seven o'clock. The whole railroad disappeared right before my eyes. By the spring of 1924 I never had to go to the outhouse once in a whole day. That fall, when I entered the eighth grade and moved to the other end of town to go to school, I no longer listened for train whistles. I was rather glad to leave the West Side school. It was lonesome over there.

The railroad was only part of a changing world. The old iron bridge had gone in 1922. The new concrete one was finished in the early spring of 1923 and placed in service when the river flooded and washed out the temporary. That May a flatcar was brought into town and placed by the unloading ramp of the freight depot. On it was a huge cement mixer. It was unloaded and within a week it was busily at work. It started at the west end of Main Street and worked down the hill, across the river flats past the lumber yard and Tony Sponto's junk yard. It moved up through the main business block and on out to the east end of town. Behind it stretched a ribbon of concrete. Main Street was paved from curb to curb and from end to end. That winter there was no coasting on the Cherry Street hill, or the Saginaw Street hill, or the McKinley Street hill, or any hill. It was considered too dangerous for us to slide across Main Street as we had always done. Our parents and the village council forbade it. Too many cars went too fast on the new pavement. There was no bob-hopping that winter either. There were no bobs any more, and no cutters.

There were changes in my own family, too. In the fall of 1922 my father sold his lumber yard in Flushing and bought a bigger one in Flint. He got up every morning and drove the ten miles to work. He didn't like it, and every day when I took my short cut through Mr. French's store, Mr. French would look up at me and say, "Are you still here? I thought you'd be in Flint by now."

There was a good reason why my father didn't move to Flint. In 1922 my mother had begun to go blind. She used to sit in the living room under a reading lamp with a magnifying glass and try to read. Much of the time she didn't feel well. As she began to fail visibly, my father began taking her to specialists in Detroit and Chicago. On one of these visits he learned that she was suffering from Bright's disease. He kept it from her and he kept it from us, but he knew she was dying and he managed to put off our moving in one way or another so that she could be among her friends. In the summer of 1924 her illness took one of those peculiar and unexplainable turns for the better. For a few months she seemed almost her old self. She could see again and she could go places again. She began to badger my father about moving. In the fall he bought a house in Flint and we prepared to move. The actual move was made on November 1, 1924. I remember the day quite well because my mother was gay and happy and felt well enough to make the trip by car all the way down to Ann Arbor with my father and me to see a football game at the University of Michigan. While we were down there the moving van came and took all our furniture to Flint. Neighbors from Flushing went over and settled the entire house so that when we came back from Ann Arbor we went to Flint rather than to Flushing. Just a month later my mother collapsed. One afternoon my brother came home from school and found her lying on the floor. She hung on into the spring, but it has always seemed to me that she was never a part of my life in Flint. She belonged in Flushing.

One can almost see the difference between her world and the world that came after her. It had already changed more than we knew. During the last month we lived in Flushing, Washington played the New York Giants in the World Series. My father and my mother and I sat in the sewing room and listened to the last game of the series. My father had bought a new loudspeaker for the radio set that Ira Sayre had given me and we were listening to it for the first time. My mother never knew radio as I knew it. She never imagined television. She never even saw a car with an automatic windshield wiper. I often wonder how she would have felt about jet airplanes.

I think it all evens out in the end. Most of the people who watch television and take a jet to Europe every summer have never known a town like Flushing either. I have a feeling that even the people who live in Flushing today don't know that kind of town.

Flushing still nestles in the big bend of the Flint River. It has 3,700 people now. All the streets are paved, not just Main Street. Most of the same houses stand where they always stood, but many of the big trees went down in a tornado that struck the town in 1934. There are new subdivisions. Houses were built in the peach orchard where we fought the Germans during the war. Brent's plantation has been restored. The buildings on the main business block are the same, but most of them are occupied by chain stores. Indeed, the people of Flushing do most of their trading in the big new shopping centers in Flint. It takes only seven minutes to run over there. Not only that, most of the people in Flushing work in Flint—in the automobile factories that the villagers ignored for so long.

The New Ideal Theater is now the old Dawn Theater. Fred Graves's barbershop is now a beauty parlor, a development that would cause Fred no end of anguish. Some of the piers of the old railroad bridge still stand and one can see the dam from Joe Gage's bridge. It is full of holes now. Bob Hart's marvelous new concrete power plant was torn down years ago, and a service station stands where Grant Reid's garage once stood, but if you know where to look behind it you can still see some of the old, twisted, rusty pipes that are left from the wreckage of the 1918 fire. The depot still crowns the hill at the top of West Main Street and Clare Fox is the station agent there. Clare was the telegrapher who took Percy Benjamin's place, but he doesn't talk on the telegraph any more. He uses a telephone. Only one train a day wanders up and down the line from Durand to Saginaw—a diesel switcher of which I never even bothered to take the number when I saw it. Wes Bird's still disappeared years ago and so did the water tank and the pumping station.

The thing I miss the most are the people. They're all up in the cemetery, even Roy Simpson. A few still live on. Tom Bulger is still alive, and Ray Budd, and Ira Sayre's daughter. He couldn't have been such a bad man to have produced such a warm, lovely woman as she is. The others have disappeared one by one. On the day after Ira Sayre died, my grandfather Love walked into the village council chambers and put down his resignation. He never participated in village affairs again. Grandpa Perry moved to Flint with us and served on countless juries and got married again. (He never lived with his third wife either.)

In 1954 I arrived in Flint for a visit with my father just as the Flint *Journal* published a feature article in the suburban section of the paper. The picture that accompanied the story showed a little old man standing beside an ancient barber chair with a somewhat bewildered smile on his face. The article was a rather noncommittal piece written by a young reporter who had never heard Joe Gage play the bones or sing a song. Joe Gage, so the story said, had finally decided to close up his barbershop and retire. He was eighty-seven years old.

Most of the old-timers who were still left read that article. A day or two after it appeared my father received a telephone call from Tom Bulger, who had left the depot in 1919. Tom wanted my father to join him and Joe Gage for luncheon the next week. My father was pleased. After he'd hung up the phone he remembered someone else who might like to have lunch with Joe Gage. He called Ray Budd, the former gay young blade who always organized the village minstrel shows. Ray was over seventy, but his memory was still good. He knew someone else who would like to have lunch with Joe. That someone else called another person. Toward the end of the week Tom Bulger called my father back. He was puzzled. Fifty people had called him. They all wanted to have lunch with Joe Gage. He had decided to rent a private dining room so that everyone could come. The telephone calls continued. The next thing my father knew the luncheon had been moved to the Masonic Temple in Flushing and the Board of Commerce had taken it over. It was too big for Tom Bulger to handle. By the time 350 tickets had been printed up, the Board of Commerce decided to change it to a dinner. The 350 tickets had not even been distributed when the plans were changed again. So many people had called the Board of Commerce for tickets that the Masonic Temple wouldn't hold them all. The dinner was moved to the Flushing Community House and the number of tickets was raised to 1,000. In the hope that not too many of these would be left over, the chairman of the dinner committee asked the editor of the Flushing *Observer* to print a small notice in his paper. The 1,000 tickets were gone the day the paper came out and the telephone calls were still coming. After making a survey of the Community House, it was found that total of 1,350 people could be squeezed in there for a meal. The extra 350 tickets were printed and sold before the ink was dry. The telephone calls still kept coming. My aunt Esther's husband, Burt Way, who was president of the village council (someone in my family was *always* president of the village council), announced that no more dinners could be served, but that anyone else who wanted to honor Joe Gage could come down to the Community House *after* dinner. When the dinner tables had been cleared, the others would be admitted to the balconies to listen to the speeches.

On the day of the testimonial dinner for Joe Gage, people began arriving in Flushing in the early afternoon. The expatriates all came home. It was the biggest single homecoming the village ever had. There were people in town who hadn't set foot in Flushing in twenty years. Loudspeakers were erected in front of the Community House and people began gathering on the lawn. When the speeches began that night, two thousand people squeezed *inside* the Community House and half as many more stood on the lawn outside. It was not only the biggest homecoming, but the crowd was the largest ever assembled in the village for any event in its history. It numbered three times the entire population of Flushing when Joe Gage first came there, in 1912. It was entirely a spontaneous event. Everyone who was there had come because he *wanted* to be there.

It was a wondrously warm and pleasant affair. There were many speeches and much reminiscing. At the very end of the evening Joe Gage got to his feet. He was a wizened little man, now, stooped and gray with his eighty-seven years, but his mind was as keen as it always had been and he still had a light in his eyes. I fully expected him to take the bones out of his pocket and go into a dance. His speech, like everything else about him, was simple.

"I don't know what I've done to deserve all this," he said. "I don't think I do deserve it. I've lived a long life and most of it's been a happy life, especially the part of it I've lived in this town. If I had it to do all over again, I'd like to change only one thing. I'd like to be born with a white skin. I just keep wondering what it would have been like. I'm not finding fault. I'm just curious. But if I couldn't change it, and if I had it to do all over again, I'd make tracks for this place just as fast as I could. God bless you, every one."

Joe Gage died in 1956 at the age of eighty-nine. He was right. The situation in Flushing *was* a good one for Joe Gages and small boys. That's why I have always loved it.

CPSIA information can be obtained
at www.ICGtesting.com
Printed in the USA
BVHW031110230722
642837BV00002B/6